ROMANTIC TIMES PRAISES
USA TODAY BESTSELLING AUTHOR
CONSTANCE O'BANYON!

DESERT PRINCE

"In the hands of O'Banyon, ancient history comes alive in this fourth book set in Egypt during the rule of the powerful Roman Caesars."

DAUGHTER OF EGYPT

"The heroine is a smart, strong woman, a perfect match for the warrior hero. Their sexual tension permeates the novel, and the culmination of their love is hot and sweet."

SWORD OF ROME

"O'Banyon continues the tale she began in *Lord of the Nile* by introducing Adhaniá. The historical facts are intriguing, and the effort of the characters to foil the plot against Caesar is heartwarming. The sensual scenes are sparse but tender and hot."

LORD OF THE NILE

"Fans of Egyptian lore and facts will find O'Banyon's historical right up their alley. She sprinkles political intrigue and love throughout the pages of this enjoyable book."

HAWK'S PURSUIT

"O'Banyon's third book in her Hawk series is possibly the best yet, with a regular little spitfire heroine, great verbal sparring and some very emotional scenes."

"My people do not think you are weak; they believe you are pitiless."

Shadowhawk took a step closer to Shiloh, as if he were compelled to do so. "What do you believe?"

She raised her head, her gaze searching his. "I cannot speak of all Comanche, but I know you to be a man of honor," she acknowledged.

He glanced away quickly, unable to meet her eyes lest he reveal too much of himself to her.

By now they had reached the river and he knelt down, cupped his hand and offered her a drink. Shiloh bent to take a sip and her lips touched the palm of his hand; she pulled back, trembling. She felt much more than respect for Shadowhawk, but she didn't know what it was. Something called her to him—something wild and beautiful—but she would not answer that call.

Shiloh's gaze moved from Shadowhawk's wide shoulders to his narrow waist. She gave an involuntary gasp when she noticed his leggings showed a fair amount of bare thigh as he bent to the river.

Shooting to her feet, Shiloh felt as if a hand had squeezed her heart. "Shadowhawk, you must let me and my brother go," she whispered.

Other *Leisure* books by Constance O'Banyon:

CONSTANCE O'BANYON

Comanche Moon Rising

LEISURE BOOKS   **L**   NEW YORK CITY

A LEISURE BOOK®

August 2009

Published by

Dorchester Publishing Co., Inc.
200 Madison Avenue
New York, NY 10016

ISBN 10: 0-8439-6265-8
ISBN 13: 978-0-8439-6265-9
E-ISBN: 978-1-4285-0710-4

Visit us online at www.dorchesterpub.com.

This is lovingly dedicated to the real Charley in my life,
Charles Allen Gee
"Happy Birthday!"

Elliott Noelle Gee, your sweetness touched my heart the
first time I met you. In marrying my son, Jason, you
became like a daughter to me. I cherish our friendship,
and I thank you for the joy you have given my son.

Acknowledgments

The valley with the spring-fed pond I mention in the book really exists near the small Texas town where I was born. My grandmother and grandfather lived and raised a family on a ranch my grandmother always referred to as "The Pretty Place." Truthfully, I would have to call it The Beautiful Place, because it is so breathtaking. When you come upon the valley, it is as unexpected as an oasis in the desert.

The site is now restricted ranch land. My sincere thanks to Mr. and Mrs. Burt Sellers, the rancher and his wife who were kind enough to allow my two brothers and me to visit, and to walk the land with us.

I was awed to find genuine Comanche artifacts lying about undisturbed. The dwelling where my family lived still stands and is now a hunting cabin. I cannot describe the feeling that came over me or the thoughts that ran through my mind as I stood at the actual fireplace where my grandmother had prepared meals for her family, my father included.

Thank you, Glenn Hoyle, my wonderful brother, who looks at the world through an artist's eyes and helped me remember the details I had forgotten about The Pretty Place.

Comanche Moon Rising
by
Constance O'Banyon

A warning given to all early settlers in Texas:

Beware of September Moon
The Blood Moon
The Comanche Moon

Author's Note

There was a time in Texas history when the mighty Comanche were lords of all they surveyed. They were a proud people, connected with nature, neither destroying the plentiful bounty the land offered up, nor misusing the gifts that sustained them throughout countless generations. It was a time when buffalo herds stretched from sunrise to sunset, and the Comanche used every part of the massive animal for their survival.

Then the white man came, slaughtering buffalo for their hides, ripping down trees, building their towns. Although the Comanche put up a valiant fight against the endless flow of white men, their voices have now been silenced; no longer can we hear the thunder of their horses racing across the Texas prairie, for these proud people have vanished from their ancient hunting grounds.

Although I have no Comanche blood in my ancestry, I am proud of the Cheyenne heritage that came down to me from my father's side of the family. Sometimes, on a cloudless Texas night when the September Moon is riding high in the sky, I can imagine the sound of proud warriors racing across the land, and for me the Comanche ride once more.

Come with me now—step back into a time when the Comanche was lord of all he surveyed.

Constance O'Banyon

Chapter One

Texas
March, 1846

The young Comanche chief raced through the raging storm, undeterred by the high snowdrifts. His spirited horse pulled restlessly against the reins and shied until the Indian's muscled legs brought the animal under control. Despite the heavy snow that swirled around Shadowhawk, he needed no landmarks to guide him home.

Shadowhawk paused atop a hill to glance down at the village located on the edge of the river that snaked across the prairie to disappear in the distance. The river was frozen, and daring young boys ventured across the ice, while women worked hurriedly, chipping away at the frozen water to fill their waterskins.

A gust of wind stirred Shadowhawk's ebony-colored hair and brushed it across his shoulders, twisting the five eagle feathers attached to his elaborately beaded headband.

Nudging his horse forward, Shadowhawk galloped down the hill while gleeful cries of welcome greeted him as he rode past a group of children. He dismounted before his horse came to a full stop and moved quickly toward the tipi in the middle of the village.

Thrusting the tipi flap aside, Shadowhawk lowered his head and stepped inside.

His grandfather, the peace chief, calmly sat with his

hands folded in his lap, a buffalo robe draped about his hunched shoulders. His face was creased with age, but his dark eyes were sharp with knowledge. Red Elk indicated that Shadowhawk should sit beside him.

"I wish my son had lived to see what a fine warrior you have become. Your wisdom in leading our people is acknowledged by all," Red Elk mused.

Shadowhawk took his place beside Red Elk. "If I have wisdom, I gained it from you, Grandfather."

"To be war chief at such a young age is a great achievement," Red Elk said, observing his only grandson. Shadowhawk was taller than most of the Comanche, his height coming from his Blackfoot mother. If anyone were to ask Shadowhawk, he would say his heart was pure Comanche, but Red Elk knew his grandson was influenced more by his Blackfoot mother than by his Comanche roots.

Red Elk realized that his grandson must have pushed both himself and his mount hard to reach the village as quickly as he had. If his grandson had a fault, it was his impatience. Even now Red Elk saw the young warrior's gaze move restlessly toward the tipi opening. Patience was the one thing he had not been able to instill in Shadowhawk. Although the information he had to give his grandson was dire, Red Elk purposely delayed what he had to say. "The storm came up suddenly and is lasting long," he observed.

Shadowhawk bowed his head in deference to the man he respected above all others. "That is so," he remarked, anxious for his grandfather to say what was on his mind. Shadowhawk's mother had been gravely ill, but she'd been recovering when he'd left for the hunt. Could her health have worsened? he wondered with concern.

Red Elk drew his robe tighter around himself. "There is no warmth in the world for these old bones," he remarked. "Winter will hang on for a time yet. The buffalo have not yet shed their thick winter coats. Your mother, who is never wrong about the weather, predicts summer will come late."

"My mother is right about many things," Shadowhawk stated, puzzled as to why his grandfather had sent an urgent message calling him back from the hunt, yet spoke of trivial things. Shadowhawk had left his warriors just as they had sighted a small herd of buffalo, and he was anxious to return to the hunt.

Red Elk took up his pipe and lit it, letting smoke curl about his head. "The river is frozen, making it necessary to break ice to get water."

"I observed the women doing so when I rode into the village," Shadowhawk replied. Experience had taught him Red Elk would speak his mind only when he was ready.

"The larger buffalo herds will be late in arriving if this weather holds."

Shadowhawk nodded. "That has always been the way of it." His grandmother, Soaring Bird, silently appeared at his side, bringing him a bowl of buffalo stew. Shadowhawk smiled at her and waited for her to depart before taking a bite of the savory meat.

"I feared your mother's fever would take her from us. I thank the Great Spirit she is now well," Red Elk mused.

"My mother is a strong woman," Shadowhawk said, relieved that it was not his mother's health that had caused his grandfather to send for him.

After a long silence Red Elk spoke. "You know Standing Bear's sister, the one who went to the white man's school with your own sister?"

"I know of her."

"The maiden returned yesterday afternoon." The old chief took a puff on his pipe before continuing. "Standing Bear's sister expected to find Moon Song in the village when she arrived."

Shadowhawk frowned. "Why should my sister be here before the other young maidens?"

Red Elk answered his question with another question. "Are you aware that Moon Song is beginning to have visions like your mother?"

Shadowhawk shook his head. "I had not been told that."

"Standing Bear's sister remarked that Moon Song had a dream her mother was grievously ill. Your sister set off from the white man's school without waiting for the warriors who were to escort her home."

Shadowhawk stood slowly. "What can this mean?"

Red Elk's gaze met his. "It means Moon Song met with something she had not expected, or she would be here by now."

Shadowhawk's eyes narrowed. "Why did you not tell me this when I first arrived?"

"You have the impatience of youth. What has happened has happened. Nothing you do now can change that. How you direct your search will reveal the answers."

"Does my mother know?"

The old man nodded. "You should go to her at once and then set out to find my granddaughter. Keep in mind the way Moon Song always traveled to arrive at our winter camp—that is probably the same way she tried to come home. Her path will lead you to the heart of the white man's settlements."

Shadowhawk stared long and hard at his grandfather. "I will send word to you as soon as I have found Moon Song."

The young war chief left abruptly, and Red Elk listened to his grandson's fading footsteps. The old man lowered his head. His grandson despised the white race, and saw the settlers as despoilers of land and water. It was true that since the swelling of the white population the buffalo herds had thinned and moved farther west, and Red Elk did not like the white eyes very much himself. Though he knew they were a threat to his people's way of life, he did not have the animosity toward them that Shadowhawk did.

Soaring Bird came to him and sat at his side. "I fear something has happened to our granddaughter," she said.

"I fear Shadowhawk's anger if his sister has come to harm at the hands of the white eyes."

Shadowhawk ducked inside his mother's tipi, finding her bent over her delicate beadwork.

In the Comanche tribe a warrior was forbidden to speak to his mother after the time of his first vision quest. But it was different with Vision Woman and her son. She was respected by the tribe as a shaman, and was the only woman who had ever been allowed to sit in on council meetings and have her voice heard. Her advice was often sought by those who needed help. There were but few who did not heed her warnings.

The young chief's mother was tall and towered above the other Comanche women. She was comely of face, her dark eyes soft and gentle. At the moment, those eyes held a worried glint.

"You have heard, my son."

"I leave immediately to find my sister."

"The storm will return with force and it will be dangerous for man and beast," she warned.

"Be at peace, my mother. I will bring her home to you."

She placed her hand on his arm. "Moon Song still lives, and I do not feel she is in distress. Look to the white eyes to be sheltering her."

Vision Woman tried to look past the curtain of darkness that hung over her son, but she could see nothing but uncertainty, and that troubled her. "Be very careful, my son, and take one of the warriors with you."

"Running Fox remained in the village. He will come with me."

"A good choice, my son."

A short time later with Running Fox at his side, Shadowhawk rode into the blinding snow, soon to be lost in a world of white.

Chapter Two

Estrella Ranch

A sudden gust of wind struck hard, and Shiloh Braden gripped the reins, steadying her skittish mare. She cast a concerned look at the deepening drifts of snow. The storm had begun that morning when she'd ridden out to help Charley drive the cattle to water in place of her father, who had gone into Antelope Wells for supplies.

Fighting against the strong wind, she finally managed to guide her nervous horse into the shelter of the barn.

Charley, one of the two hands who rode for Estrella Ranch, galloped in behind her, shaking his head as he dismounted. "Unless I'm wrong, Miss Shiloh—which I ain't—this Blue Norther will last all night."

Shiloh had heard old-timers speak of the danger of such storms, but she'd never been in one herself. Unsaddling her horse, she backed the animal into a stall. "I hope Papa decides to stay in town," she said, picking up a bucket to water her horse.

Charley took the bucket from her. "Don't you worry none 'bout the boss. He knows how to take care of himself. You'd best get into the house now and let me finish up here."

Sleet stung Shiloh's cheeks and she shivered with cold, as she hurried up the steps to the porch. The wind was so strong it almost wrenched the doorknob out of her hand. Once inside, she leaned against the door and took in a deep breath.

This storm was bad, and her father might be out there somewhere, unprepared for such severe weather.

Sleet hit the window as Shiloh looked out across the yard at the small, three-room house where the *gran* vaquero, Hernando, lived with his wife, Juanita, and their two young sons. Beyond their cabin stood the bunkhouse. At one time, when Estrella was thriving, twelve men had lived there; now Charley was the lone occupant.

Although the sleet and snow were so heavy she couldn't see very far, Shiloh's troubled gaze searched the road that led to town for any sign of her father.

Trying not to worry, she concentrated on the chores that needed to be done before her father got home. With a last glance toward the road, she moved to the kitchen, tying an apron about her waist. Luke, her fourteen-year-old brother, was seated at the table and cast an expectant look in her direction.

"No sign of Papa yet," she said, attempting to sound cheerful. "Looks like he'll be late." She saw the history book open before Luke. "Did you do your lessons?"

Luke nodded, looking glum. "Except for history. But I did build up the fire, and I put the stew pot on the stove, like you told me to. You sure took your time getting back."

Shiloh smiled to herself. Luke was miffed because he was recovering from a sore throat and she had refused to allow him to ride out with Charley that morning.

She placed her hand on his forehead. "Your fever is gone. You should be able to leave the house tomorrow."

"I'm starved," Luke muttered, staring hopefully at the pot of stew that bubbled on the iron cookstove. He sniffed, taking in the delicious aroma that wafted through the kitchen. "Do we have to wait for Papa? Can't we eat now?"

Shiloh shook her head. "The stew won't be ready until later."

"But I'm hungry."

She placed a bowl in front of him. "There's still some mush left over from breakfast, but you'll have to eat it cold." Lifting a pan from a corner of the hearth, Shiloh scraped the bottom, frowning at the mush that clung to the wooden spoon. With a determined set to her mouth, she tapped it hard, until a thick glob fell into her brother's bowl.

"I don't much like cornmeal mush," Luke stated morosely.

Shiloh sighed, looking into his huge blue eyes. He was tall for his age, with dark hair like their father's, and at the moment, he needed a haircut. "Eat the mush, Luke—it's nourishing."

Luke took a bite and grimaced, then shoved the bowl away. "I'll just have a bit of bread and a cup of milk."

Shiloh reached for the loaf she'd baked the night before and sliced a thick piece for Luke, spreading it with apple butter. She poured him a cup of milk and set it before him, arching her brows. "Satisfied?"

Luke paused with the cup halfway to his mouth. "What if Papa got caught in the storm and can't find his way home?"

"I don't think that's likely to happen." Still, Shiloh wrapped her woolen shawl about her shoulders and headed out the kitchen door. Standing on the wraparound porch, she shivered, pulling her shawl tightly about her, staring into an endless sea of white. Unease stirred within her. The temperature had dropped drastically since she'd gotten home. Before she realized what was happening the wind kicked up, whipping the sleet into a frenzy so thick she could barely make out the barn.

"Still no sign of Papa," Luke said, coming up behind her, buttoning his woolen coat and pulling his cap down over his ears.

"Papa wouldn't want us to worry. He probably decided

to remain in town until the storm passes," Shiloh said encouragingly. She took her brother's arm and pulled him back into the kitchen. "You don't need to be out in this weather."

Luke moved to the window, staring into the storm. Turning, he looked at his sister, and for a moment, she reminded him a little of their mother, with her auburn hair and a sprinkle of freckles across her nose. "Shiloh, do you ever miss Mama?"

"Every day, Luke. We live in the house where she grew up, and I sleep in the bed that belonged to her as a child. I feel her presence in every room."

At the time their mother had inherited Estrella, the family had lived in Williamsburg, Virginia, where their father was a successful attorney. At their mother's pleading, their father had left his practice and moved them to Texas.

After their mother died of typhus, their housekeeper Molly, who had accompanied them from Virginia, suddenly died of the same disease. Out of necessity, Shiloh had taken on Molly's cooking and cleaning chores. It was no secret to anyone that Shiloh would rather be on horseback, helping with the cattle, than cooking. His sister might look delicate but she wasn't. She could ride herd at branding time, toss hay, and chop wood.

Luke looked at Shiloh, seeing her as others might. Even if she was his sister, he thought she was pretty. Her hair was braided and wound about her head, and her eyes were dark blue.

Luke's brow furrowed. "Papa told me he was worried about you because you don't have much of a social life. You never have fun like some of the other girls your age. Papa says we take advantage of you."

Shiloh slid her arms about Luke's shoulders. "I don't

miss anything. I'm happy as long as we are together as a family. That's what I think is important."

"Do you ever wish we hadn't left Virginia?"

"Why would I wish that, Luke? Texas is our home. I sometimes feel like Mama left this place to us as a trust. She loved Estrella."

Luke looked puzzled for a moment. "We had many servants when we lived in Williamsburg. And we only had Molly when we came here. Are we so poor we can't have servants now?"

Shiloh laughed. "Whatever do you mean?"

Luke shrugged. "Don't you want someone to help with the household chores?"

Shiloh ruffled his hair. "Are you volunteering? Maybe you think you're a better cook than me because you put the stew on today."

"Not me! I'm not doing women's work. But you didn't answer my question. Are we poor?"

Frowning, Shiloh tried to think how to answer. "I don't really know, Luke. Papa never discusses finances with me. But we are doing fine without servants." She gave him a devilish smile. "Don't you think my mush has improved?"

Luke, knowing she was teasing him, wrinkled his nose. "Not so much as you could tell it."

With mock sternness, she shook a wooden spoon at him. "Careful what you say or I'll put you on a mush diet and see how you like that."

"Mush seems to be one of the staples in Texas—I know Charley likes it, but Hernando doesn't seem too fond of it."

"Mush and gravy," Shiloh remarked with a sigh. "Most Texans put gravy on every cut of meat they serve."

"Do you remember when Mr. Tyree wanted to buy Estrella?" Luke suddenly asked.

"Of course. And Papa told him the ranch wasn't his to sell—that it belonged to us." Shiloh nodded at the open book on the table. "You need to read the chapter on Roman history, because I'm going to test you on it tomorrow."

"I don't see why I need to know what the Romans did hundreds of years ago," Luke said glumly. "How can that help me now?"

"When you're older Papa expects you to attend William and Mary in Williamsburg like he did. You'll need knowledge in many subjects to be accepted there."

Luke looked troubled. "I don't want to be an attorney like Papa. What good does it do him here in Texas?"

"Silly," Shiloh said affectionately. "Papa wants you to have every advantage, and so do I. A man is often judged by what he knows. Papa wants you to be able to stand toe-to-toe with anyone."

"Charley never went to school and neither did Hernando, and they're doing all right."

"They work for us, Luke. They don't even own the horses they ride."

There was a sharp rap on the back door and Shiloh nodded for Luke to see who it was. "It's probably Papa," she said, feeling a rush of relief.

But it wasn't their father who stood on the doorstep. It was Charley.

The old man stomped his feet to remove the snow before he stepped inside. He snatched off his battered hat and slapped it against his thigh. His grizzled white hair stood on end, and he had so many deep wrinkles, his face looked like an old map; his knuckles were gnarled and his hands callused from hard work.

"I was thinkin' on feedin' the stock, Miss Shiloh, and I figured I'd check on you and young Luke." He closed the door and inched toward the warmth of the hearth. "It's turned mighty cold out there."

Shiloh poured Charley a cup of hot coffee and handed it to him. "I'll feed the stock," she said, needing to keep busy so she would not worry about her father. "You get warm, and then if you don't mind, I'd like you to bring in a load of wood."

"I surely will," he said, casting a glance at the pot of stew on the stove.

Shiloh looked into Charley's soft brown eyes. "What about the cattle in the south pasture—will they survive this storm?"

Charley scratched his head. "Well, I can't rightly say for sure. This storm's worse'n the one we had back in thirty-nine; that one killed hundreds of head in this part of the country."

Luke look worried. "I wish Papa was home right now."

"Well, youngster, don't you fret none 'bout your pa. Likely as not, he put up in town, or he's holed up somewhere until the blizzard's passed." Charley sniffed the air. "That stew surely smells good, Miss Shiloh."

Shiloh took her coat from the coatrack and wrapped her shawl about her head. "Why don't you have supper with us?"

"Why, thank'e kindly. I'd surely like that."

When Shiloh opened the door, the wind almost tore it out of her grasp. Moving down the steps, she sank into snow to the middle of her boots. It was snowing so hard she could barely make out the shape of the barn. Shiloh could not remember a time when she'd felt so cold.

With relief Shiloh hurried inside the barn, slamming the door shut. For a moment she leaned against the door, blowing on her fingers to warm them, and waiting for her eyes to adjust to the darkness. Finally she could see vague outlines, and lit the lantern, hanging it back on a hook.

There were twelve stalls, five of which were occupied. Two of the empty ones were for the red mules her father had driven to town. Stopping at the first stall, she rubbed the ear of the snow white filly her father had given her for her last birthday. She had named the horse Perla, the Spanish word for *pearl*.

As Perla nudged Shiloh's shoulder she reached in her pocket and offered a handful of oats. Giving the horse a final pat, Shiloh took the pitchfork from a hook and began scooping hay and tossing it into the first stall.

A faint sound caught Shiloh's attention and she paused to listen. It was difficult to hear anything with the wind howling, so Shiloh decided it had been her imagination.

Then she heard the sound again. Turning toward the tack room, which was cast in shadows, she decided the noise had come from that direction. Unease tightened in her chest as she raised the pitchfork to use as a weapon. Taking a cautious step toward the darkened corner, she paused and waited.

There. She heard it again.

Waiting for her eyes to adjust to the darkness, Shiloh asked in a trembling voice, "Who's there?"

This time she heard a distinct moan as if someone was in pain. Tossing the pitchfork aside, she snatched up the lantern, holding it high overhead so muted light fell across the scattered hay. Shiloh gasped when she saw a small huddled figure. Placing the lantern on the floor, she went to her knees.

"Who are you?" Shiloh asked. "Are you ill?"

The girl didn't respond; instead she moved her head back and forth as if she were in a lot of pain. Each breath the poor creature took seemed to be an effort. Touching the girl's forehead, Shiloh discovered she was burning with fever.

Standing, she bit her lower lip, trying to think what to do. "Wait just where you are while I go for help." She wasn't sure if the girl heard her. "I can't carry you into the house by myself. Don't worry, I'll be right back."

Quickly hanging the lantern back on the peg, Shiloh dashed out of the barn calling for Charley, who was heading toward the house with an armload of wood.

"I need your help," she cried. "There's a sick girl in the barn!"

Chapter Three

Once in the house, Shiloh removed her coat, tossing it onto a kitchen chair. Pausing at the hearth, she quickly placed a warming stone among the smoldering embers and stoked them into flames. Hurrying into the small bedroom off the kitchen, she folded back the colorful pinwheel quilt that had once belonged to her grandmother.

By the time she returned to the kitchen, Charley was carrying the girl through the back door.

Luke's eyes widened in surprise. "Isn't she an Indian?"

"Yep," Charley said. "Looks like Comanche to me."

"I don't care who she is. We need to get her in a warm bed," Shiloh stated, motioning them forward. "She would have frozen to death if I hadn't found her."

Charley laid the girl on the bed and stepped back, studying her face. "She's Comanch' right enough. Wait and see, she'll bring nothing 'cept trouble. Somebody'll come looking for her, and nobody can track like the Comanch'. Miss Shiloh, you don't want to tangle with those people." He shook his grizzled head. "No-sir-ee, you surely don't."

The poor girl was bundled in a buffalo robe, which Shiloh quickly removed and tossed aside. Her gaze settled on a fringed doeskin dress and knee-high moccasins, and she felt the color drain from her face as she realized Charley was right. "What do you think she was doing in our barn?"

The old man looked speculative. "I'm a-thinking she was hoping to shelter there 'til the storm passes."

Luke stepped closer. "She sure is young. Do you think she's alone?"

"There was no one else in the barn, as far as I could tell," Shiloh said firmly.

"You can't keep her here, Miss Shiloh." Charley pointed to the girl's beaded headband. "Look closely at the markings. She ain't just any Comanche—she's from the family of a chief."

"She's sick, and I refuse to leave her in the barn to freeze," Shiloh stated, removing the Indian girl's wet moccasins.

Charley shook his head. "Nope. I don't 'spect you coulda left her to die." He squinted his eyes. "We're gonna be in a heap of trouble when the Comanch' come lookin' for her, and they will."

Luke stared long and hard at the girl, then moved closer so he could see her face. "What if she dies, Charley?"

"Then we'll still be in a heap of trouble," the old man said with certainty. "Nothing stirs up the Comanche like one of their own in the hands of the white man."

Shiloh looked worried when she touched the girl's forehead. "Luke, put the kettle to boil, and see if the warming stone is hot. Wrap it in a thick towel and bring it to me."

Charley ambled toward the door. "I'll be on the lookout for trouble, 'cause it'll be coming. Let me tell you, when those Comanch' come looking for her, they'll not stop to ask questions."

Shiloh turned to the old man. "You said your piece, Charley, now I'll say mine: the girl stays here until she's well enough to leave on her own."

Luke had been staring at the Indian girl, and Shiloh pushed him toward the door. "Hurry. Get the stone and bring in more quilts."

Charley shook his head, lowering his voice so only the

boy could hear him. "When your sister gets her mind set on something, we'd better just get out of her way."

"You're right about that," Luke agreed as he followed Charley out the door. "But I don't know what Papa will say when he comes home."

Shiloh worked the girl's wet buckskin gown off and dropped it on the floor. It was a bit of a struggle but she finally managed to pull one of her own flannel nightgowns over the girl's head. The poor creature was so cold she was shivering and her teeth were chattering.

Luke returned with a flannel-wrapped heating stone. His features were solemn as he stared down at the girl. "Don't you think she's too young to be wandering about alone?"

Shiloh placed the warming stone at the girl's feet and added two extra quilts. "She is young, and I'd like to know her story. But, Luke, I would like to think if Papa is out there somewhere caught in this storm, some kindhearted person would take him in."

Luke looked uneasy. "I wish Papa was here."

Shiloh gathered her brother close, trying to fight off her own fears. "So do I, Luke."

Snow drifted earthward, and the wind was strong as Shadowhawk motioned for Running Fox to dismount. In the distance they could see the lights of a ranch house.

Gripping his horse's reins, Shadowhawk looked troubled. "My sister would never have allowed herself to be caught out in a snowstorm." As he glanced up at the dark clouds that covered the moon, his concern grew. "I will not give up until I find her."

Both warriors led their horses into a dry wash, alert to everything that went on around them. Although the snow worked to their advantage, because not many men would venture forth in such weather, the two of them were still aware that they were in enemy territory.

"Everything feels wrong to me," Shadowhawk remarked. "My sister is clever and would never put herself in a dangerous situation."

Running Fox turned his attention to his chief, the man he admired above all others. "Then you believe she is dead?"

Shadowhawk took a moment to answer. "Either that, or someone is holding her captive." He thought of his sister's gentle ways, and how everyone in the tribe loved her. He could not bear to think of anyone mistreating her.

Running Fox braced his back against his horse's haunches. "There are three more ranches between here and our village."

Anger rose inside the young chief. "If someone has harmed my sister, I will bring all the power of the Comanche down on them."

Running Fox nodded, knowing how deeply Shadowhawk cared for his sister. "And I will help you."

Chapter Four

Shiloh watched the mantel clock in the parlor as it ticked off the seconds with the slowness of hours. She was waiting and listening for some sign that her father had arrived home.

Around midnight she made her way to the small bedroom off the kitchen to check on the Indian girl; she was still unconscious. The room was cold, and the girl had kicked off the bedcovers. Shiloh rearranged the quilts, then sat down in her mother's rocking chair, pulling a quilt over herself, determined to keep vigil in case the girl needed her. She was so worried about her father, she would not be able to sleep in any case.

Shiloh watched the Indian girl's labored breathing, wishing she could breathe for her. Sometimes the girl's whole body would be racked with coughing spasms. Shiloh manage to spoon a bit of wild honey down her patient's throat, and it seemed to calm her a bit.

Dampening a cloth, Shiloh laid it across the girl's feverish forehead. Her black hair was braided, interwoven with colorful beads. Her skin was the color of honey. With her high cheekbones, she would be considered lovely by any standard.

It was nearing dawn when Luke tapped lightly on the door. "I couldn't sleep for worrying about her. How's she doing?"

Shiloh stretched her stiff muscles and rolled her shoulders. "There's been no change that I can see."

Luke spoke softly. "I never saw an Indian this close before. She looks harmless, don't you think?"

"It's cold, Luke," Shiloh remarked, casting a worried look toward the window, where sleet and snow continued to pepper the glass. "You should go back to bed. I'll let you know if she wakes."

"I can't sleep. I keep worrying about Papa."

Shiloh met her brother's gaze. "I know. Me too. No doubt he'll be home in the morning and expect you to help him unload the supplies, so get your rest."

Luke yawned. "I suppose," he said before trudging off to bed.

For the next few hours Shiloh continued to apply cold cloths to the girl's forehead. Though weary, Shiloh remained at her bedside, doing whatever she could to make her patient more comfortable.

Just before daylight, the girl opened fever-bright eyes and thrashed about, crying out in her language. Shiloh managed to spoon more honey down her throat and she fell asleep once more.

Concern for her father's safety was never far from Shiloh's mind. As the wind intensified, she feared for any poor creature out in such weather.

Shadowhawk glanced at his friend. "This winter promises to be as harsh as the one three years past when food was so scarce," he said.

"The other Comanche tribes lost many people that year," Running Fox agreed, "but your wisdom carried our people through that awful winter."

"Take your rest," Shadowhawk said, staring toward the ranch house. "We leave this place before sunup."

Gathering his buffalo robe tighter about him, Shadowhawk listened to the howling wind. Running Fox had fallen asleep, and Shadowhawk was alone with his troubled thoughts. What if he never found his sister and never knew her fate?

Hearing a sound, he whipped his head to the right, and he watched a wolf slink into the scrub brush. If the storm did not end soon, the wildlife would suffer and many of them would die.

His heart was heavy, and his fear for his sister was growing with each moment that passed without any sign of her.

A shiver ran down his back, and he drew the buffalo robe tighter about him. He had only two more ranches to search, and it was hard not to despair of ever finding Moon Song.

Having fallen asleep in the chair, Shiloh awoke with a start. She slowly stood, stretching her cramped muscles, her gaze going quickly to the Indian girl. Placing her hand on the girl's forehead, Shiloh was relieved to find it a bit cooler, although she was still unconscious.

Stepping quietly to the window, Shiloh opened the curtains a crack, watching the morning sun strain through the heavy cloud cover. It was no longer snowing, but high snowdrifts were piled along the walkway and against the barn.

She closed the curtains and walked purposefully out of the room and through the kitchen. It was possible, she told herself, that her father had come home during the night and she hadn't heard him. She crossed the parlor, heavy trepidation settling on her shoulders as she stopped at the doorway to her father's bedroom. Gripping the handle, she shoved the door open, only to find the room empty.

More worried than ever, Shiloh made her way to the kitchen. She stoked the cookstove before filling the blue galvanized coffeepot with water. After adding more wood to the hearth, she gathered her shawl about her and hurried to the front door.

The sun was hidden by clouds and the wind whipped snow into her face.

Still no sign of her father.

Hearing laughter, Shiloh turned to watch Hernando's two sons making snowballs and lobbing them at each other until their mother's scolding sent them scurrying toward their house.

"Señorita Shiloh," Juanita asked in heavily accented English, "has the *patrón* not returned?"

Even as she answered, Shiloh's gaze went to the road. "Not yet."

"Do not worry. The *patrón* knew he must wait out the storm."

Nodding, Shiloh realized the high snowdrifts would impede her father's progress. She watched Juanita hurry toward her small house, shooing her sons inside.

Leaning her head against the porch post, Shiloh fought the urge to give in to despair. Charley came out of the barn, whistling, and walking in her direction with a milk bucket.

"I thought I'd do the chores for you, Miss Shiloh. It's mighty cold for a young woman to be about."

She took the offered bucket. "Thank you, Charley. Would you like to come in and have breakfast?"

"Thank'e, but I've already et. Thought I'd ride out and have me a look-see 'bout the cattle."

"It would relieve my mind somewhat to know if we lost any during the storm." She caught and held Charley's glance. "What about Papa?"

His gaze quickly swept toward the road. "Ain't no reason to fret none. Most likely he'll be home afore supper."

Anxiety crept into Shiloh's tone. "I hope so, Charley."

"Hernando made it home before the storm got bad last night."

That gave her hope. If Hernando could make it through the storm, then so could her father.

"How's the little Comanche gal?"

"I believe she's a little better."

Charley nodded. "It's best to get her up and gone as fast as you can, Miss Shiloh. Not many folks know this, but I passed a couple of winters with the Comanch' when I was young. Picked up some of their lingo, and got to know their ways. They'll soon come looking for her, and her trail will lead right to Estrella."

"I know that, Charley, but what can we do?"

Shiloh watched Charley shrug his frail shoulders and move away mumbling, his bowlegged gait taking him toward his horse. As he mounted and rode past the barn, she was still thinking about what he'd told her. She had not known he'd lived with the Comanche. But then, Charley never talked much about his past.

She looked once more down the road to town, wishing for the sight of her father's red mules heading home. Hernando called out to her and climbed over the fence of the paddock, heading in her direction.

She hurried toward him. "Did you have any trouble with the storm last night?"

He was a handsome man, his face unlined, with a mustache and long sideburns. His dark hair was only lightly sprinkled with gray. Hernando had been Estrella's *gran* vaquero in her grandfather's day and had raised a family on the ranch. His eldest son, Francisco, was buried on the hill not far from the grave of Shiloh's mother. Hernando had the gallant manners of his Spanish heritage, and his eyes lit up when he smiled. At the moment, he wasn't smiling, and his dark eyes reflected concern.

"Señorita Shiloh, your papa will come home." His questioning gaze met hers. "Yesterday, the *patrón* asked me to ride to the valley to pick up the bull he bought there. I will be gone for five days. Would you rather I wait until he returns?"

She considered for a moment. "If Papa wanted you to get the bull, and if you think the weather permits, you should go."

"Very well. I should be home no later than Sunday."

"Be careful, Hernando. Dress warmly."

When he smiled his dark eyes sparkled. "The cold does not bother me, and I am always careful."

Watching Hernando mount his horse, she was tempted to call him back. If Charley was right about the Comanche, with Hernando leaving, she would be one gun short.

When she saw Luke heading toward the house with an armload of wood, she hurried to hold the kitchen door open for him. While her brother stacked the logs neatly in the wood bin, Shiloh placed the bucket of milk on the table and went into the parlor. Reaching up, she removed the rifle from where it hung over the mantel. Releasing the catch, she looked into the chamber to make sure it was loaded.

It was.

"I fed the animals and gathered the eggs, Shiloh. And guess what?" Luke didn't wait for his sister to guess before he said, "I found the Indian girl's horse behind the barn, so I put the poor animal in a stall and fed it. It must be a hardy breed to have survived the storm."

Shiloh realized the Comanche might be able to track the horse to Estrella, but she didn't see any reason to worry Luke. "I suppose Indian ponies are accustomed to the weather. I don't think they have barns."

Luke came up behind his sister, holding his hands out to warm them over the open fire. "It's a white horse with black markings. Charley said they don't shoe their—" He stopped in midsentence when he saw the rifle. "What are you doing?"

"Just being prepared, Luke," Shiloh said, leaning the rifle against the wall. "Come to the kitchen, and I'll feed you."

Watching Shiloh break eggs into a bowl, Luke grinned. "So you decided not to poison me with more cornmeal mush this morning?"

Shiloh bit down on her trembling lip and managed to smile. "Not today."

"Charley said after he checked on the cattle, he'd ride down the road to see if he can meet up with Papa," Luke said, sitting down at the table.

"He wouldn't do that unless he was worried," Shiloh said thoughtfully. When she saw fear in her brother's eyes, she quickly amended her statement. "Charley probably thinks the wagon got stuck in a snowdrift and Papa needs his help to free it. Now start studying while I finish breakfast."

It was past the noon hour when Moon Song finally opened her eyes. At first she stared at the ceiling, and then blinked her eyes in confusion that quickly turned to fear.

Seated in the rocking chair, Shiloh witnessed the very moment terror crept into the young girl's dark eyes. Trying to rise, the Indian fell back weakly against the pillow.

Shiloh placed her hand on the girl's arm and spoke gently. "I know you can't understand me, but you must not try to get up. You've been very ill."

The girl shoved Shiloh's hand away and tried once more to rise, but the exertion was too much for her and she closed her eyes, breathing deeply.

"You have nothing to fear from me. I found you in our barn and want only to help you."

Dark eyes stared at Shiloh.

Noticing the girl's lips were dry and cracked, Shiloh poured a glass of water and held it to her mouth. At first the Comanche shook her head, refusing to take a drink, but thirst finally won over fear and she reluctantly took a few sips.

"I'll bring you something to eat—you must be hungry."

Shiloh smiled and adjusted the quilt about the girl's shoulders. "Rest for now."

Mistrust was plain in the girl's dark eyes. Shiloh wondered how she'd feel if she woke up in the bed of a stranger who didn't speak her language. "I promise, you are safe here," Shiloh assured her gently.

A short time later Shiloh sat beside the bed, spooning mush into the girl's mouth. "I added a little wild honey to make it more appetizing." Shiloh nodded at the heaping spoon. "Please try a little more."

When the girl clamped her lips together tightly, Shiloh frowned. "This is nourishing, and will help you regain your strength." She held the spoon to her lips and mimed taking a bite. "Like this. Mmm, delicious."

Luke suddenly appeared at the doorway, then came slowly toward the bed. "She's scared, isn't she?"

"It would seem so. I wish there was some way I could convince her we mean her no harm."

Luke nodded at the bowl of mush. "You chose the wrong way to gain her trust. She'll think you're trying to poison her with that concoction."

Shiloh laughed. "Get out of here, you scoundrel. Surely you have chores that will keep you from pestering me."

They both heard the Indian girl make a sound and they turned to find her smiling.

"She must have understood us," Luke said, stepping closer.

Shiloh shook her head. "I don't think so. She just responded to our laughter."

Luke shrugged. "You're probably right. If you need me, I'll be in the barn."

Shiloh nodded, listening to her brother's retreating steps. Turning her attention back to the girl, she held the spoon out and the girl took a small bite.

When Shiloh was satisfied the girl had eaten enough,

she watched her close her eyes and drift into a peaceful sleep. With a weary sigh, Shiloh rose and left the room.

A short time later Luke rushed into the house, finding his sister in the kitchen. "Charley didn't find Papa on the road, so he's going to ride farther out. I'm going with him."

"Dress warmly," Shiloh responded worriedly. "The wind is still sharp, and you're just getting well."

Luke grabbed his heavy coat from the coatrack and hurried outside to join Charley.

A short time later Shiloh returned to check in on her patient and found her still sleeping. Standing by the window staring at the clear blue sky, she noticed the snow was melting.

"Oh, Papa, please be safe," she said softly.

"You are worried."

Shiloh's eyes widened with shock as she whirled around to look at the Indian girl. "You understand our language?"

"I understand you are concerned about your father," the girl said in near-perfect English. Her dark eyes were filled with sympathy; the hand that rested on the quilt trembled. "Perhaps your father was caught in the same storm I was."

Shiloh dropped down in the rocking chair. "Where did you learn to speak English?"

"My mother taught me many words. Then Mrs. Samuelson, the wife of the missionary, was my teacher."

"Did you attend the Samuelsons' school in Antelope Wells?"

The young Indian girl nodded.

"My name is Shiloh. My brother is Luke. What is your name?"

"Most white people cannot pronounce my name. It translates to Moon Song. That is what Mr. and Mrs. Samuelson call me."

Shiloh frowned. "You are aware you have been very ill, and are still far from well, Moon Song?"

"I must go home." Moon Song lowered her dark eyes. "My mother may be dying." When the Indian girl looked at Shiloh, tears shimmered in her eyes. "I must get back to my village."

Shiloh took one of Moon Song's hands in hers. "I lost my own mother when I was about your age. And now my father . . ." Shiloh shook her head. "Your family must be worried about you by now."

"Even now, my brother will be searching for me." Moon Song lifted dark eyes to Shiloh. "I left the school without permission when I learned my mother was ill. My brother will be angry with me because I disobeyed his orders."

The thought that Moon Song's Indian brother would come looking for her, and that he would be angry, filled Shiloh with dread.

"How old are you, Moon Song?"

"This year I will have seen twelve summers."

"So young. You should never have been out alone."

Moon Song lowered her head. "I had to try to get home."

It was midafternoon when Luke and Charley returned. As they rode toward the house, Shiloh pulled the lace curtains aside and watched Charley dismount and lead the horses to the barn, while Luke came toward the house, his footsteps heavy.

Shiloh met him at the door, her gaze sweeping his face. "You found no sign of Papa?"

"We rode as far as the Hellman place, and saw nothing. Charley is going to change mounts and ride into town and find out when Papa headed home."

Shiloh looked into her brother's eyes. "Papa wouldn't linger in town knowing we would be worried about him."

Luke lowered his head. "I know."

Shiloh reached for her shawl and hurried out of the house. The sky had darkened once more and her heart shuddered with apprehension. As she stepped off the porch her shoes sank in the slushy snow, and she felt chilled to the bone. Once inside the barn, Shiloh found Charley saddling a fresh horse.

"Do you think there is any hope?"

"Missy, there is always hope." He yanked on the cinch, drawing it tight. "Don't you go getting in a fret 'til we know what's what. I'll be back 'afore midnight."

Shiloh placed her hand on his arm. "There is another storm gathering and I don't want to worry about you. Unless you meet Papa on the road, remain in town tonight."

He pushed the bit between the horse's teeth and pulled the reins over its neck. "I'll see you when I see you."

Shiloh watched him mount up and ride out of the barn. Feeling a chill wind stirring, she shivered. Glancing up at the darkened sky, she estimated the storm would strike before sunset.

Shiloh fed and watered the stock, giving the Indian pony an extra pitchfork full of hay. By the time she headed toward the house, a bone-chilling wind had struck.

Now she had Charley to worry about as well as her father.

By nightfall, wind and snow slammed against the windows. Shiloh sat beside Moon Song while the girl ate a buttered biscuit. She had many questions to put to her guest, but didn't want to tire her.

"Your father has not returned?" Moon Song asked.

"Not yet." Shiloh glanced down at her hands, which were clasped in her lap. "I'm worried, but I don't want my brother to know."

"I have prayed to God that He will see your father safely home."

Shiloh looked into soft dark eyes filled with compassion. This girl did not fit what she had been told about the Comanche. "You pray to our God?"

"I have discovered your God is not so different from ours. I believe He led me to you and your brother when I was lost in the snowstorm. Perhaps God has led your father to a kind family who took him in."

"I hope so." Shiloh was fascinated by Moon Song's insight and compassion. "Tell me more about yourself."

Moon Song smiled. "I have been attending the missionary school for three years. I go home in the summer to be with my family. My mother insisted I attend the school."

"And all your family approved?"

"Not at first. My mother convinced my grandfather it was a wise decision. Then he convinced my brother." She paused to reflect. "My brother would never go against my grandfather's advice."

"Is this the same brother who will be angry when he sees you?"

"My brother is to be obeyed in all things."

"Why is that?"

"He is head chief."

"Why did your mother want you to attend the mission school?"

"My mother is from the Blackfoot tribe. Her people have been at peace with your race for years. She says the Blackfoot learned long ago if they understood the white race, there would be far less conflict between us."

Wishing she had a mother to advise her, Shiloh felt a lump in her throat. "There is much wisdom in what your mother says."

Moon Song sighed. "And there will be much anger in my brother when he finds me."

Chapter Five

Shiloh scraped ice crystals off the inside of the window so she could see out. With relief she saw the dark storm clouds had moved away and a weak sun was straining through tattered clouds.

Still her father had not come home.

Luke banged the front door shut and Shiloh heard his footsteps as he hurried into the kitchen.

"Charley's coming! He's got two men with him and they're leading a packhorse."

Shiloh was at the kitchen table kneading bread dough. Quickly wiping her hands on a cloth, she removed her apron and draped it over a chair. "Is Papa with them?"

Luke shook his head. "I didn't see Papa, or our wagon."

They both rushed outside, waiting on the porch for the men to approach. When they were close enough for Shiloh to make out their features, she didn't recognize the two men with Charley.

Fear tugged at Shiloh's mind as she watched the men solemnly dismount. It didn't escape her notice that Charley looked grim, and she felt her heart lurch when he finally looked at her and she saw distress in his eyes.

Shiloh's gaze flew to the other two men. The one who respectfully snatched his hat off his head was tall and lanky, and appeared to be in his forties. The second man was younger, perhaps in his late twenties. He was taller than his companion, and walked with a long gait as he headed toward her and Luke.

The younger man paused on the bottom of the steps, his blue gaze fixed on Shiloh before it shifted to Luke. When he removed his hat, his coffee-colored hair tumbled about his rugged face. At that moment the wind whipped the flap of his coat open, and Shiloh saw the Texas Ranger badge pinned to his vest.

Charley's gaze quickly slid to the tip of his worn boots rather than looking at Shiloh or Luke. "This here's Captain Clint Gunther and Corporal Earl Briggs of the Rangers. Captain Gunther's got something he wants to tell you."

One look into the Ranger's face quelled any hope Shiloh had that her father was still alive. Although she didn't want to believe it, she saw the truth in Captain Gunther's eyes.

Gunther looked as if he'd rather be anywhere than where he was at the moment. "Ma'am, Luke—" He paused as if he were weighing his words. "It saddens me to have to be the one to tell you your pa's dead."

Wrenching pain tore through Shiloh and she felt as if a black cloud had gathered around her. Her gaze flew to the packhorse with the realization that the tarp covered her father's dead body. Her hand went to her mouth and she shook her head, not wanting to believe what she knew to be true.

"Please, not my father!"

The Ranger was still finding it difficult to meet her gaze. "Miss Braden, Luke Braden, there's no easy way to say this: me and Earl came upon your pa early this morning, and that's when we met up with Charley here."

Shiloh hurried down the porch steps with the intention of going to the packhorse when Captain Gunther caught her hand, dragging her against him to restrain her.

"Ma'am, you don't want to see him until we've prepared the body. And maybe not even then."

She laid her head against his rough coat, closing her eyes. "I need to see him. So does my brother."

"No, ma'am, you don't. Not yet." Gunther enfolded her in his arms, trying to ease her pain.

Heartbroken, Shiloh wrenched her body away from the Ranger and hurried to Luke. Grabbing her brother in her arms, she held him close. She felt him tremble, and it took all her strength to keep from crying. Her throat burned with sobs that were building deep inside, but she couldn't give in to grief—she needed to be strong for Luke.

Still, unwelcome tears flooded her eyes and she wiped them away with the pad of her hand. "I guess we knew all along it had to be something bad that kept Papa from coming home to us."

Luke laid his head against Shiloh's shoulder and gripped her about the waist, his tears soaking her gown. "I hoped Papa was only delayed because of the weather."

Shiloh was consumed by grief, but she had questions that needed to be answered. "Where did you find . . . our father's body?"

Gunther nervously twisted his hat in his hands, apparently affected by their grief. "We located his body . . . about four miles from here. The wagon had been pulled into a gully, so you wouldn't have seen it from the road. The mules were cut loose—there was no sign of them."

Tears swam in Shiloh's eyes. "How did he die?"

"He . . . it appears your pa was attacked by Indians. We took an arrow out of his back." He hesitated. "And he was scalped."

Shiloh felt the world spinning and reached out to clutch the porch post to steady herself. She felt strong hands span her waist and Captain Gunther turned her toward the door. "Lean on me, ma'am. You've had a shock."

Shiloh allowed him to lead her into the parlor, where

she dropped down onto a chair, while Luke followed, sitting close beside her.

Gunther watched Shiloh carefully. "You aren't going to faint on me, are you, ma'am?"

She shook her head. "I don't think so."

"I'm right sorry to be the bearer of such sad news for you and the boy. I'm . . . real sorry."

Gripping Luke's trembling hand in hers, Shiloh tried to think what they would do without their father to guide them. He had been her strength, and she had always felt as if nothing bad would happen to the family as long as he was watching over them.

An awkward Charley knelt beside Luke to comfort him, so Shiloh stood and moved into the kitchen, while Gunther followed, watching her with concern. She floured her hands and began kneading the bread dough she had left when the men had arrived.

Unconscious of what she was doing, Shiloh slammed her fist hard into the dough, motivated by the need to hit something. Then rolling the dough with a wooden roller that her father had carved for her mother, Shiloh tore off bits and shaped them into biscuits, placing them into a buttered pan.

Captain Gunther watched her closely, his eyes filled with pity. "Miss Braden, maybe you should go lie down for a bit—you look mighty pale. Can I get you anything?"

"Thank you, no. I'm just—" She lowered her voice and nodded at her brother, who had just entered the kitchen. "You must see I have to be strong for Luke. I can't give in to grief—not yet."

The Ranger nodded. "I sent one of my men to tell the neighbors. Some of them should be arriving at any time, so you and the boy won't have to face this alone." Again he twisted his hat. "I'll set Earl to digging the grave, if you'll tell me where you want . . . him to dig."

Shiloh raised her head, staring at the overhead beams, trying to understand what must be done. The pain was too new, the ache too deep for her to sort out her thoughts. She expected her father to walk through the door at any moment, proving these men wrong. But reality hit her hard—her father would not be coming back. She swallowed several times before she spoke.

"First, I want Papa dressed in his best suit," Shiloh said in a voice that trembled. "Luke and I never thought we'd have to—" She met the Ranger's gaze, trying to tell him what he needed to know, but hardly knowing herself. "My mother is buried on the rise at the back of the barn. Papa would want to be buried beside her. There is a tall cottonwood tree that shades the grave in the summer." She wiped away tears, smearing flour on her cheeks. "In springtime it's covered with wildflowers."

Captain Gunther took a cup towel and wiped her cheek. "Put your mind to rest, ma'am," he said kindly. "We'll see to it for you."

Shiloh saw pity in the captain's blue eyes and she wanted more than anything for him to hold her while she cried out her grief. Without knowing she was doing so, she took a step in his direction and soon found herself clasped in strong arms.

Gunther let her cry, patting her shoulder. "Now, now, miss. You just cry it all out."

Neighbors had been arriving all morning. They came laden with food and heartfelt sympathy. The women gathered about Shiloh, while the men stood in a tight group debating why the Indians would be on a raid so early in the year. Luke moved among them as if he were in a daze. Captain Gunther had advised Shiloh not to mention the Indian girl she had rescued to anyone, and she and Luke agreed it was good advice.

All Shiloh could think about was how much her father would have enjoyed visiting with all the neighbors who had gathered in their home.

It was a chilly afternoon as they congregated around the grave. Shiloh gripped Luke's hand and they bowed their heads while Mr. Samuelson spoke words that were meant to comfort. His platitudes did nothing to help the pain Shiloh felt. Luke stood beside her stoically, and she drew him closer, tears filling her eyes.

This bleak hard land yielded no comfort as the cold wind whipped snow across the hillside. There were no flowers to place on the mound of frozen earth. It flashed through Shiloh's mind that she would need to have the stonecutter in town carve a monument for her father.

After the service they all trudged back to the house. In her haze of grief Shiloh managed to make the right responses when neighbors voiced their sympathy and offers of assistance.

Mrs. Greely, an elderly woman who lived with her son and daughter eight miles from Estrella, took Shiloh's hand. "The good Lord knows these are hard times for you and your brother. But you have strength in you, Shiloh Braden, you'll get through it. I buried a husband and two sons here in Texas. But if you've got the gumption to ride it out, you won't be sorry."

"They can't ride this out," disagreed Mrs. McNair, the banker's wife. "They're too young to survive without help." The woman's eyes were small and black as she pursed her small mouth when she looked at Shiloh. "You've got to sell and move into town."

All Shiloh could manage was a weak smile. "That is a choice my brother and I will make."

Mr. and Mrs. Curruthers, the storekeepers in Antelope Wells, expressed their sadness, and explained to Shiloh how they had tried to prevent her father from leaving town. Not knowing what to say, Shiloh could do no more than stare back at them. It did not escape her notice that their neighbor, Mr. Tyree, stood alone. She wasn't sure whether he didn't want to socialize with the others, or whether they were snubbing him.

She didn't much care.

Most of the neighbors had already taken their leave when Surge Tyree approached Shiloh and Luke. Instead of offering his condolences as the others had, he swept Shiloh's face with a bold gaze that shocked her. Although the man could be considered handsome, something about him had always repelled her. He was somewhere in his fifties, with brown hair that was free of gray except at his temples. He was a bit stocky and not very tall, but it was impossible to ignore him.

Tyree brushed up against Shiloh, and she quickly stepped back.

"I'll give you time to grieve, little gal, before I come back with an offer to buy Estrella."

Luke stepped between Tyree and his sister. "Don't come back, if that's your reason. Papa wouldn't sell to you, and neither will we. You aren't welcome here, Mr. Tyree."

Tyree stared long and hard at the boy. "You'll be glad for my offer before too many weeks pass. Mrs. McNair was right about one thing, you're both too young to run this place alone. Your father was no good as a rancher; do you two think you can do any better?"

There was a chill to Shiloh's voice. "My brother meant what he said. You are not welcome here. Good day, Mr. Tyree."

The boss of the Crooked H took an exasperated breath before pushing past them and stomping toward the door, slamming it behind him.

Luke moved off to talk to Charley, and Shiloh stood in the middle of the parlor, not knowing what to do next.

"How are you holding up?" Captain Gunther asked, as he took her arm and steered her to a chair.

"I'm not sure," she answered with fresh tears swimming in her eyes.

"I overheard Surge Tyree. Pay no mind to him. He won't be satisfied until he owns all the land within a hundred miles."

Her eyes narrowed in concentration. "My father didn't trust him."

"Neither do I. The Rangers suspect Tyree is operating outside the law, but we haven't been able to catch him at it. Yet."

Shiloh was grateful for Captain Gunther's comforting presence. She glanced at the window, watching the sun sink low in the west. She and Luke had gotten through this day.

How would they get through tomorrow and all the days after without their father to guide them?

Shiloh found Moon Song asleep. Placing a tray of food within reach should the girl awake hungry, she tiptoed out of the room.

When she returned to the kitchen she found Captain Gunther and Corporal Briggs had gathered around the table with Charley, waiting for her.

"We need to talk," Captain Gunther said.

"Yeah," Corporal Briggs agreed, motioning for Luke to join them. "We need to know everything about that little Indian gal you've took in."

"Miss Shiloh and Luke's got enough trouble without you two stirring up the Comanche," Charley said firmly. "They surely do."

Shiloh saw the worried expression on her brother's face and decided to delay talking about Moon Song until later. "We'll discuss her after we've eaten," she said, reaching for a bowl of mashed potatoes, and scooping a heaping spoon-ful onto Luke's plate.

Captain Gunther frowned, wanting to argue the point, but he caught Charley's warning gaze and changed his mind.

The subject could wait until after they had eaten.

Chapter Six

Ranger Briggs speared a chicken leg with his fork and placed it on a plate that was already heaped with food that the thoughtful neighbors had provided. "You'd best eat something, Miss Braden," the Ranger advised. "Young Luke here says you haven't ate anything all day."

"I'm not hungry," she said, pushing a slice of chicken around the plate with her fork. Her gaze slid to Luke as he scooped a forkful of corn into his mouth. Charley seemed to be relishing a biscuit dripping with butter. "I couldn't swallow a bite."

"How about a piece of peach pie?" Captain Gunther said, shoving her plate away and placing a slice of pie before her.

Reluctantly she took a bite, but it stuck in her throat. How could she eat when her father would never taste food again? Laying her fork beside her plate, Shiloh shook her head. "I'm sorry. I can't."

Captain Gunther cleared his voice. "That's all right. You'll eat when you feel up to it."

Luke looked at his sister, guilt written on his face. He put his fork down. "I don't guess I want anything either."

"You must eat," Shiloh urged him. Then she said more firmly, "Being the man of the family, you'll need your strength. I'm going to depend on you to . . . to . . . take Papa's place."

After a long silence, Captain Gunther spoke. "Miss Braden, Luke, we need to talk. Me and Earl think it's best if the two of you move into town until you decide about your future. If you like, we'll stay and help you pack up your belongings. It isn't safe for you to stay here."

Shiloh absorbed the Ranger's words. "My brother and I have not yet decided what we are going to do. After we've talked, I'll let you know our plans."

Captain Gunther frowned. "Let me impress upon you the danger of remaining here without a man to protect you. To be sure, you have Charley and Hernando to help out. But Charley, here, would be the first one to tell you, the two of them can't protect you if the Indians decide to raid your place. What happened to your father might just be the beginning of Indian trouble."

Suddenly Shiloh shot to her feet. For all she knew it could have been the Comanche who'd killed her father. She thought of Moon Song and anger boiled inside her. "Do you think this has anything to do with the Indian girl staying under our roof?"

"I don't know," Gunther replied. "Who can say?"

"Excuse me," Shiloh said, acting on her anger. She pushed her chair back from the table and stood. "I'm going to talk to her."

"I'd like to ask that gal a few questions myself," Gunther said, standing. "Luke said she could speak English."

"I can't allow you to do that; you might scare her, and she is only twelve years old. I'll ask her what needs to be asked."

Shiloh stormed out of the kitchen to find Moon Song sitting up in bed, the plate of food on her lap.

Moon Song looked at Shiloh sadly. "Your brother told me they found your father. I weep for your sorrow."

Shiloh shook her head. "I don't want your pity. I just want you out of my father's house as soon as possible!"

Tears crept into Moon Song's eyes. "I will leave now if you wish," she said with great dignity.

Shiloh examined the girl's tear-bright eyes and felt remorse. Moon Song was so young and she had been so ill. "Not until you're well enough to travel. Maybe you'll understand my anger when I tell you my father was killed by an arrow, and then scalped."

Moon Song's hand went to her throat. "And you think it was one of my people who killed him?"

"What do you think?" Shiloh demanded.

Moon Song lowered her head. "It is possible," she admitted. "I long for the day when there will be peace between our people. Mr. Samuelson says it will happen in time." She raised her gaze to Shiloh. "What did the arrow look like?"

"I don't know. What difference can it make?"

Moon Song reached out to Shiloh. "Would you find out about the markings? It is important to me to know who did this to your father."

"How can you know that?"

"Each tribe has its own markings and so does each warrior. I will know if it is Comanche."

"I'll ask Captain Gunther," Shiloh remarked, turning away and stalking out of the room. She had taken Moon Song in and nursed her, saving her life. Now she just wanted her gone.

The men had moved into the parlor, and Captain Gunther was speaking quietly to Luke. He glanced up when Shiloh approached.

"I was just telling your brother, Miss Braden, that if it's all right with you, we'll bed down here tonight."

Shiloh felt a rush of relief. "Of course it's all right. I'll have Charley carry quilts and pillows to the bunkhouse, Captain."

"Then it's settled," Gunther said.

"Captain Gunther, there is one thing I would like to ask you. Do you still have the arrow that . . . killed our father?"

"Of course. I kept it for evidence. I don't think you need to see it, though, Miss Braden."

"Is it a Comanche arrow?" She waited tensely for him to answer.

"You know, I've just been thinking on that, and I don't believe so. If I was to speak what I feel, I'd say it has Kiowa markings. And that's a fact I find troubling."

"Why troubling?" Shiloh asked.

"The Kiowa fear the might of the Comanche. They don't usually raid this deep into Comanche territory."

Shiloh didn't realize she'd been holding her breath. "Thank you, Captain." Her gaze met her brother's. "Luke and I are glad to hear that."

"That doesn't diminish the danger you'll face when the Comanche come calling. Tell me everything you know about the Indian girl."

"She attends the missionary school in Antelope Wells."

"Even so, she could be a danger to you, Miss Braden."

"Now that I know it wasn't her tribe who—" Shiloh broke off. "I'm not afraid of having her here, Captain."

"It's not her that worries me, Miss Braden. The Comanche are dedicated to family—they will go to any length to recover one of their own. Don't you doubt it for a minute."

"Moon Song is not going anywhere until she is well."

Captain Gunther's sun-browned face turned pale. "Say her name again."

Shiloh felt a prickle of uneasiness, and exchanged glances with her brother. "Moon Song."

Gunther turned to Briggs. "Ain't that the name of Shadowhawk's sister?"

"I believe it is, sir."

Turning back to Shiloh, Gunther shook his head. "Whether you like it or not, I have to question the girl at once. If she's who I think she is, you've got real trouble." He started out of the room, but Shiloh called him back.

"I don't want you upsetting her."

"Miss Braden, you and your brother remain here. I'll just stand in the doorway of her room and ask her if Shadowhawk's her brother. There's no harm in that."

Moments later Captain Gunther came back to the parlor. "No doubt about it—she's Shadowhawk's sister all right."

Luke moved closer to Shiloh. "Who is Shadowhawk, sir?"

"No one knows much about him, except he's a young buck as ruthless as they come. Since he became war chief, most of the other tribes have all but abandoned this part of Texas. Believe me when I tell you, Miss Braden, you do not want to meet up with him. Why don't I take the girl back to the missionary school in the morning?"

"There's another storm coming, and if you take her out in this weather, it will be hard on her. What do you say, Luke?" she asked, trying to include him in her decision. "Does Moon Song go or stay?"

The young boy didn't hesitate. "It seems to me she's too sick to leave her bed, and definitely too sick to leave the house. Wouldn't this Shadowhawk be angrier if we let her die?"

Captain Gunther looked disapproving. "I think you're both making a mistake, but I can't force you to send the Indian gal away. Shadowhawk's most likely looking for his sister right now. I'd like you two to move into town until this Indian trouble is settled."

So much had happened in the last few days that Shiloh was incapable of making any life-changing decision until she had time to think about it. "My brother and I will decide tonight and give you our answer in the morning."

Luke touched the Ranger's sleeve. "Can you tell me more about Shadowhawk?"

"No one knows much about him, son. Some say he's myth, and some say he's real. I think he's real, 'cause something has sure scared the other tribes away from this area."

Shiloh felt a shiver dance down her spine. What kind of man was this Shadowhawk?

Chapter Seven

The three men sat around the potbellied stove that stood in the middle of the bunkhouse, each lost in his own thoughts.

Charley was the first to speak. "I don't 'spect you'll get them to move to town."

"Ain't they got no family they could move in with?" Briggs asked.

"None 'cepting an old maid aunt, lives back in Virginia, that they've never met—leastwise that's what the boy once told me."

"Miss Shiloh is a pretty little gal. What's her life gonna be like without her father to protect her?" Briggs speculated. "I watched her struggling today, trying to be strong for the boy. They can't make it out here by themselves, Charley. You know they can't."

"You may think that's the way of it," the older man said, rubbing the bridge of his nose. "But this here family's known hard times afore, and they've worked their way through 'em."

"But, Charley," Briggs stated, "that was when their pa was alive. They wouldn't even last through spring without a man to look after them."

Captain Gunther had been lost in his thoughts, remembering misty blue eyes that had struck him to the heart. Shiloh Braden had stirred something to life within him, something he'd only felt once before. He'd cared for a woman up Austin way, but because he didn't make enough money on a Ranger's pay, she'd married a rancher down in Nacogdoches.

With Shiloh Braden, he'd be willing to give up being a Ranger and settle down. She brought out the protectiveness in him, but he didn't want to figure out why. Not yet—he'd scare her if he admitted how he felt about her after such a short acquaintance. "Miss Braden will do the wise thing," he said with assurance. "She'll do what's best for her brother, and what's best for him is moving into town." He was thoughtful for a moment. "'Course we don't want them to lose Estrella. It sets on the best land around this part of Texas."

Briggs shifted in his chair, grinning at his boss. "I saw right away you were taken with her, Captain. You can't deny you was."

Gunther stood, walking to the window and staring at the lights shining from the ranch house. "Yeah. I like her. At the moment, Miss Shiloh Braden's alone, with no one to turn to. But she's a fighter—I like that about her."

"And it don't hurt none that she's the prettiest gal you ever did see," Briggs remarked, smothering a grin.

Gunther turned back to his subordinate, fixing him with a dark look, but his words were for Charley. "What's the story on Shadowhawk's sister?"

Charley explained to the Ranger how Moon Song had come to be in the Bradens' home, and how Shiloh had insisted on taking care of her, although he had cautioned against it.

"When dealing with a Comanche, kindness will only bring trouble in the end," Briggs said, adding his views. "Yes-sir-ee, nothing but trouble."

Charley rubbed his rheumatic hands down the legs of his trousers. "I said as much to Miss Shiloh, but she done it anyway."

The captain set his chin in a firm line. "They've not

only got the Comanche and their pa's death to contend with, but Tyree will soon come calling. I saw him talking to them today—he won't wait long before he tries to make them sell Estrella."

Charley rocked back on his chair, staring into space. "I've been studying on the arrow that kil't Mr. Braden. I ain't so sure it was Kiowa." He glanced at Gunther. "Like you pointed out, this is too far west for Kiowa."

Captain Gunther studied the old man, amazed that they had both come to the same conclusion. He'd heard that when Charley was young he'd spent a few years living with the Comanche. He didn't know if it was true, because the old man never spoke of it. "I've been turning that over in my mind as well. I asked myself who has the most to gain by Braden's death. And do you know whose name comes to mind?"

"Tyree!" Charley interjected, nodding his head. "That man's lower than dirt," Charley added.

"Of course, we're only speculating here," Gunther said flatly "At this point we can't prove anything. But I'll be paying Tyree a visit and asking him questions all the same."

Briggs nodded in agreement. "Good idea."

Gunther glanced back at the ranch house, which was now dark. "She can't win against Tyree. This one night is all we can stay, Briggs. In the morning we have to head on up to Val Verde."

The night sky shimmered with stars as the two Comanche rode up a rise that overlooked a ranch house and several outbuildings.

Shadowhawk dismounted and dropped to his knees, his eyes focused on the barn. Then his gaze flickered to the bunkhouse. He motioned for Running Fox to keep the horses quiet when a man came out of the bunkhouse, lit a cigar, and stood gazing at the ranch house. With no cloud cover, it was easy to see the moonlight reflecting off a shiny badge.

Shadowhawk's mood darkened. "A Ranger," he said with contempt.

He focused on a second man who had just come out of the bunkhouse. Another Ranger. "Why are they here?" he wondered aloud.

Motioning for his companion to lead the horses down the embankment so they would not be seen, Shadowhawk waited until a cloud covered the moon before he inched forward. Cautiously, he approached the barn, grasped the handle, and eased the door open, moving silently inside the dark interior.

Shadowhawk paused until his eyes adjusted to the darkness. He had been taught to rely on his other senses when he could not see. Shadowhawk heard horses stomping their hooves, and he surmised there were several of them, one of which was unshod. Understanding the implication, he felt as if a dagger had pierced his heart.

Silently, he crept toward the fourth stall, opened the gate, and gripped the horse's mane. Glancing upward to the small opening in the hayloft, he waited for the moon to emerge from the cloud bank. He had to be certain it was his sister's horse. Soon he was rewarded by a sliver of light that swept away the darkness.

Shadowhawk recognized the horse he'd given his sister during her last visit to the village. He laid his head against the horse's sleek neck, almost sure Moon Song was dead. Why else would her horse be stabled at the white man's ranch?

After a while, he turned to leave, but he heard someone approaching. Softly closing the stall gate, he ducked behind Moon Song's pony, waiting. The barn door creaked open and he watched a Mexican man unsaddle his horse and toss his saddle across the stall partition.

After the man fed and watered the horse, he left. Shadowhawk made his way out of the barn and up the hill, where Running Fox waited for him.

"I do not know if Moon Song is here, but her horse is in that barn. It would be unwise to attack with the Rangers on guard." His dark gaze swept the area. "I am forced to wait until they leave."

Running Fox stood. "There are horse tracks and many wagons tracks that show people have recently come to this house and departed." Shadowhawk's companion lowered his head. "I discovered a fresh grave on the small rise."

Shadowhawk fought the urge to rush into that house and demand to know what had happened to his sister.

That would be unwise.

His grandfather had always warned Shadowhawk that his spirit was too restless. And Red Elk was right. It had been hard for Shadowhawk to learn to be patient, and he was not certain he had even now. He gazed up at the moon, hoping his sister was still alive. "We will remain here tonight and watch the house."

Running Fox had been friends with Shadowhawk since boyhood. They had trained together to become warriors. Like others of the tribe, he had learned to trust Shadowhawk's instincts. "I will not leave your side until Moon Song is found. I will take the first watch. You sleep."

Shadowhawk nodded, as weariness weighed heavily on him. "Observe everything. Be alert at all times. Wake me when the moon is full in the sky."

"You have not slept in two nights."

"I will sleep when I find my sister."

Running Fox nodded. "I believe you will find her alive."

The young chief disagreed with a shake of his head.

"How can my sister be safe if she is among the white eyes?"

"Because Vision Woman thinks she is safe."

Shadowhawk spread his blanket and lay on the hard ground. "Tomorrow night, even if the Rangers are still there, I will get closer to the house. The ones who dwell there will know my anger if they have harmed my sister. I saw a woman and a boy, but I could not tell much about them from such a distance. It could be that they belong to one of the Rangers."

"I do not think so," Running Fox said skeptically. "Otherwise the Rangers would sleep in the house instead of bunking with the old man."

Shadowhawk glared at his friend. "I do not know how the people fit together, and I do not care. I only need to know what I will come up against before I act."

Running Fox grinned. "Then this is a new Shadowhawk. When we were boys, you acted first and asked questions later."

"Before the sun rises in the morning, I shall venture into the barn. You will wait here for me."

Running Fox yawned and shook his head to clear away the need to sleep. "It will be as you say."

Chapter Eight

Later that night, when Shiloh was sure her brother was asleep, she gathered her shawl about her and quietly left the house. The weather had warmed enough to melt the snow, but she hardly noticed as she trudged up the hillside.

Once Shiloh reached her father's grave, she bent down on her knees, feeling the night chill reach all the way to her heart. She grasped a handful of newly turned earth and squeezed it in desperation. Shiloh felt desperately alone.

There was nowhere she could turn for the answers she needed—her father could not help her now. Bowing her head, she cried as she prayed for divine guidance. After a while, she stood and made her way back down the hill toward the house, never knowing that two fierce Comanche warriors had observed all her movements.

When Shiloh reached the house, Captain Gunther was leaning against the porch railing, his arms crossed over his chest. "I saw you go to your pa's grave, so I waited here for you."

A sob tore from her throat. "I can't seem to give up my father, not even to death."

Gunther drew her into the shelter of his arms. "Miss Shiloh, you shouldn't be out here in the cold."

"I . . . wanted so badly to know what Papa would expect us to do. But he can't help us now," she said, placing her head on the Ranger's shoulder.

"What have you and Luke decided to do about Estrella?" Although she felt comforted by Captain Gunther, she moved out of his arms. "We are going to stay . . . if we can."

He was quiet for a moment, as if he were weighing her words. "I must be leaving tomorrow. I want you to be aware of the danger you face without your pa to protect you. Mrs. Curruthers, in Antelope Wells, is a nice lady, and I know she'd agree to take you and Luke in for a while."

"Captain Gunther, I appreciate your concern, and I can never thank you and Corporal Briggs enough for your help. But Luke is all I have now, and I must consider his wishes. He wants to stay here, so that is what we're going to do."

Gunther saw her shiver and removed his coat, placing it about her shoulders. "That's not wise—you know it's not."

Shiloh stared into the distance. "Of course I know that. But Luke just lost his father. I'm not going to take Estrella away from him too."

Hearing the conviction in her tone, Gunther was quiet for a moment. "Is there nothing I can say to change your mind?"

"No, Captain, there isn't. We're the third generation of this family to own Estrella. And that means something to us."

"If that's how you feel, I'll say no more at this time. Briggs and I will be leaving before sunup. I want you to remember, if you need my help, just send Charley to fetch me—I'll come to you as fast as I can."

She removed his coat and handed it back to him. "I'll take comfort in that, Captain Gunther."

When she would have turned away, he caught her hand. "Could you call me Gunther? Most folks do; most certainly my friends do."

"Gunther." She felt a prickle of sadness that he would be leaving. "I do consider you a friend. I feel safe with you and Corporal Briggs nearby. Luke and I don't want the two of you to disappear from our lives. You'll always find a welcome on Estrella."

His voice was deep with feeling. "I will check in on you and your brother from time to time."

Shiloh's hand slid out of Gunther's grasp, and as she watched him move down the steps, loneliness assailed her.

Gunther had only just met Shiloh but there was something about her that called out to him. He'd actually thought of asking her to be his wife. Of course, now was not the time to approach her about his feelings. Not when she was suffering from her father's death.

Gunther was a patient man when the prize was worth waiting for. Estrella and Shiloh would indeed be worth waiting for.

He would give her time.

Shadowhawk had been watching the woman when she cried at the grave site, and he watched the exchange between her and the Ranger. He was puzzled by the bond between them. He noticed how tenderly the Ranger treated the woman. But she went into the house at the end of their exchange, and the Ranger went to the outbuilding. They did not seem to share a life.

Shadowhawk stood over the grave where she had knelt. Bending down, he touched the soil that had been recently turned, wishing he knew who was buried there. He did not understand the white man's custom of burying those they loved. The Comanche raised platforms as monuments to their dead, dressing them in their finest clothing, and allowing them to rest beneath the open sky.

As his gaze settled on the light coming from the ranch house, Shadowhawk felt a surprising twinge of sympathy deep inside. The woman was hurting, and he did not know why.

Gazing up at the star-filled night, Shadowhawk wondered why he should care.

She was his enemy!

* * *

The driving force in his life was finding his sister, so in the early morning hours, after Shadowhawk watched the Rangers leave, he made his way to the barn and hid in the hayloft, hoping to find some clue to Moon Song's whereabouts.

He had not been there long when the old man and the young woman entered. From what he could tell, the man worked for the woman.

With a frown, he watched the woman feed and water the animals. Shadowhawk had always been told that white women were puny and idle, leaving their men to do the work. That was not true of this woman. Already this morning he had watched her chop wood, tend the animals, and shovel snow.

She moved toward the lantern, and he stared in wonder as flickering flames reflected off hair that rivaled the glow of fire. When she paused and glanced up at the loft, it was as if she knew someone was there. Shadowhawk hunkered down, not wanting to be discovered.

He watched as the woman moved to his sister's horse, taking special care to feed and groom it. Startled, Shadowhawk felt an unfamiliar connection with her when she laid her face against the animal's neck, just as he had done the night before.

Against his will, his gaze kept returning to the fiery hair that curled about her face. She continued to defy everything he had been told about white women, and Shadowhawk was surprised to find himself wanting to know more about her.

After a while, she and the old man left the barn and Shadowhawk heard the latch shoot into place. He silently climbed through the opening in the loft and dropped to the ground. He had still seen no sign of his sister. The answers he wanted were in the woman's house.

Chapter Nine

Shiloh removed the apple pie from the oven, placing it on top of the stove. She had followed her mother's handwritten recipe, but it had been a challenge. If only someone could have explained to her the difference between a pinch, a dash, and a dab, it would have been easier. She only hoped the pie would be edible.

Hearing a sound behind her, Shiloh turned to see Moon Song enter the kitchen. To her surprise, the girl was fully dressed in her buckskin gown and knee-high moccasins.

Shiloh asked with concern, "Do you think you are well enough to be out of bed?"

"Thanks to your care, I am feeling much stronger," Moon Song said shyly. "I was drawn to this kitchen by that wonderful smell. What can it be?"

Shiloh smiled. "This, Moon Song, is an apple pie. I only hope it tastes as good as it smells. My attempts at cooking aren't always successful."

Moon Song sat down at the table, tracing a flowered pattern on the tablecloth. "In my village, females are taught to feed the family as soon as we can toddle about and pick berries. But the food we eat in my village is different from what I had at the missionary school, and here in your home."

Shiloh placed a heavy iron skillet on the stove and began gathering the ingredients for corn bread. "Perhaps you could teach me to cook some of your favorite foods."

Moon Song giggled. "I do not think you could make

the food I like best. You would first have to bring down a buffalo—then you would need to clean and prepare the animal. And that is just the beginning."

Shiloh laughed as she poured cornmeal into a bowl. "Maybe I will just stick to my mother's recipes. What else did you learn in your village?"

Moon Song shrugged. "When I was young, I played games with the other children. As I matured, I was taught to prepare buffalo robes and soften doeskin for clothing and moccasins. My mother does beautiful beadwork . . ." Moon Song dropped her head. "I miss her, and I still do not know if she has recovered from her illness."

Shiloh wanted to comfort Moon Song, but did not know how. "Tell me about your family," she said gently.

"We of the southern Comanche live apart from the other Comanche tribes, and have since my brother became chief. My mother is called Vision Woman, and she is a shaman. She was born Blackfoot, but left her tribe because of her love for my father. We have spent many summers among my mother's people, in the Blackfoot tribe where her brother is chief."

Shiloh listened intently, all the while continuing her work. Luke had ridden out that morning with Charley and Hernando, and he would be hungry when he got home. "Charley says there is a mystery surrounding your people. Why is that?" she asked Moon Song as she added milk to the cornmeal and started stirring the batter with a wooden spoon.

Moon Song was lost in thought as she formed her words. "I believe it is because my brother is like no other Comanche warrior. He walks two conflicting paths—that of the Comanche and that of the Blackfoot."

"I don't understand."

"My mother explains it like this: the part of my brother that is Comanche is dedicated to driving the white race off our land, while the part of him that thinks like a Blackfoot yearns for peace with all people. At times it is difficult for him."

Shiloh shivered, wondering whether she would meet the ruthless side or the reasonable side of Moon Song's brother should he come calling. "Charley said you are from a family of chiefs."

"That is so. My brother is war chief of our tribe, my grandfather is peace chief."

"Does that not put them on opposite sides?"

"In your world it might. But not among the Comanche. Each seeks advice from the other."

"What if they disagree?" Shiloh asked.

"My brother is—" Moon Song broke off what she was about to say and jerked to her feet, standing stock-still, listening.

"What is it?" Shiloh asked, hearing nothing out of the ordinary.

"Do you not hear it?"

"No, what?"

"Someone is here. There are two of them. Their horses are unshod." The young girl's face glowed with happiness. "It is my brother! He has come for me!"

Shiloh rushed to the window and pulled the lace curtains aside, her blood turning to ice. Moon Song was right—there were two mounted Indians in the front yard, sitting stoic and still upon their horses. If the wind had not been rippling through their long hair, she would have thought they were made of stone.

Moon Song saw Shiloh stiffen and her face go deadly white. "You will have nothing to fear from my brother when I tell him how you saved my life," she said, hoping to reassure Shiloh.

Pulling back with a gasp, Shiloh watched as one of the men dismounted. He moved with easy grace as he ascended the steps, searching the area. He was tall, but Shiloh could see very little of his face as he moved into the shadow of the porch.

"I have to get the rifle!" Shiloh cried, wishing the Rangers were still there. What could she do against those two Indians when she didn't know how to shoot all that well?

Moon Song placed her hand on Shiloh's arm. "Do not," she cautioned. "Shadowhawk will react with anger if he sees you with a weapon."

There was no time to consider because the door burst open as if the Indian had kicked it instead of turning the knob. Shadowhawk's dark gaze swept across the room as if he were taking in every detail. He looked at Shiloh for a moment before his gaze settled on Moon Song.

If Shadowhawk was happy to see his sister, it did not show in his fierce expression. He appeared angry and threatening, and Shiloh was terrified. She took a step backward, thinking she might be able to grab up the iron skillet to use for a weapon if the Comanche advanced in her direction.

In contrast, joy spread through Moon Song when she saw her brother. "I knew you would come!" she cried excitedly in their language. "How is our mother?"

"She is worried about you." Shadowhawk's expression was dangerous. "I feared you might be dead. Why are you here with these people?"

Since her brother was angrier than she had expected, Moon Song was uncertain how he would react to Shiloh. "I would have died if this compassionate white woman had not taken me into her home. I was very ill and she nursed me back to health."

Shadowhawk turned his attention to the white woman. His dark eyes focused on her, and he regarded her with curiosity. Though he had been watching her from a distance, he was not prepared for the delicate beauty of her face up close. Although her eyes were filled with fear, it was as if their color had been drawn from the bluest sky. Her skin was a creamy white, her face the most arresting he had ever seen. Her body was in the full bloom of womanhood. But Shadowhawk despised the race that had spawned her, so he forced himself to turn away from her.

The Indian looked at Shiloh so long, she felt prickles across her skin. She didn't know what his intentions were, but they couldn't be good.

Moon Song was watching him with concern. "My brother," she said, moving to his side and placing herself between him and Shiloh. "You are frightening my friend, who has done nothing but good for me."

Shadowhawk glanced down at his sister. In truth, his heart was gladdened that he had found her. Despite his mother's faith that Moon Song was alive, he had feared never to see her again.

A sudden thought hit him hard—a thought that made his anger flare anew. Since the white woman had saved his sister's life, he owed her a debt of honor that must be paid.

Shiloh watched every move the Indian made, fearing he would come after her. For a moment their eyes met, and his were filled with pure dislike. She stepped back quickly, eyeing the iron skillet.

Shadowhawk's anger spiked. The white woman was afraid of him, but he knew what she did not—he could do her no harm; he owed her for his sister's life.

Suddenly Shiloh raised her chin defiantly. She had done nothing to merit the Comanche's anger, and she was not going to cower before him.

Shadowhawk glared at her while he spoke harshly to his sister. "We are leaving," he said, grasping Moon Song's arm. "Now!"

Moon Song spoke hurriedly to Shiloh in English. "Do not fear for your life, you will not be harmed. I must leave with my brother. I will always remember you were my friend. Please tell Luke I said good-bye."

Shiloh finally found her voice. "Will you be all right?"

"My brother will take me home. Seeing my mother will be the best cure for me."

Shadowhawk urged Moon Song toward the door. "Tell Running Fox to get your horse from the barn," he said in harsh Comanche. "Then wait for me."

Moon Song was reluctant to leave him alone with Shiloh, not because he would harm her, but because her friend was frightened by him. However, Shadowhawk was head of the family, as well as the all-powerful war chief of her people. He must be obeyed without question, so she left.

Shiloh avoided looking at the Indian, but she knew he was watching her. At last she could stand the silence between them no longer and met his eyes. His dark gaze was hard as he stared back at her.

Five feathers were woven into thick hair that was black as midnight and hung past his shoulders. His skin was the color of warm copper, his face smooth, with no sign of stubble. He wore fringed buckskin trousers and shirt, and his muscles rippled with every movement.

Where the thought came from, she did not know, but he reminded her of a beautiful wild animal that could not be tamed.

Shiloh thought how strange it was that they were standing silently in her kitchen observing each other. Suddenly she watched Shadowhawk's expression harden even more, and she read contempt in his eyes.

"Please go away," she said through trembling lips, doubtful that the Comanche even understood her words.

Shadowhawk took a step backward, dipped his head the merest bit, and before she realized what was happening, he was gone.

Shiloh dropped into a chair. Her whole body was trembling, and her heart was beating so fast she could feel it in her throat. Luke would not believe her when she told him she had stared death in the face and lived to tell about it.

Later, Luke, Charley, and Hernando gathered around the kitchen table while Shiloh told them about the incident with Shadowhawk.

Noticing she was pale, Hernando asked with concern, "Are you all right, Señorita Shiloh?"

"I will be when I can stop shaking. If Shadowhawk is as deadly as people say, I wonder why he allowed me to live." She looked to Charley for the answer.

The old man scooped a forkful of apple pie and said, "That's 'cause he either decided to let you live, or he felt obligated to you. If it's the first, you're not likely to see him again; if it's the second, he'll be back."

"I hope it's the first," Shiloh said fervently. "I don't ever want to see him again."

"I hope it's the second," Luke said, his eyes wide.

Charley rocked back in his chair. "No, you don't, boy. Your sister's maybe the only white person ever to see Shadowhawk."

"Why would he come back, Charley?" Shiloh asked.

"I'd only be guessing, but I think he feels he's obliged to you for saving his sister's life. He won't like it none, but he's bound to you by this debt. He can't harm you or yours, and he can't allow anyone else to." Charley paused with a scoop of apple pie dripping from his fork. "That's what I'm hoping anyway."

"I have heard of this custom among the Comanche," Hernando said.

Shiloh shuddered when she remembered Shadowhawk's dark eyes colliding with hers, sending shock throughout her body. "I was afraid of him."

Charley leaned in on the table, looking from Shiloh to Luke. "No matter what the reason, we've got us a passel of trouble, and that's the gospel truth."

"I'll tell you what I know of the Comanche," Hernando said. "Not Shadowhawk's tribe, because no one knows about them. The Comanche are as ruthless as they come, and who can blame them? This was their land long before my people, or yours, came to Texas. I can also tell you this: they kill without guilt and strike when you least expect it."

Charley nodded in agreement. "You see, the Comanche I lived with was meaner than dirt. I was but a young man when they came upon me lost and half starved. I fell on my knees, trembling and saying what I could recall of the Lord's Prayer. Well, sir, they took it in their heads that I was crazed, and for reasons I never did know, they let me live— even took me to their village. I was hardly old enough to shave. They weren't 'zactly good to me, and beat me a lot. I spent two winters with them, and when I thought it was safe, I hightailed it out of there. They didn't even try to stop me. Guess we'd all had enough of each other."

"And they didn't come after you?" Luke wanted to know.

"They was happy to see me gone." Charley held out his empty plate for Shiloh to serve him another piece of pie. "You met with a legend, Miss Shiloh," he told her, reaching out awkwardly to pat her arm. "Like I said, no one else can say they've met him."

"He didn't seem old enough to be a legend," Shiloh said.

"Well, the way I see it," Charley remarked, taking another bite of pie, "it ain't the years that make a man a legend, but how others see him."

Chapter Ten

Shadowhawk dismounted and turned to Moon Song. "Go to our mother's tipi and ease her mind," he commanded, taking the reins of her horse. He regretted speaking so sharply to his sister when he saw the hurt in her eyes.

Anger still dwelled within his heart, and he knew the cause. For the first time in his life, he had found a woman he wanted to claim as his own, and he could not have her. Long were the nights on the journey home when sleep had eluded him. He had been tormented by unfamiliar and unwelcome thoughts of the white woman. Even now, though he had just returned home, some force was pulling him back to her. Thinking of the white woman's blue eyes, he felt his heart constrict. His desire for her had come upon him deep and quick, and try as he might, he could not rid his mind of flame-colored hair falling against pale cheeks.

The two of them were from different cultures. Their paths should never have crossed, but they had.

So much had happened in such a short time that Shiloh was reeling. Though her days were full, she was lonely and sometimes wished she could be carefree again. But her secure world had crumbled with her father's death. She was now father and mother to Luke, head of a failing ranch, and terrified that the Comanches would return at any time. She had to be strong for everyone around her, but sometimes she wished for a shoulder to lean on and someone to take care of her.

She thought of Captain Gunther. She knew he had been attracted to her, but she wasn't sure what she felt for him. He had been strong, and had helped her get through a very difficult time. But thinking of him did not ease the aching loneliness in her life.

Dark eyes flashed through her mind. Shadowhawk. She had often thought about their encounter and anticipated his return, but was it with fear, or something else?

Shiloh dried the last of the dishes and put them away, then hung her apron on a peg. Going into the parlor, she picked up one of Luke's shirts that needed mending. Luke was stretched out on the floor with his head bent over a book.

Looking up, he observed his sister for a moment as she sewed. "I remember Mama doing the mending." His gaze met Shiloh's. "I never thought Papa would . . . we would lose him too."

Shiloh put her mending aside and gave her brother her full attention. "It's a bitter thing we must endure, Luke. But we have to look for the good things in our lives and get past the hurt. The most important thing I can think of is we still have each other."

He nodded and was quiet for a moment, pondering. "Shiloh, Papa wanted to build up the herd, and that's what we need to do."

"You're right. It was his dream to make Estrella prosper, and it should be our dream as well."

Luke sat up. "It will take a lot of work—and a lot of money. Do we have enough money, Shiloh?"

Leaning back in the rocking chair, Shiloh rested her head against a delicate scarf her mother had tatted. "I don't know," she said, frowning. "Papa never talked about finances." Watching her brother for his reaction, she said, "If we are forced to, we could always sell to Surge Tyree."

Luke's eyes widened with fury as he jumped to his feet.

"Never! We already decided we wouldn't sell to him. I remember Papa saying he'd give this ranch back to nature before he'd sell to that man."

Luke had spoken with such vehemence that it brought tears to Shiloh's eyes. It seemed he had grown several inches in the last few weeks. Standing there with the firelight playing on his face, she imagined he must look much as their father had at the same age. "Then what do you suggest we do, Luke?"

He started pacing. "I know it won't be easy to keep the ranch, but we still have Charley and Hernando to help us."

"But Charley is getting old and we can't expect him to keep working so hard, Luke. How much longer can we depend on him?"

Luke nodded. "We need to find out how much money we have before we make any plans."

"I suppose we should go into town and speak to Mr. McNair about that. If we have no money in the bank, we'll have to make some painful decisions."

The shadow of sadness lingered in Luke's eyes. "You and me can do it, Shiloh. I know we can."

"You and I," she corrected.

"You and I," he repeated.

Cold reason enveloped Shiloh while doubt plagued her mind. Without their father's guidance, it would be difficult to keep Estrella. But she had to try for Luke's sake.

Luke stood, yawning. "I'm going to bed."

She watched him leave, then picked up the lamp and walked toward her father's bedroom. Opening the door, she could smell the soap her father had always used and the slight hint of his pipe tobacco. Her heart ached as she picked up his coat and held it close to her.

Moving restlessly about the room, she touched her father's stack of law books, ran her hand over the back of his favorite chair, then moved on to pick up his shaving mug. Pausing, she considered whether she should rearrange the bedroom so Luke could use it since he was now the man of the house.

No. Not tonight.

It was too soon.

Shiloh blew out the lamp and curled up on her father's bed, pulling his coat over her. Wrenching sobs shook her body and she cried until she was exhausted.

With sorrow weighing her down like an anchor, she finally fell into a dreamless sleep.

Chapter Eleven

Sometime during the early morning hours it had rained, and as if by magic, wildflowers dotted the pastures. It was a beautiful day, with blue skies stretching across the heavens as far as the eye could see.

Shiloh stood on the bottom rung of the paddock fence, watching dappled sunlight pierce through the leaves of a lone mesquite tree that stood near the barn. Turning her full attention to Charley, she watched as he attempted to instruct Luke in lassoing a calf.

Thus far the lessons had been disastrous.

Luke had fallen off his horse the first time he threw the lasso, and he'd fallen again when his lasso slid over the calf's head and the animal jerked Luke to the ground.

Not to be deterred, Luke dusted himself off, remounted, and made a slipknot as Charley had showed him. Slinging the rope above his head in a wide circle, he tossed it toward the calf. The loop flew past the animal's head, and Luke glared at the calf in disgust.

Charley grinned, taking the rope from Luke, loosening the knot, and handing it back. "Ain't nobody ever gets it right on the first few tries. Do 'er again, but don't make such a wide loop next time 'cause you can't control it if you do." To Charley's way of thinking, Luke's pa had set too much store in book learning and had neglected to show his son how to work a ranch. Of course, nobody could have guessed the boy would have to take the reins of control so young.

When Luke's rope finally slipped around the calf's neck, he gave a loud whoop. Shiloh clapped her hand over her mouth to smother a laugh and almost fell off the fence.

Hearing the sound of horses approaching, she turned to the north road. Shading her eyes against the glaring sun, she didn't recognize the riders at first. There were four of them. As they drew near, Shiloh had no trouble picking Surge Tyree out from the group, nor his foreman, Tip Rawlins.

Shiloh waited for them to approach, and Charley came over to the fence to stand beside her, while Luke watched from the back of his horse.

"Trouble," Charley muttered in disgust, spitting out a stream of tobacco juice. "I can guess what they're here for."

Shiloh felt bile rise in her throat. With a trembling hand, she reached out to Charley. "Stay beside me. Don't leave me alone with those men."

Charley glared at Tyree. "Don't you fret none, Miss Shiloh, I ain't goin' no place. And I seen Hernando duck behind the barn with his rifle."

Surge Tyree rode high in his saddle and gave the impression that he wouldn't let anything, or anyone, stop him from getting what he wanted.

The man who rode at Tyree's side was tall, his face angular and as tanned as boot leather. There was a gap between his front teeth, and if Shiloh were to judge from the two bumps on the bridge of his nose, she'd guess it had been broken several times. She'd heard Rawlins was quick with his fists, and that he never walked away from a fight.

The other two cowhands remained on their mounts while the owner of the Crooked H dismounted, smiling, and his foreman followed his lead. Rawlins remained by his horse, while Tyree approached Shiloh.

"Howdy there, little gal. I came by to see how you're making out without a man around the place."

He stuck out his hand to shake Shiloh's, but she didn't want to touch him, so she clasped her arms behind her back. Shiloh's mother had taught her that a gentleman would never offer his hand to a lady unless she first offered hers to him—but then, Surge Tyree was no gentleman.

"We appreciate your concern," she said woodenly. "As you can see, we are making out just fine."

"Well now, little lady, I just wanted to remind you that 'round here, we kinda look out for one another. I was thinking you might be needing help since you're short-handed."

"If we need your help, we'll let you know, Mr. Tyree."

"Pretty little gal, you don't have to ask. I'm offering."

Tyree's words might sound polite, but his eyes held a threatening expression, reminding Shiloh of a snake preparing to strike—the fact that Tyree's tongue kept flicking out to moisten his lips compounded that feeling. The air was thick with malice, and it was directed at her.

"Let's not play games, Mr. Tyree," Shiloh said coldly. "We both know why you're here. Say what's on your mind and then leave."

Tyree's eyes narrowed to pinpoints. "And what is it you think I have on my mind?"

Shiloh didn't hesitate. "Everybody knows how you force folks off their land so you can buy their property cheap. Take heed—that won't happen with us, Mr. Tyree."

Instead of being angry, Tyree gave a loud belly laugh. "Call me Surge," he said, admiringly. "I believe I've met a woman of my own caliber. You stand up to me, little gal, and I like that."

Shiloh glared at him. "I'm nothing like you."

Undaunted, Tyree nodded at his foreman. "I think you already know Tip, here—you can call him by his given name too."

Shiloh stood her ground, and looked at him contemptuously. "And you can both call me 'Miss Braden.'"

The boss of the Crooked H shifted his weight, while a muscle jerked in his jaw. "Little gal, folks like your family come to Texas thinking they can make a go of it—most of you don't have enough grit to last out the first winter. When they fail, they come crying to me to buy their land. If I get it cheap, as you said, it's because folks'll take any amount of money when the land defeats them. Out here only the strong survive—all I see here is an old man, a young woman, and a boy."

Shiloh made no reply.

"What do you say?" Tyree asked. "Are you ready to sell Estrella?"

Shiloh was watching Tyree's foreman, whose hand was resting on the handle of his gun. "I say 'get off our land.'"

Tyree took a menacing step forward. "I came here today with good intentions. If you want to play hard, I can play harder. You'll sell to me in the end. Waiting won't bring you nothing but trouble."

Shiloh's chin went up a notch. "The answer is no today—it will be no tomorrow, and every day thereafter. You're wasting your time—and mine."

Tyree's eyes turned stony. "You Bradens came out here with your superior ways, thinking we're dirt beneath your feet." He shifted from one foot to the other, as if he were trying to beat down his anger. "Your ma grew up on this ranch, and was the same as the rest of us, and although your pa might have been a fancy lawyer in Virginia, he was a failure out here."

Shiloh's anger flared. "My father was no failure."

"Yeah!" Luke said. "He was a better man than you'll ever be."

Ignoring the boy, Tyree looked straight at Shiloh.

"There ain't no call for insults. I'm willing to admit you got yourself a prime bit of land here 'longside the Brazos. I don't usually do this, but I'm prepared to give you a fair price for Estrella. Maybe more than it's worth. I'd advise you to take it, or you'll regret it."

"Sounds like a threat to me," Charley remarked, spitting a stream of tobacco juice that landed near Tyree's boot.

Tip Rawlins stepped toward Charley, grinding his jaw before he spoke. "Ain't nobody disrespects Mr. Tyree like that," he warned, his hand going to his gun.

Hot fury coursed through Shiloh as she stepped in front of Charley, knowing what Rawlins was capable of doing. "I'm asking you nicely to leave, Mr. Tyree, and take this fool with you."

"You'll see me again, only next time I won't be so polite," Tyree snarled.

"Save your threats," Charley warned. "This family's protected by Texas Rangers. You know 'bout Captain Gunther. He'd take it poorly if he knew you was making trouble here."

Saddle leather creaked under Tyree's weight as he remounted. He leaned over the saddle horn, his gaze on Shiloh. "I made my offer once, and you saw fit to refuse. You'll regret it, little gal—you surely will."

Hernando came from behind the barn, cocked his rifle, aiming at Tyree's heart. "Don't try your threats here, Señor."

Tyree and his men turned their horses and rode away in a cloud of dust.

Shiloh leaned against the fence, drawing in a deep breath. Charley stood on one side of her and Luke on the other, both looking worried. "What are we to do?" she asked.

"I wish I could tell you to hold out against that man," Charley said. "But he's plumb mean. He'll stoop as low as the ground just to put on his boots."

"I don't like the way he was looking at you, Shiloh," her brother said. "Papa would have shot him for being so disrespectful."

"I don't believe he intended to be respectful, Luke. He meant to insult us in every way possible." Shiloh glanced at Charley. "Why would he do that?"

"To scare you off."

"Well, it won't work," she said, setting her chin stubbornly. Then with less bravado, she asked, "What do you think he'll try next?"

Charley's brow furrowed. "I can only tell you what he's done to others. Someone poisoned the well at the Mince place, and drove their cattle over a cliff. Nothing was ever proved, but folks think it was Tyree. Someone burned down the house at the Cramers' ranch, and a baby died in the fire. Both families sold out real cheap to Tyree."

"Well, we won't," Luke said, reminding Shiloh of their father when his eyes glistened with determination.

"No, we won't," Shiloh agreed. But in her heart she wondered how long they could hold out against such a vile man.

Shiloh clasped her brother's hand. "Don't worry, Luke. When we band together, no one can defeat us."

It was just before dawn when Shiloh set the coffeepot on the stove. Yawning, she tied her apron about her waist before reaching into the wood bin and finding it empty. Luke had been helping drive the cattle to the river the day before, and when he'd returned home, it had been after dark. Her poor brother had almost fallen asleep while eating, and she'd shooed him off to bed. Certainly he'd been too tired to bring in wood.

Opening the back door, Shiloh hurried toward the woodpile and stopped short when she saw a dead elk lying near the chopping block. She backed up the steps, fear racing through her when she saw it had been brought down by an arrow.

Who had left the dead animal so near the doorstep? she wondered. And why?

Hearing Charley whistling as he made his way toward the barn, she hurried in his direction. When he saw Shiloh, the old man stopped, waiting for her to catch up with him.

"Morning, Miss Shiloh. Sure looks like a nice day." Hernando's two sons were trailing along beside Charley.

Juan, who was twelve, and Alejandro, who was Luke's age, looked at Shiloh eagerly. They knew she had baked their favorite cookies the day before.

"Go into the kitchen and you'll find a plate of ginger cookies," Shiloh told them. "Take all you want."

As the boys raced away, she turned her attention to Charley. "Someone left a dead elk in the backyard. It was killed by an arrow."

Charley looked startled. "Let's just have a look," he said, urging her back the way she'd come.

The sun was creeping over the barn as Charley bent to examine the carcass. He stood, shaking his head. "It's still warm, so it's a recent kill. But that ain't what befuddles me."

Shiloh bent down beside him. "It's the arrow, isn't it, Charley?" she asked anxiously.

With a twisting jerk, Charley withdrew the arrow and studied it for a moment. A slow smile lit his eyes. "Well, I declare. Just as I thought—it's Comanch'."

Shiloh's hand covered her throbbing heart as fear climbed up her spine. "What can it mean?"

"If I was a-guessing, I'd say Shadowhawk just made his first payment on the debt he owes you."

"You mean he was this close to the house and no one saw him?" Shiloh was filled with dread. "I had hoped he'd leave us alone."

"I have a notion he's been watching the place for a time. Mayhaps he's been trying to figure out how best to help you. You gotta understand, Shadowhawk's plenty mad 'cause he's owing a white woman for his sister's life. He'll want to get the debt paid as soon as he can."

"I hope he considers the debt paid *now*. He frightens me, Charley."

"No need to be scared just yet, Miss Shiloh. Shadowhawk won't do you any harm 'til he figures his debt is met, and probably not even then." Charley studied the arrow. "I'll skin and clean this elk for you and hang the carcass in the smokehouse. This here bull must weigh nigh on seven hundred pounds. The meat should last through the summer."

Shiloh was dazed as she gathered an armload of wood and hurried back into the house. She was trembling as she lifted the lid on the cookstove and added several chunks of wood to the fire.

Pausing, she remembered Charley speculating that Shadowhawk had been observing them. For the last few days she had been uneasy, as if someone was watching her, but she had dismissed the feeling as so much nonsense.

Could it have been Shadowhawk?

Shiloh remembered how angry he had been when he came for his sister. No one had to tell her Shadowhawk could be ruthless, she had read that in his eyes.

If Charley was right, and she had no reason to doubt he was, the only way they would be rid of the Comanche would be when he considered his obligation had been met.

Shiloh prayed for that day.

Luke came out of their father's bedroom, which he'd now taken for his own. Yawning, he leaned in the doorway. "The cattle we bought from Mr. Graves should be arriving today."

Shiloh cracked eggs in a bowl, while she told her brother about the elk.

He sat down at the table, looking glum. "I never get to see Shadowhawk. I'd like to talk to him. I wish he'd come back."

Shiloh shuddered, hoping he wouldn't.

Chapter Twelve

Antelope Wells

The town was situated on a slight rise within sight of the seemingly endless prairie. Buffalo hunters rubbed shoulders with ranchers and even an occasional farmer. The blacksmith shop, owned by Ken Johnson—who also served as the town barber and occasionally a dentist—was at the end of the dusty street. Across from the smithy stood the general store, a bank, a hotel, two saloons, and a cantina.

At the edge of town stood a crumbling structure that had been Santa Teresa Mission, built by early Spanish settlers. The abandoned building had been recently taken over by a missionary and his family of eleven offspring. Mr. and Mrs. Samuelson were dedicated to educating Indian children, and Moon Song had attended their school.

Luke stopped the wagon in front of the bank and helped Shiloh to the ground. Pausing to tighten the reins, he glanced at his sister. "I'm nervous. What if there's no money?"

"Let's take this one step at a time, Luke," she said reassuringly. As he stepped onto the boardwalk, Shiloh noticed her brother had outgrown his trousers. "One thing we need to do is buy you new clothing that fits."

"What about you—don't you need new clothing?"

She arched her brow at him. "I haven't outgrown my gowns."

Laughing, they entered the building together. Harley

Miller, the bank teller, greeted them with a smile and led them directly to Mr. McNair's office. Mr. McNair greeted them warmly and asked them to be seated.

Fearing to hear the worst, Shiloh sat on the edge of a chair studying Mr. McNair's bland expression. The banker was white headed, his face plump, his mouth generous. "I've been expecting you," he said, flashing a smile.

Reaching into a drawer, he took out some papers and thumbed through them. The bifocals that rested on the bridge of his nose magnified his hazel eyes. Turning a page, he continued to read, while Luke squirmed in his chair.

Meeting his sister's worried frown, Luke waited for Mr. McNair to finish rifling through their father's documents.

At last the banker raised his head and studied each of them in turn. "Your father placed a copy of his will in my care since we have no lawyer in Antelope Wells. As I understand it, the original was drawn up by your father's attorney in Williamsburg, Virginia. I assume the original copy is with this Mr. . . ." He looked down at the page. "Mr. Managan, attorney-at-law. I have already written to Mr. Managan, informing him of your father's death. I'm sure he'll be contacting you with all the pertinent details."

Shiloh adjusted her bonnet and nervously pressed the crease out of one of her white gloves. "Can't you tell us what it says?"

"I surely can, Miss Braden. I don't have the complete breakdown, but I can tell you what the codicil to the will, made after your mother's death, contains. I'll give you a copy to take home with you so you can study it at your leisure."

Mr. McNair adjusted his glasses, cleared his throat, and began to read: "I, Jonathan Luke Braden, being of sound mind and body, do bequeath all my holdings, properties, and monetary investments to be divided equally between my daughter, Shiloh Anne Braden, and my son, Luke

Jonathan Braden." Mr. McNair ran his finger over the paper, skipping the parts that were unclear to him. After all, he was a banker, not an attorney. "Oh, here it is," he said at last. "Should either my son or daughter precede the other in death, the entire holdings shall go to the remaining child." Mr. McNair frowned. "I see he left you property back in Williamsburg, Virginia. It says here it's an estate being managed by this Mr. Managan."

"I didn't know about that, did you, Shiloh?" Luke asked.

"No. I had always assumed our father had sold our home in Virginia when we moved to Texas."

McNair raised his head, his gaze moving from the face of the young woman to her younger brother. "As I told you, this is a simple version of the actual will, but accurately drawn. After all, your father was a lawyer."

Shiloh frowned as she leaned forward. "Our father never spoke to us about the will." She ducked her head so the banker wouldn't see the tears gathering in her eyes. "He did not expect to . . . die." She slowly raised her gaze to Mr. McNair, resting her hands on the edge of his desk. "Mr. McNair, only twenty head of our cattle survived the storm—five of those are calves that Charley managed to rescue. My brother and I are wondering if there is enough money to buy more stock. It is what our father had planned to do . . . if he had lived."

"And we would like to hire more wranglers to help out on Estrella," Luke added anxiously.

Mr. McNair stared at the two young people with growing concern. "Surely you don't intend to remain on Estrella? If I may speak candidly, you're both too young and inexperienced to make a go of it without your father to guide you. If your father were here, I believe he'd advise you to sell Estrella. If I could take the liberty to speak to you like a father, I'd advise you to sell it as soon as possible."

Luke stood, shoving his hands in his pockets. "Mr. Mc-

Nair, begging your pardon, but Papa would expect us to stay at Estrella. It's our home and we aren't going to leave."

The banker frowned. "You are just beginning to discover how hard life can be without your father. Texas is an inhospitable land, even in the best of times. It takes strength and endurance to make a go of it here." McNair leaned back in his chair, cleaning his glasses with a snowy white handkerchief. "Word's out that Surge Tyree has made you an offer."

Shiloh motioned for her brother to be seated. "It wasn't exactly an offer—Mr. Tyree threatened us if we didn't sell. One thing he needs to know about us Bradens is if someone tries to push us, we push back."

McNair smiled at the beautiful young woman, who had spent the first part of her life in the polite society of Williamsburg, Virginia, and the last few years on an unproductive ranch in the middle of nowhere. "I don't see how you can keep Estrella." He lowered his voice and it was tinged with sympathy. "Don't give this town the grief of having to bury the two of you, like you buried your father."

"The way I see it," Luke said stubbornly, "Papa died for this land, and we're keeping it. Me and my sister are tired of people telling us to sell."

Mr. McNair was quiet for a long time, then asked: "What can I do to help you?"

"We need to know how much money we have in the bank," Shiloh said pointedly.

The banker turned another page of the document. "You have on deposit in my bank ten thousand dollars. In the Williamsburg Bank, your father has twenty-five thousand dollars, some bonds and bank notes that amount to another twelve thousand dollars. Your father has left you what amounts to a fortune." He observed the brother and sister above his bifocals. "Is Charley still working for you?"

Luke was stunned by the banker's revelation, but he managed to nod. "Yes, sir. He and Hernando Sanchez."

"They're both good men. Take my advice and don't hire any wranglers unless Charley approves of them. He may be getting on in years, but look to him for guidance whenever you can."

"We trust Charley," Shiloh informed him. "Now," she said, turning the conversation back to the matter at hand. "To begin with, sir, we need money for supplies."

McNair stood. "Then come with me. I'll walk you to the Currutherses's store and help you set up an account."

A short time later, Willard Curruthers, the owner of W. C. Farm and Ranch Supplies, handed a bag of potatoes to Luke, then stepped back to watch him hoist it into the wagon. What Curruthers lacked in height he made up for in girth. His hair was thinning on top and sprigs of gray hung over his ears.

"Lad, how are things going on Estrella?"

Luke glanced toward the store, where Shiloh was speaking to Mrs. Curruthers. "We are getting on fine, sir."

"You know, I saw the storm coming up the day your pa came to town for supplies. The wife and I tried to talk him out of leaving, but he wanted to get home to you and your sister."

Luke turned, giving the store owner his full attention. "Papa told us when he came to Texas, he decided Estrella would either beat him or he'd conquer it. I guess it beat him, Mr. Curruthers, but he would expect me and Shiloh to win through."

"You're so young. What can you do against the elements, the Indians, and Surge Tyree?"

"The best we can—that's what we'll do. Me and my sister want to buy at least a hundred head of cattle and hire more hands to work the place." He looked earnestly into the storekeeper's eyes. "Do you know where we can find help?"

"No. I don't. And Surge Tyree will threaten anyone who even thinks about hiring on to your brand."

"We'll find some hands that aren't cowards to work for us."

Curruthers studied the young boy who wanted so badly to hold on to what belonged to him. But Curruthers had seen grown men give up and abandon their homes. "It's going to be hard without your pa, Luke."

"Everyone keeps telling us that. But we will do it, sir. You just see if we don't."

"Well, you've got grit, and you have Charley and Hernando, and that counts for something."

Luke lifted a fifty-pound bag of flour and placed it in the wagon, then slammed the tailgate shut and latched it. "It looks like Shiloh is ready to leave, Mr. Curruthers."

Shiloh climbed into the wagon and waited for Luke to take up the reins. As they drove away she turned and waved at Mrs. Curruthers, who had come out of the store to stand beside her husband. "Everyone expects us to go back to Virginia, Luke."

"I know it," he said, setting his chin at a stubborn tilt. "But we won't. We have money now."

Mrs. Curruthers linked her arm through her husband's. "Lord help those two young people, alone in the world."

"Amen, Martha," her husband said. "Still, they're determined, and that just might get them by."

Spring advanced across the land, and the days seemed to pass quickly for Shiloh. Charley had made a trip to San Antonio to hire wranglers who hadn't heard about Surge Tyree and wouldn't be intimidated by him when he came calling, as he surely would.

Now that they had money, Shiloh was more hopeful about the future; they had purchased a hundred head of cattle from far West Texas, and drovers were driving the cattle to Estrella. To her relief, Mr. Tyree hadn't come around, and so far, no Comanche had come calling either.

The new hands appeared to know what they were doing, and Charley assured Shiloh they were hardworking. The oldest, who went by the name Flint, appeared to be somewhere in his late forties. He had a pock-marked face and a tall, lean frame. The second wrangler, Bud Rankin, was somewhere in his twenties. He was a quiet man, and seemed to be more comfortable with cattle than people. The third man, Horace Beck, Charley referred to as a saddle bum and a drifter, who only stayed in one place long enough to make sufficient money to move on to another. But Charley hoped the young man might change his ways if given the chance.

Shadowhawk crouched next to a broken-down wagon, watching the white woman planting seeds in her garden. He found himself returning to this place against his will, just so he could have a glimpse of her. He would be in his village or on the hunt, trying to live his life as if he had never seen the white woman, when he would be stricken with an overpowering urge to look upon her once more. He fought for control of his emotions, reminding himself he was a chief—a Comanche—a strong man. Why then could he not purge her from his thoughts?

Shadowhawk watched the young woman remove her bonnet. A ray of sunlight struck her hair, and he considered it the most beautiful sight he had ever seen. Closing his eyes, he imagined how it would feel to touch her hair, to touch her face. Never had a woman stirred him as deeply as she had.

In watching the house, Shadowhawk had witnessed the brother and sister struggle to hold on to their land. They faced troubles that even a Comanche family who had just lost their father would find difficult to endure.

Shadowhawk lingered until long after the woman had

entered the house before he left. As he rode away in the gathering dusk, he had to fight the urge to return to her. Something was happening to him—this woman was becoming too important in his life. He ached to touch her, he yearned to look into her eyes, and his body wanted to know hers.

Urging his horse forward, he raced the wind, trying to distance himself from his thoughts and the woman who pulled at his heart. A Comanche was not meant to love someone of the white race. Surely not he, the war chief. If the two races met, it should only be in battle.

It was a moon-bright evening as Comanche warriors gathered around the campfire, while the women served them roasted buffalo meat.

Moon Song served her brother, confused by his strange withdrawal of late. Just now one of the other warriors had spoken to Shadowhawk, and her brother had not even heeded the man's words. She watched Yellow Bird, a beautiful maiden of marriageable age, hand Shadowhawk a slice of berry cake sweetened with wild honey. He took the cake, but he neither tasted it, nor heeded the young maiden.

Moon Song intended to speak to Shadowhawk about what was troubling him. Perhaps he was worried about the rogue band of Apache that had been raiding in their territory. She watched as her brother stood and move away from the others. Troubled, she decided to follow him.

When Moon Song found her brother, he was standing on the riverbank, staring into the distance.

"May I speak to you, my brother?"

He gave a nod indicating she could.

"I have seen that you are troubled about something. Is there anything I can do for you?"

Always before, Shadowhawk had refused to ask the

white woman's name, thinking it would be even more difficult to forget her if he could put a name to her face.

But now he must know.

With his gaze still fastened on the darkness, he said, "Tell me her name."

Moon Song knew immediately whom he meant and the realization made her uneasy. "Her name is Shiloh."

"Shiloh. Her name is like music." Shadowhawk closed his eyes. "I do not know what grips me, but I shall overcome it," he said with conviction. Then he walked toward his horse, already losing the battle.

Moon Song followed him and stood silently watching him unhobble his horse.

"Have you finished the deerskin robe I asked you to prepare for me?" Shadowhawk wanted to know.

She nodded. "I finished it yesterday."

"Bring it to me and tell the others I will not return to the feast tonight."

Shadowhawk watched his sister disappear into her tipi—she was worried about him, but he could give her no words of comfort—he could not even find comfort for himself. He waited impatiently for Moon Song to return. Taking the deerskin from her, he tied it to the back of his horse and mounted. "I do not know how long I will be away."

"Wait," Moon Song called, touching his horse's flank. "I would speak to you on an important matter."

Shadowhawk reined in his horse and looked down at her.

"You have been distracted tonight or you would have noticed how Yellow Bird tried to catch your attention."

He looked at his sister in puzzlement. "Why should she? I have given her no encouragement."

"She is my friend, and you may not have noticed she is sought after by other warriors. If you do not notice her soon, one of them will take her for his wife."

Shadowhawk glared down at his sister. It was not seemly for a young girl to speak thus to her brother, especially if he was a chief. "Why do you tell me this?"

Moon Song ducked her head, knowing she had overstepped the bounds that were set for Comanche females. "Yellow Bird favors you."

Shadowhawk was silent for a moment while he considered his sister's words. "I do not see her."

"No," Moon Song said sadly, "you do not notice many things that are happening around you these days."

Without answering, Shadowhawk nodded to his sister and rode swiftly into the night. Moon Song was right—his mind was too often with . . . Shiloh, and he could not turn his thoughts away from her. A sharp pang of loneliness hit Shadowhawk. He had no place in Shiloh's life. If she ever thought of him at all, it was probably with fear.

Several nights later Shadowhawk stood on a small rise that overlooked the ranch house where Shiloh lived. Cattle were milling about, grazing on the sweet grass, and he could see how this would be a good life for the white man. For himself, he would not like to live in such a place. He would feel enclosed. Suffocated. He needed the vastness of the plains to feel at home.

Hearing riders approach, Shadowhawk quickly took his horse's reins and led the animal behind a tall clump of scrub brushes. He clamped his hand over his horse's muzzle so the animal would not make a sound.

The men stopped no more than fifty paces from Shadowhawk's hiding place. There were five of them, but only three dismounted to talk among themselves. "I don't like doing this to cattle," one said. "H'it just don't seem right to me."

"You'll do what the boss says," another answered.

Shadowhawk's instincts warned him these men had

come to make trouble. As he watched two of them string bows and aim at the cattle, anger exploded inside him. Why would they slay the cattle, and why use bow and arrow when they had guns?

The wounded cattle bellowed and some of them dropped to their knees, then fell dead. It was a senseless slaughter. Those cattle belonged to Shiloh.

"If this don't scare them Bradens off, the boss'll get tougher," one of them remarked.

"What will he do if they refuse to leave?"

"You'll see. When the boss wants something, he gets it."

"And he don't care who he hurts?"

"Nope. Long as he gets his way."

Most of the cattle were dead, but a few had stampeded in fright. By now those that had survived would be halfway to the river.

Shadowhawk watched the men mount up and ride away. Once they were out of sight, he moved to the first dead carcass and withdrew an arrow.

Staring at it in confusion, he wondered why they had used arrows with Kiowa markings.

Shadowhawk's head swung in the direction of the house and he saw no lights. Shiloh and her brother had gone to bed, not even knowing how near danger had come to them.

Fury tore though his mind. Shiloh was in danger and he had to know why, and from whom. He would have to set up a vigil to make sure no harm came to her.

Shadowhawk rode toward the ranch house, and dropped the soft deerskin across the railing of the back porch.

His gift for Shiloh.

She was his to watch over, to keep safe, but not to keep.

Chapter Thirteen

The weather was hot, and with the cookstove the heat in the kitchen was almost unbearable, so Shiloh stepped out onto the porch for a breath of fresh air. A slight breeze brought the sweet smell of the honeysuckle bush that twined its way through the porch railings.

Shiloh turned to Luke, who stood beside her. The eastern sky was painted in bright crimson, reminding her that sunrises in Texas were almost as spectacular as the brilliant sunsets.

She started to say just that to Luke when she spotted something hanging over the porch railing.

"What is that?" Shiloh asked Luke, clutching his hand and venturing closer.

"It looks like a deerskin," Luke said, excitement creeping into his voice. "Who could have hung it here?"

Shiloh laid her hand on the deerskin, rubbing her fingers over its softness.

Luke grinned widely. "I'd say Shadowhawk was here again last night." He touched the deerskin, and nodded. "If I didn't know about his debt of honor, I'd say he was courting you, Shiloh. First he gives you a fine elk, now a beautiful robe. He never leaves anything for me."

"Silly," she laughed, ruffling his hair affectionately. Then Shiloh became serious. "This deerskin is beautiful," she admitted, folding it across her arm. "Maybe after this, Shadowhawk will leave us alone. It's unsettling to have a Comanche leaving me gifts." As the words left Shiloh's lips she realized that she was losing her fear of the Comanche chief. Something about his generosity touched her heart.

That thought frightened her.

Shadowhawk kept a vigil from the hillside. Shiloh would soon learn what had happened to her cattle, and he wanted to be nearby when she did. It was a strange feeling he was experiencing, knowing she was in trouble, yet not understanding how to help her.

He watched as Shiloh and her brother laughed together. It had never occurred to him that white people had some of the same feelings his family shared, though he could not imagine him and Moon Song laughing together.

His throat tightened when he saw Shiloh caress his gift; he knew that it pleased her.

Shadowhawk's attention was suddenly drawn to the old man who was riding in swiftly from the pasture. He would wait to see what transpired.

Watching Charley ride toward them at a full gallop, Shiloh turned to Luke. "Something's wrong," she said. "He'd never ride his horse that fast otherwise."

Brother and sister waited anxiously for Charley to dismount.

"We got us a passel of trouble!" Charley exclaimed, bending to catch his breath. "We lost nineteen head of cattle last night." He handed Luke the arrow. "It has the same Kiowa markings as the one that killed your pa. But it weren't no Kiowa that did this. I found hoof marks—the horses were shod, so they didn't belong to no Indian."

Shiloh gripped the porch post and stared at Charley in disbelief. "When will this ever stop? Who is doing this to us?"

"Like afore," Charley said with suspicion creeping into his tone, "I think it's Tyree's doing."

Shiloh held out the deerskin for Charley's inspection. "This was left on the porch during the night. I'm sure it's from Shadowhawk. Do you think he's responsible for the dead cattle?"

Charley glanced at the deerskin. "Nope. Don't think so. Why would he leave you a gift, then turn 'round to kill your stock?" Charley scratched his head, trying to put his thoughts into words. "You see, an Indian lives by reason— he won't give with one hand and take away with the other, 'cause it don't make sense."

Angrily, Luke met the old man's gaze. "We need to ride over to the Crooked H and confront Mr. Tyree, and tell him we know what he's doing."

"I don't 'zactly want to accuse anyone 'les I can prove for sure they done it."

Shiloh glanced at the bloodstained arrow and shuddered. "If it was Mr. Tyree, he might also have . . . killed Papa." She frowned and looked from Luke to Charley. "Papa was shot by the same kind of arrow. Captain Gunther and Mr. Briggs didn't think it was Kiowa, even though it looked like it." She was trembling inside. "Is it possible that he . . ."

She shook her head, unable to continue. "Mr. Tyree wants Estrella. Would he stoop so low to force us to sell?"

Charley glanced in the distance. "I don't rightly know. I think it's time for me to talk to Captain Gunther."

Shiloh nodded. "Be careful, Charley. I don't want anything happening to you."

"You two stay close to the house, and make sure the rifles are handy 'til I get back. I'll tell Hernando to keep an eye out. I'll be back afore sundown."

But Charley did not return by sundown, and Shiloh paced the floor, worrying about him. The inside of the house was stifling; even with the windows open there was no relief from the heat. Walking out to the porch, she lifted the weight of her hair off her neck. Flint was sitting on the steps of the bunkhouse, and the sound of his harmonica drifted back to her. It was a lonesome sound that struck at her heart.

Luke came out of the barn and flopped down on the steps. "If Charley doesn't come home soon, I'll ride toward town and search for him."

For the first time Shiloh noticed the buzzards circling the sky—the scavengers were feeding off the dead cattle. Coldness surrounded her heart and she was afraid. "No. You certainly will not ride toward town. It's just like when Papa didn't come home."

Before Luke could answer, they heard riders approaching. The harmonica fell silent and Shiloh's heart slowed until she heard Charley's voice. She also heard Captain Gunther being introduced to Flint.

Shiloh quickly swept her hand through her hair, capturing a stray curl and pushing it behind her ear. Captain Gunther was such a welcome sight, she smiled as he rode toward the house.

Dismounting, Gunther removed his hat. "Miss Braden, I'm glad to see you again, but not under these circumstances. Charley took me to the pasture where the cattle were slaughtered. Whoever did it is ruthless. They weren't rustlers, because they left the dead carcasses. It was done for a reason. I asked around and none of the other ranchers had similar attacks on their herds."

"Please come inside," Shiloh said, opening the screen door. "You must be hungry. I have beans and some corn bread with green chilies warming on the stove."

The Ranger smiled down at her. "I'm powerful hungry, ma'am."

After Gunther and Charley were seated, Shiloh served them supper. Then she and Luke sat down at the table with them.

"What are your thoughts about what happened to our cattle, Mr. Gunther?" Shiloh asked.

The Ranger buttered a slice of corn bread, while watching Shiloh. "I thought we had an understanding that you would call me Gunther."

Shiloh felt a blush climb up her cheeks. "I remember, Gunther."

The Ranger stared down at the bowl in front of him, as if choosing his words carefully. "I walked the pasture, and looked at the hoof marks. The horses were definitely shod. Just like before, someone is trying to make us believe it is Kiowa, but we know better. An Indian would have taken the meat."

"What about the Comanche?" Shiloh asked, explaining about the gifts left by Shadowhawk. "Could their war chief have done this and tried to implicate the Kiowa?"

"I'd say not. Comanche take credit for what they do. I can't see them trying to put the blame on another tribe." He took a bite, then chewed before he remarked, "It takes a white man to be that devious."

Shiloh ladled more beans into Charley's empty bowl, watching his eyes widen with appreciation.

"Even so, I wish this Comanche would leave us alone," Shiloh said wistfully.

Gunther set his fork aside. "You can't stop Shadowhawk until he's satisfied his obligation. As strange as it may sound to you, I doubt his tribe will do you any harm, now or in the future. The Comanche have a strong code of decency they abide by. He would not have his sister if not for you."

"How will we ever know who slaughtered our cattle?" Luke asked. "If we buy more, they will just do it again."

"Proof may be hard to come by, Luke. But whoever did this will eventually be caught. I have to leave for San Antonio in the morning, but I'll be back as soon as I settle my business there. Meantime, don't go far from the house. Whoever is doing this may become bolder."

Shiloh met Gunther's gaze. "Let me ask you this: is there some way we can set guards around the ranch?"

Gunther placed his fork on his plate. "There's just too much land to cover. What we could do is have men watch the house. I'll talk to Hernando about that."

"Thank you for coming all the way out here," Shiloh said, standing to stack the dirty dishes, then sinking them in the soapy dishpan.

Gunther stood, coming up behind her. "Miss Braden, if it's all right with you, I'll sleep in the bunkhouse tonight. I'll be gone at first light."

She smiled bleakly, wishing he didn't have to leave, but knowing his duty took him elsewhere. "Luke and I are always glad to see you, Gunther."

His eyes sparkled. "And you can bet it won't be too long before I show up again, asking for your hospitality."

It had been quiet for over a week and Shiloh was beginning to relax a bit, hoping whoever had killed the cattle had decided to leave Luke and her in peace.

In the late afternoon dark rain clouds gathered in the distance, and although they needed the rain, Shiloh knew it could mean trouble if the Brazos ran its banks. Already it was raining in the hills and gullies, and the cattle would be trapped on the other side of the river if they weren't driven across as soon as possible.

Hernando hurried toward the barn, and Shiloh ran after him. The three hands had already saddled up and were waiting for the *gran* vaquero. Luke threw his saddle over his horse and a short time later, they all rode out together.

Rounding up the cattle was not an easy task since lightning streaked across the sky, scattering the beasts in every direction. Finally they had rounded up the bigger part of the herd, and drove the animals across the river, which was already beginning to swell and churn.

Since she was riding in the rear, Shiloh was the only one who heard the calf bellowing in a gully. Turning her horse, she rode to its rescue. Dismounting, she found the animal caught among a clump of thornbushes, making her glad she'd worn her gloves. The poor calf couldn't be more than two days old, and it was too weak to free itself.

Shiloh heard a rider approaching and assumed it was her brother. "Help me. Its hind leg is caught."

"Yes, ma'am," a deep voice said. "Let me free him for you."

Shiloh shrank away when she saw the foreman of the Crooked H. "What are you doing on my land?" she asked, backing toward her horse.

"Now, now, ma'am, I'm just being neighborly." He freed the calf and gave it a slap on the rump, sending it running toward the river.

To Shiloh's dismay she saw her own riders were halfway across the river, and she was alone with this man. Hearing other riders approaching, Shiloh hoped Hernando had missed her and come back to look for her. But when the rider was close enough to see his face, she recognized Surge Tyree and two more of his men. Tyree dismounted and walked toward her, his eyes boring into hers.

"I heard about the cattle you lost the other day. Now, ain't that an awful shame?"

Shiloh was trembling, but she didn't want Tyree to know she was afraid of him. "Yes, it was an awful thing to do. Someone would have to be pretty low to kill helpless cattle."

"Little gal, you don't need to be out here in the rain," Tyree said, stepping closer to her. His gaze followed the raindrops that ran down her cheek and plopped onto her blouse, drawing his attention to the swell of her breasts.

"First of all, Mr. Tyree, I told you to call me Miss Braden. And if you'll move so I can mount my horse, I'll leave."

Tyree stepped closer to her, backing her toward the thornbush that had trapped the calf. He looked at Shiloh with a malicious expression. "I ain't stopping you."

They both knew Shiloh would have to brush against Tyree's body to get to her horse. And she wasn't about to do that.

"Boss," Rawlins said, "even out here in the rain she smells powerful sweet, don't you think?"

Shiloh pushed against Tyree. "And I can smell the stink of cowards. How many men does it take to bully one woman?" Anger drove her further, and she shoved Tyree aside. "Mr. Tyree, you are no gentleman if you allow your men to speak to me with such disrespect."

She must have struck a nerve because Tyree motioned for the others to mount up and ride away.

After his men had disappeared down a gully, the boss of the Crooked H turned back to Shiloh. "Surely you don't want to stay in this god forsaken place that has already robbed you of so much. How many cattle did you lose the other night?"

As the rain slowed, Shiloh met Tyree's gaze. "I'm sure you know the exact count."

His eyes narrowed. "Are you accusing me of something? I wouldn't like it if you were." Tyree reached for her and attempted to draw her into his arms, but Shiloh fought and struggled to free herself from him.

The Comanche moved so quietly that neither of them heard him approach. Shiloh smothered a startled scream when all of a sudden Shadowhawk appeared from out of nowhere and yanked Tyree away from her, placing the blade of his knife at the terrified man's throat. Shiloh didn't know which was the greatest threat, Tyree or Shadowhawk, but instinct drove her to do the right thing and she reached out to stay the hand that held the knife.

"Don't do this," she said decisively, hoping he understood her.

Shadowhawk gazed into Shiloh's eyes and she saw the fierceness of his spirit in them. She was relieved when he flung Tyree to the ground and sheathed his knife.

Tyree didn't waste any time scrambling to his feet and mounting his horse, riding away and leaving Shiloh to face the Indian alone.

She swallowed deep, her eyes widening. "Please go away."

In that moment, a streak of lightning struck nearby and Shiloh's horse bolted, leaving her alone with Shadowhawk.

His eyes almost begged her not to fear him as he lifted her into his arms and carried her the few paces to his horse. He mounted with her in his arms.

Frozen with fear, Shiloh wondered if he was kidnapping her when he rode farther downstream to cross the river.

"Where are you taking me?"

Shadowhawk's dark gaze fell on her, and he shifted her weight, holding her close.

Shiloh's clothing was soaked and she was so cold she couldn't stop trembling. Shadowhawk gathered her against his warmth and she buried her face against his shoulder. "Take me home."

When they crossed the river, the swirling water was halfway up the horse's haunches. Shadowhawk guided his mount to the riverbank and it soon became clear to Shiloh that he wasn't going to harm her—he was indeed taking her home.

When they reached the hill where her mother and father were buried, Shadowhawk dismounted and lifted her to the ground.

Her gaze locked with his, and she saw questioning in

his dark eyes. "Thank you," she said, reaching out to place her hand on his arm. "I will never forget what you did for me today."

Shadowhawk moved back as if her touch had stung him. Mounting his horse, he stared at Shiloh for a long moment before whirling the animal around and disappearing into the rain.

Although Shiloh could no longer see him, she stood there, her heart thundering in her breast. How strange it was that the Indian she had been terrified of had become her savior.

Shivering with cold, Shiloh made her way down the hill to the house, too weary to think.

She found Charley pacing on the porch. His face lit up when he saw her. "Everyone's gone looking for you. I stayed here in case you came home." He looked around. "How'd you get here? I didn't hear you ride up."

Shiloh stepped beneath the shelter of the porch. "Shadowhawk brought me home." She explained to Charley what had happened, and how Shadowhawk had rescued her from Tyree.

"You don't say? Looks like Shadowhawk's still looking after you."

Tyree considered himself fortunate to be alive. That Comanche had come upon him so quickly, he hadn't had time to draw his gun. He thought about the Braden girl. He'd left her to her own devices, and the Comanche had probably kidnapped her or killed her. He shrugged. If she was dead or gone, he'd have one less Braden to deal with.

The next morning when Shiloh was cooking breakfast, Charley ambled into the house. "You ain't gonna believe this—someone rescued the calf from the other side of the river and put it in the barn. Your horse is there too."

Warmth filled Shiloh. "Shadowhawk brought them home."

"That's what I'm thinking."

"There's something more," Charley said, shaking his head. "Tip Rawlins rode by this mornin'. It's kinda strange. He wanted to know if'n you made it home yesterday."

Shiloh knew exactly why Rawlins had come calling. Tyree wanted to know what had happened between her and Shadowhawk. "Did he say why he wanted to know?"

"Nope. But when I said you was fine, he lit out."

As the days passed, Shiloh found herself watching for Shadowhawk. If only she could make him understand how grateful she was to him for saving her from Tyree.

At times, she had a feeling he was nearby, but he didn't show himself to her. She began to wonder what his life was like, and one night she even dreamed of him.

Trouble came one day when Shiloh was least expecting it. She was sitting at her father's desk, trying to make sense of the account books, when Flint knocked on the door.

He twisted his hat in his hands and cleared his throat. "Miss Braden, I hate doing this, ma'am, but when I signed on, I didn't expect to have to fight Tyree and his men."

"Has he threatened you?"

"Yes, ma'am, he did. And if it's all the same with you, I'll be drawing my pay and heading out today."

"I need you here, Flint. I wish you would reconsider."

"I ain't no coward, if that's what you're thinking, ma'am," Flint said. "I just want to live long enough to marry Betty Sue and have kids, maybe have a place of our own someday."

"I understand," she told him.

And she did.

Chapter Fourteen

July swept across West Texas, bringing sweltering heat in its wake. The grass turned straw-colored and even leaves on the hardy mesquite trees seemed to droop from the constant need of rain.

Life was hard, and each day was a challenge—another hill to climb.

Shiloh tossed and turned on her bed, unable to find a comfortable position. In frustration she swung her legs to the floor, slid her arms into her robe, and belted the waist. In the kitchen, she poured herself a glass of water and carried it out onto the porch, not understanding why she was so restless.

A barn owl called to its mate, and a coyote's lonely wail echoed across nearby Wild Horse Canyon.

Shiloh had never felt so alone.

On impulse, she stepped off the porch and headed up the hill where she had last seen Shadowhawk. A half-moon illuminated her path. When she reached the grave site, she stood quietly for a long time, yearning for something that was just out of reach.

Shiloh wasn't sure what alerted her to the fact that she was not alone; there was no sound or movement to warn her, she just felt someone's presence. Turning slowly, she found herself standing face-to-face with Shadowhawk.

Her heart sang with joy, but she was still nervous around him. Taking a quick step away from him, she wondered how long he'd been watching her.

At last she found her voice, although it trembled when she spoke, "I know you don't understand my words, but I was hoping you would be here."

Shadowhawk just stared at her searchingly.

"I wish I could tell you how much I appreciate what you did for me at the river that awful night." Shiloh frowned, trying to put her thoughts into words. "I guess what I want to say is you don't owe me anything. You protected me from Tyree, so please consider your debt to this family paid."

Shadowhawk took a step toward her, and she stood her ground. With a gentleness that took her by surprise, he lightly touched her hair, his dark gaze tracing the lines of her face.

In that moment, Shiloh knew she would never fear him again.

He placed his hand over his heart and then nodded toward her father's grave with a sympathetic glance.

Warmth washed over her as she realized what he was trying to convey to her. "I understand. You are expressing your sorrow for my father's death," she said softly, her grief piercing.

Shadowhawk took her hand. Reaching up, he plucked two feathers from his hair and placed them in Shiloh's palm, closing her fingers over them. Before she could react, he turned away, disappearing into the shadows.

Shiloh opened her hand to look at the two white feathers.

What could they mean?

Her gaze swept the shadows, but she knew she was alone. Shadowhawk was gone.

It was still hours before dawn as Shadowhawk galloped across a ravine, carefully guiding his horse up the other side. He had gone to the ranch, as he often did, to keep watch over Shiloh. He had been drawn to the hillside, never expecting Shiloh would go there as well. He had thought to leave the feathers on her father's grave, but he had been fortunate to be able to place them in her hand.

She would have no way of knowing that in giving her the white feathers, he had pledged his protection and a lifelong commitment. It was a solitary path he had set for himself. He would never give another woman the white feathers.

Tonight Shiloh had greeted him with pleasure, and her reaction had taken him by surprise. He had left quickly because he had been overcome by a strong desire to hold her to him. In all honor, he could not act upon those feelings.

Why was this happening to him?

Her hair. He closed his eyes. It had been soft to the touch, and the sweetest scent had clung to her. Even now he could smell the fragrance that was Shiloh.

A deep yearning tore at his heart, and he slammed his heels into his horse's flanks.

She had released him from his debt tonight, but he would not leave her. For reasons he could not understand, she was in danger. Not comprehending the white man's ways, he found it difficult to know how to help her.

Shadowhawk had no answers, but he would.

Racing his horse across the prairie, Shadowhawk could not outrun his yearning. He had been amazed when Shiloh had allowed him to touch her. He had seen the exact moment when she gave him her trust.

Pulling on the reins, he halted his horse, staring up at the same moon that had shone upon Shiloh's beautiful face.

Her name sang in his mind like a melody on the wind.

Scorching winds continued to blow across the prairie, while wildflowers withered and died. The Brazos was low, and the cattle had to wade in mud to satisfy their thirst.

It had been three weeks since Shiloh had encountered Shadowhawk that night beside her father's grave. He had been strangely gentle, and without speaking a word, he had brought her a measure of comfort.

She opened the small ebony case her father had given her for her sixteenth birthday and touched the white feathers that lay on the velvet lining. She removed a feather and raised it to her cheek. As she closed her eyes, the softness against her skin revived the memory of Shadowhawk's gentle touch. She had told no one about the incident. It had been a moment to cherish, a moment that belonged to her alone.

The next morning the family had another reason for concern.

Luke had risen early and headed toward the barn, only to find an Indian lance had been driven into the ground near the back door. Hurrying to find Charley before Shiloh discovered the lance, he found the old man coming out of the bunkhouse.

Hearing voices in the backyard, Shiloh came outside and saw Charley circling some kind of Indian lance, while Luke waited anxiously. The weapon had strange markings on it, and two white feathers were tied to the end with a beaded leather strap.

"What does this mean?" Shiloh asked, fighting back tears of anger and frustration.

"This here ain't no threat," Charley said, grinning. "We don't want to remove it—let it stay as it is. This here's a message from Shadowhawk, warnin' everyone, Indian and white man alike, not to trespass on this ranch. I can tell you this for fact—there ain't no Comanche or Kiowa gonna go agin' Shadowhawk."

"Charley, what do white feathers mean to the Comanche?" Shiloh asked, thinking of the ones Shadowhawk had given her.

"It means Shadowhawk's become your protector." Charley squinted his eyes and took a closer look at the lance. "I think he knows you're in danger, and he's sent his warning to anyone who comes to Estrella with bad intent, that they'll have to deal with him. Course, it seems to me, he should consider his debt paid by now, seein' as you released him from it. I just can't figure why he's still 'round."

This was Shiloh's chance to tell Charley about the feathers, but she was reluctant to share that special moment with anyone. "It means protection?"

"It do. Course, Tyree don't know that, but you surely won't have to worry 'bout any Indians coming to call."

Shiloh's gaze went to the hillside where she had last seen Shadowhawk. Two other nights she had gone up the hill, hoping to find him there. But he did not come.

As days rolled into weeks, the family settled into an uneasy routine. Acting on Charley's advice, Shiloh and Luke left Shadowhawk's lance where it was. Every time Shiloh saw the lance, it was a reminder that she was under Shadowhawk's protection.

Often when she stepped out of the house, her gaze would sweep the area. But Shadowhawk was like a ghost—if he was nearby, he was invisible to her.

One morning Luke found the tracks of an unshod horse near the barn. Charley thought Shadowhawk had purposely left the tracks to let them know he was still there.

He certainly would not have left such a visible sign of his presence otherwise.

Chapter Fifteen

Disaster struck again.

This time Shiloh was really scared. Someone had come up to the house during the night and put a rattlesnake in Luke's bedroom.

Luckily, Luke had just dressed for the day when he saw the rattler slither under his bed. "Shiloh," he shouted, "bring the broom. Hurry!"

Hearing the desperation in her brother's voice, Shiloh reacted right away. Between the two of them, they managed to hook the broom around the snake and toss it out the window.

"This was no accident," Shiloh said, falling back on Luke's bed as she waited for her heartbeat to return to normal. She sat up, thinking. "Let's check for footprints," she suggested, already starting for the door.

Brother and sister hurried out of the house. Once they reached the window that led to Luke's bedroom, they dropped to their knees, examining the area.

"Boot prints," Shiloh said, pointing to a fresh set of tracks.

"When will this stop?" Luke asked angrily.

"If it's Tyree, and we both know it was, he won't stop until he drives us off Estrella."

"We'll just see about that," Luke said. "He thinks because I'm not grown, I can't protect you. But I won't let anything happen to you, Shiloh."

"I know that," she said, hugging him to her, grateful he

had not been bitten by the rattler. "Like I always say, we have each other."

Charley had told her that the Comanche Moon would rise in September. He'd explained that during that time most Comanche went raiding across the land. Although it was late August, and September was approaching, Shiloh felt no fear of their ranch being raided: she was under Shadowhawk's protection.

"Shiloh!" Luke called as he ran through the house, searching for her. He paused in the doorway, breathing hard to catch his breath. "Charley's and Hernando's horses are missing from the paddock!"

She looked at Luke with concern. "How did it happen?"

"Charley says he checked on them before he went to bed last night, and they were fine. Whoever took them came during the night."

"It's got to be Tyree again."

Luke's eyes were filled with anger. "If I was older, I'd ride right up to his house and demand he give us back those horses."

"Why just take two horses? Why not take them all?" Shiloh turned, whispering beneath her breath. "I don't understand that man's thinking."

"Charley thinks it's Tyree's way of reminding us he hasn't given up."

"I think you're right; it's time we pay that man a visit," Shiloh stated, stalking across the kitchen floor, and out the back door toward the barn. "Now!"

Luke's eyes glinted with excitement. "You mean we're going to confront Mr. Tyree?"

Shiloh paused inside the barn and looked at her brother. "I doubt he'll admit to taking our horses. We'll just let him know we think it was him."

Charley and Hernando had seen the brother and sister enter the barn and hurried to joined them.

Charley watched Shiloh saddle her horse. "So ya decided to do somethin'. We're going with you."

Shiloh agreed with a nod.

By the time Shiloh and the others reached the perimeter of the Crooked H ranch, several of Tyree's wranglers fell in behind them.

"Don't pay them any mind," Charley said dismissively. "They won't do nothin' without their boss's orders."

They rode for miles before they sighted the ranch house. The house was a large two-story structure with a bunkhouse almost as large as the ranch house at Estrella. Blooded horses whinnied behind whitewashed fences, and several colts frolicked beside them.

By the time they reined in their horses, Tyree came out of the house to greet them. His wife, whom Shiloh had never met, came down the veranda steps behind him. She was slender, with dark hair and fine features. Mrs. Tyree was having a difficult time meeting Shiloh's gaze, and she appeared frightened about something.

Surge Tyree stopped at the hitching post, his gaze going from Shiloh to Luke. "This is an unexpected pleasure," he said sarcastically. "Dare I hope you're here because you want to sell me Estrella?"

"Mr. Tyree, you're a mean man," Luke said, sitting tall in his saddle. "We know everything you've done to us, and we don't like it. Last night some of your men took two of our horses. We're here to get them back."

"Now, youngster, that's a mighty insulting accusation, and I don't like it much," Tyree remarked, as his gaze hardened. "Matter of fact, I don't like it at all."

"Surge," Mrs. Tyree said, touching his sleeve tentatively.

"It's hot. Shouldn't we invite our guests in for a cool drink?"

Tyree spun around to his wife and she shrank back. "When I want your advice, I'll ask for it. Get back in the house, woman, and leave men to do a man's work."

Shiloh watched Mrs. Tyree's eyes close with shame as she hurried up the steps and entered the house. She felt a sudden rush of pity for the woman, who was apparently frightened by her own husband. "It seems you don't treat your own any better than you treat your neighbors," Shiloh remarked insultingly, meeting Tyree's angry gaze with a look of contempt.

"You have no right to say that to me. My wife and daughter have everything money can buy." Tyree's gaze swept from Shiloh to Luke and back again. His tone softened, and he smiled slyly. "One day I'll give my daughter Estrella for a gift."

Shiloh was aware that the Crooked H riders that had followed them were drawn up in a circle behind them. She was too angry to be afraid. "You can't give what doesn't belong to you. I'm warning you," Shiloh said. "Don't come on our land again, and don't send others. We have been tolerant up to now—but that stopped last night when you stole our horses. There won't be any more stock killed, horses stolen, or snakes in our house. Do we understand each other?"

"Yeah," Luke said. "Do we?"

Tyree was furious. "Now, look here—"

Undaunted, Shiloh held up her hand. "I don't want to hear anything you have to say. I'm just warning you to leave us alone." She glanced at her brother. "Let's go home."

Tyree's face was red with rage as he watched the sister and brother turn their backs on him and ride away.

Charley and Hernando had hung back with their rifles across their laps in case there was trouble.

Charley was proud of how Shiloh and Luke had stood up to Tyree. "You'd best take Miss Shiloh's warning for gospel. There'll be hell to pay if any of your men step one foot on Estrella."

"You're as good as dead, old man." Tyree's outraged gaze swept over Hernando's face. "And so are you."

The Mexican laughed. "Maybe so, Señor. I have already lived longer than I expected to."

Two days had passed since Shiloh and her brother had visited the Crooked H. Each man on Estrella wore a gun and carried a rifle, waiting for Tyree to retaliate. The man certainly would not let their challenge go unanswered for long.

It came as no surprise to Shiloh when Bud Rankin decided to leave. He told Shiloh he was sorry to desert her, but that he didn't want to be part of a fight between Tyree and two untested young people. At least Horace Beck had stayed on. That gave them three guns against the dozens from the Crooked H.

Hernando and Charley had devised a plan to guard the place. One of them would take the night watch, and the other would patrol by day. They'd make sure they were visible to anyone who decided to trespass.

Everyone waited, with the knowledge that a showdown would surely come. They would be ready for it when it did.

Chapter Sixteen

Shiloh awoke as if she'd been jerked out of sleep.

Turning her head toward the window, she watched the curtain ripple in the wind against a red glow.

Something was wrong!

Terribly wrong.

Smoke.

She smelled smoke.

Scrambling out of bed, she grabbed her robe and hurried across the kitchen, flinging open the back door. Her heart skipped a beat when she saw the barn was on fire.

Shiloh didn't pause to think as she hurried down the steps, knowing she had to get the horses to safety.

By the time she entered the barn, she could already feel the intense heat against her face. Flames were licking at the dry hay and spreading toward the animals. She could hear the frightened horses rearing and kicking against their stalls.

Shiloh knew she could never lead the horses past the fire unless she covered their eyes. Ripping her robe off, she went to the first stall, which held Luke's horse. The animal was terrified, but she managed to throw her robe over its head, and finally led it outside, sending it galloping with a slap on its haunches.

Hurrying back inside, she unlatched the next two stall gates and reached for her own horse. Perla had always been skittish, and at the moment the mare's eyes were walleyed with fear. Fighting to cover Perla's head, Shiloh stumbled and struck her head on the stall, just as a crashing timber fell beside her. Sobbing, she tried one more time to rescue her horse, but the mare kept rearing, making it impossible to control her.

Flames curled all around Shiloh, and smoke stung her eyes. She had lost her sense of direction and she was finding it difficult to breathe.

When another burning plank fell at her feet, she realized the danger she was in. Despite the flames that whooshed in her direction, Shiloh forced her way forward. Hearing a crackling over her head, she ducked just in time to miss the burning timber that swung down toward her. To protect her face, she instinctively raised her arms over her head. But the flames hit the palms of her hands and she felt a searing pain.

Crying, she turned around in a circle, trying to get her bearings. Just when she thought all was hopeless, a shadowy form came through the flames, scooping her into his arms.

Shiloh cried out with relief when she saw Shadowhawk. Without ceremony, he threw a wet blanket over her head and carried her outside. He pushed her into someone else's arms, and Shiloh fought to throw off the blanket. She was startled when she realized another Indian held her in a tight grip.

Taking in a cleansing breath, Shiloh fought and clawed in an attempt to get away from the Comanche, but he refused to release her. "The horses—I have to get to them," she cried.

Shaking his head, the Comanche issued an order, and she grasped his meaning even though she did not understand his words.

There was a horrible sound of pain, such as Shiloh had never heard from an animal, and her eyes filled with tears.

The Comanche's grip tightened and she fell helplessly back against him. With a sob building inside her, Shiloh watched Shadowhawk rush back inside the burning barn.

Minutes passed with the slowness of hours. The whole barn was engulfed in flames and Shiloh feared the entire structure would come crashing down with Shadowhawk inside. Distraught, she tried once more to pull free of the Comanche, but he issued another curt order.

At last Shadowhawk emerged from the smoke, leading her horse to safety. By now Luke was beside her, and the Comanche released Shiloh and joined his chief.

"Are you hurt?" her brother asked, looking her over carefully. "Are you burned anywhere?"

"The palms of my hands are burned a little, but it's not bad," she said, hardly feeling the pain. She didn't know she was crying until she felt tears on her cheeks. "Papa's horse is still in the last stall."

Luke saw it was impossible for anyone to go into the barn. His gaze went from the Indian standing beside them to the one who had led Shiloh's horse to the paddock. "That's Shadowhawk, isn't it?"

"Yes, it is."

Luke's eyes widened in awe as he stared at the legend. "He saved your life, didn't he?"

"Yes, he did," Shiloh said, glancing at Shadowhawk, who was speaking quietly to his companion.

Shiloh's eyes widened in horror as she heard the unmistakable sounds of their father's horse in its dying thralls. At that moment the whole barn collapsed in a heap, sending out a cloud of burning ash and bright flames that licked at the darkened sky.

Shiloh fell to her knees and buried her face in her hands. "Why did Tyree do this? What kind of monster is he?"

Charley came hurrying toward them, his rifle across his arm. "Hernando's been knocked on the head, and he's out cold." The old man's gaze fell on the Comanche, and he spoke a few words of greeting to them in their tongue. "I saw what they did. They saved your life."

"Charley," Shiloh cried, shaking with grief. "Papa's horse . . . I couldn't save him. We were fortunate half the horses were out to pasture."

"I'm damned mad—begging your pardon, Miss Shiloh, for speaking so plain. When I woke, it was too late to save the barn. I found Hernando slumped on his porch, where he'd been standing guard. Whoever did this snuck up behind him and clobbered him." He nodded at the two Indians. "'Less I miss my guess, that tall one's Shadowhawk." Charley turned his attention back to the brother and sister. "Looks like you owe him your life, Miss Shiloh."

Shiloh stood, her knees almost too weak to hold her weight. "Yes, he did. And he went back inside to save Perla."

"Will the Rangers arrest Tyree now?" Luke asked between clenched teeth, trying not to cry. "He did this, didn't he, Charley?"

"I know it for sure now. When I found Hernando outside his house, I saw Tip Rawlins ridin' away, like the skunk he is." He nodded in Shadowhawk's direction. "We're lucky he was here tonight."

"Yes," Shiloh agreed.

"I knowed he'd been watching the house for several nights. I wonder if he suspected something was 'bout to happen? The Comanche is smart about reading signs."

Feeling defeated, Shiloh suddenly realized she wore only her night shift, and it was damp and clinging to her, but modesty didn't seem to matter at the moment. "Shouldn't we send for Gunther? This time you actually saw Rawlins riding away. We have our proof now."

Luke unclenched his fists and put an arm around his sister. "I'm just glad you weren't hurt worse."

Watching flames shooting in the night sky, Shiloh thought of her father's horse and said nothing. One more connection to their father was broken.

Luke's eyes widened as he watched Shadowhawk approach. "I can't believe it's really him."

With his companion at his side, Shadowhawk spoke to Charley in Comanche.

Charley in turn told Shiloh what was said. "Shadowhawk wants you to know the other horse did not suffer long."

It was small comfort to Shiloh, but she appreciated Shadowhawk's kindness in trying to comfort her.

Before Shiloh knew what was happening, the other Comanche grabbed Luke, while Shadowhawk swept Shiloh into his arms.

"What do you think you're doing!" she cried, trying to twist out of Shadowhawk's arms.

Shadowhawk spoke quickly to Charley, and Charley said something back to him. She could tell by Charley's tone he was angry.

"What did Shadowhawk say?" she demanded.

Charley glanced at her. "He says you and the boy are in danger here, and he's not too happy that I ain't kept you safe, so he's takin' you both with him."

"Is he crazed? We aren't going with him. Tell him to put me down," she insisted.

Charley saw Shadowhawk's fierce expression. "No, I don't believe I'll be tellin' him that, Miss Shiloh. But don't fret none; he gave his word you won't be harmed, and I believe him."

Terror tore through Shiloh's mind. "Do something, Charley. I don't want to go with him!"

Again Charley spoke to Shadowhawk, then translated his response. "Shadowhawk says you *will* go with him."

"No!" she said, pushing against Shadowhawk's broad

chest. His gaze locked with hers, and she saw in that moment, he would not relent.

"Ain't no use in struggling, Miss Shiloh. He's got his mind set."

Shadowhawk said something more to Charley and then mounted his horse, settling Shiloh across his lap, while the other Comanche swung Luke up behind him on his horse.

Luke glanced at Charley, trying to understand what was happening. "Where are they taking us?"

"Someplace safe—leastwise that's what Shadowhawk told me," Charley assured the boy. "No need to be afeard. I'll get Captain Gunther and we'll come after you."

Shiloh reached out to Charley, just as Shadowhawk whirled his horse around and raced away into the night.

"No," she cried, watching Charley until he was no more than a shadow against the reflection of the burning barn. "Please take me home."

Shadowhawk ignored her.

Before they rode out of sight, Shiloh turned back to look at the smoldering ruins, her body trembling violently with fear.

So much had happened in the last few months, Shiloh could hardly sort it all out in her mind. Tears welled in her eyes and then coursed down her cheeks.

She turned to her brother, wanting to reassure him. "You heard Charley say he and Gunther will come after us."

Luke nodded, his eyes filled with confusion. "I heard."

Shadowhawk kicked his horse in the flanks and it pulled ahead of his companion's horse.

Shiloh had the feeling Shadowhawk didn't want her talking to Luke. She thought she'd try one more time to reason with him. "I don't know if you understand me, but I need to know why you're doing this. I want to go home."

Shadowhawk did not respond to her. Instead, he called to his companion in words Shiloh didn't understand. But he must have told him to keep up, because the two of them soon rode neck and neck at a gallop.

Shiloh fell into a glum silence. Her words to her brother had been meant to comfort him, but for herself, Shiloh could find no solace. They were being taken deeper into the wilderness of Texas, far from white settlements, into a land where the Comanche ruled.

Staring into that vast wilderness, Shiloh felt insignificant. A person could disappear in this vast expanse and never be found.

Shadowhawk was angry at a nameless, faceless enemy. What would have happened to Shiloh if he had not been watching out for her tonight?

The wind picked up a lock of her hair, blowing it across Shadowhawk's face, and he closed his eyes as it brushed against his lips. He glanced at her hand; her fingers were long and tapered, and it was clear she had never worked the same way Comanche women toiled for their families.

He felt the curve of her body as she moved in his arms, and his heart leapt in his throat. He wanted her—his body ached for her—but he could never have her.

Until he knew she was safe, Shiloh would be under his care. But the moment the danger had passed, he intended to take her home. His duty was to his people, not to her.

Shadowhawk stared straight ahead. But his heart knew her, and he would never forget how she felt in his arms.

Chapter Seventeen

As the moon shone down on the craggy hills, Shadowhawk guided his horse into a shallow creek and they rode through the water for miles.

Any hope Shiloh had of being rescued plummeted. Although Charley had promised he would find them, it didn't look like Shadowhawk would leave a trail to follow.

Shiloh had been holding herself rigid, but in her exhausted state, her head fell back against Shadowhawk's shoulder. She felt the muscles in the arms that circled her, and in that moment, she felt safe. Lately, whenever she had been in danger, he had come to her. She felt his arms tighten. Something was stirring in her heart—a new emotion—a disturbing sensation.

At last Shadowhawk guided his horse up the embankment and the animal picked its way across rocks and hard-packed ground.

Shiloh glanced up at the moon, unable to distinguish which direction they were traveling. When she glanced at Luke, she saw he'd fallen asleep with his head resting against the other Comanche's back.

With surprising gentleness, Shadowhawk's arms tightened about Shiloh, and her face was brought against his soft buckskin skirt. Shiloh was so weary she too closed her eyes, finding a measure of comfort in his arms. Ever so softly she felt him touch her hair; then he said something in the Comanche language, his tone deep, and she thought he might be attempting to comfort and reassure her.

The heavy hand of fatigue settled on Shiloh, and she nestled against Shadowhawk, not wanting to dwell on the horrible events of the night. Weariness swamped her, beckoned her to surrender to the forgetfulness of sleep—and she finally succumbed to that invitation.

She had no way of judging how long she'd slept, but when she finally awoke, it was late morning. She immediately turned her head toward Luke to make sure he was safe. He appeared to be asleep.

Shiloh had little doubt that if their father's horse hadn't died in the fire, her brother would have looked upon this as a great adventure.

Pulling away from Shadowhawk, she glanced up at him to find him watching her. "How can I make you understand that you need to take me home? That if I don't go back, I could lose Estrella?"

His gaze turned fierce and unrelenting, forcing her to lower hers. The distance between her and Estrella was widening with each step the sure-footed pinto took, and she was going into the unknown.

Suddenly Shadowhawk pulled his mount up and raised his hand for his companion to do the same. He helped Shiloh dismount, then slid off his horse while the other Comanche obediently followed his lead.

Taking Shiloh's arm and gripping his horse's reins, Shadowhawk led them down a steep incline and pushed Shiloh behind a cluster of mesquite bushes, while Running Fox and Luke hid in the shadows of an overhanging rock.

Shiloh searched the expanse around them, puzzled. "I didn't hear anything. Why—"

Shadowhawk clamped his hand over her mouth and shoved her to the ground. Sharp rocks bit painfully into her knees, and when she tried to rise, Shadowhawk held her in place.

Trembling with fear, she didn't dare utter another word. It wasn't long until she heard the sound of riders.

Shiloh cringed when Shadowhawk's free hand went to the knife attached to his belt. She saw ruthlessness shadow his face, and his dark eyes became piercing. In that moment, Shiloh knew he would kill without hesitation. He was primed and ready to meet danger in combat.

Shiloh heard the riders rein in their horses, and their voices carried on the wind. She pressed against the ground as terror poured through her body. Not ten paces away from their hiding place, a group of Indians had stopped to water their horses in the river.

Since Shadowhawk did not greet the Indians, she guessed they were not from his tribe. He knelt beside her, his gaze fastened on the intruders, tension radiating from him. Deciding she wanted to get a better glimpse of the other Indians, Shiloh moved forward.

Shadowhawk broke off his surveillance long enough to shove her back into the shadows. Tense moments passed before the intruders rode away.

Still Shadowhawk did not move, so Shiloh didn't either.

At last Shadowhawk stood, pulling Shiloh up beside him. He said something to the other warrior, and the man climbed cautiously up the ravine. When he returned, he hunkered down near Shadowhawk and the two of them conversed.

Shiloh expected them to leave right away, but Shadowhawk went to the ground and pulled her down beside him. The other Comanche led Luke to Shiloh and she pulled her brother close.

"Why aren't we leaving? Who were those other Indians?" Luke whispered.

"I don't know," Shiloh answered. "Perhaps they have camped somewhere nearby."

Shadowhawk did not try to silence them, so she gathered the other tribe was not near enough to hear them.

"Do you think Charley is tracking us?" Luke asked, standing to his full height.

"I think he would have gone straight to the Ranger station and enlisted Gunther's help." Her hand sought her brother's. "Don't worry, they will find us."

Feeling Shadowhawk's seeking gaze on her, Shiloh refused to look at him, and was relieved when he moved up the embankment. She felt throbbing pain in her hands, and turned the palms up to examine the angry blisters on them. They were so painful she gritted her teeth to keep from crying.

She had not heard Shadowhawk return. She flinched when he bent down beside her, taking her hands in a firm grip.

Looking at her for a long moment, he stood and quickly disappeared again up the embankment. He was gone for quite a while, and when he returned, he knelt beside her, once more taking her hands in his. Crushing the stems of a milkweed plant, he wiped the sticky substance on her burns. After a moment, she did feel some relief.

Shadowhawk pulled Shiloh to her feet and offered her a waterskin, which she readily took and drank thirstily. The other Indian offered Luke a drink of water too. Shadowhawk climbed on his horse and held his hand out; grasping Shiloh by the arm, he swung her around behind him.

In the gathering heat of midday, they once again galloped across the prairie. To keep from being unseated, Shiloh was forced to lock her arms about Shadowhawk's waist. She could feel every breath he took, and soon the rhythm of her breathing matched his. Somehow it felt right for her to be with him. She pressed her face against his back, feeling the honed muscles beneath her cheek.

She should be afraid of him, and she was, but she did not fear that he would hurt her—rather that he would take her into the great unknown and she might never see her home again.

Hour after hour passed and the sun began its long descent into the west. Hungry, thirsty, and too weary to think, Shiloh finally fell asleep. She slept the night through, hardly stirring when Shadowhawk pulled her in front of him and held her in his arms.

Shadowhawk halted his horse. He swung Shiloh to the ground, and she sleepily glanced about. She could hardly believe she had slept so long, but it was dawn, and golden streaks stretched across the eastern sky, announcing the approach of day.

Shiloh was still trying to shake herself awake when Shadowhawk rode off, leaving her and Luke with the other Comanche. The man motioned for them to be seated, and they did as he indicated.

Luke leaned his head against his sister's shoulder, and they both took comfort from each other's nearness.

"Where do you suppose they are taking us?" he asked.

Shiloh glanced at the Comanche, who seemed to be ignoring them. "I don't know. Maybe to their village."

A burst of sunlight hit the tree-lined creek and spread its light across the land. Shiloh glanced down at her nightgown. Although it covered as much of her body as her dress would have, it was made of thin muslin, and she felt exposed. There wasn't anything she could do about it, though.

"Do you think Tyree will take over Estrella if we aren't there to stop him?"

"No, I don't, Luke. The law would never allow him to take over without our consent." She smiled, pushing a dark strand of hair off his forehead. "I can only imagine Surge Tyree's confusion when he learns we've been abducted by Comanche. He can't cause us any more mischief if he doesn't know where we are."

"Are you afraid?" Luke asked.

She glanced up at the sky, noticing it promised to be a clear day. "I know I should be, and maybe I am a little," she answered as honestly as she could. "But I believe we can trust Shadowhawk."

Shiloh noticed the smudges on Luke's face and imagined hers must look the same. "Let's wash ourselves," she said, moving down the riverbank, and dipping her hands into the water.

The Comanche merely glanced at them and then took up his stance as guard, staring into the distance.

Since Shiloh was barefooted, she felt sharp rocks pierce her feet. Bending, she took a deep drink and then washed as much of her body as she could reach without exposing herself. Holding her hands in the cool water felt soothing to her burns.

Nodding to her brother, she guided him back up the bank and they both settled beneath the sheltering branches of a tall mesquite.

Luke compressed his lips. "I'm hungry."

"I know. So am I." Then she smiled at him mischievously. "Wouldn't you like a bowl of my cornmeal mush right about now?"

He laughed. "I'd even take that if it was offered to me."

They became subdued when they saw how curiously the Comanche looked at them.

With nothing to do but wait, Luke yawned and laid his head in her lap, his eyes closing as he drifted to sleep. With her back braced against the trunk of the tree, Shiloh also fall asleep, but she jerked awake moments later when she heard voices.

Shadowhawk had returned to camp and was conversing with his companion, all the while staring at Shiloh.

Didn't that man ever need sleep? she wondered in agitation.

Moments later he walked toward the river and bent to cup his hands, taking a deep drink.

When Shadowhawk stood, staring into the distance, Shiloh took the opportunity to study him. He was a most handsome man, in a dark, sensual way. His ebony hair fell past his shoulders, and he wore no adornment other than a leather band and three feathers woven through the strands. He was tall, and his beaded shirt was stretched taut across his broad shoulders. His features were chiseled, his dark eyes expressive.

Shadowhawk had come to represent everything noble to her.

He must have felt Shiloh's scrutiny because he turned, his gaze colliding with hers. The effect sent a shock through her. There was no disrespect in the way he examined her attire, merely curiosity. After a moment, he turned back to his companion.

Even though he was no longer watching her, Shiloh's heart was pounding. Shadowhawk affected her as no man ever had. Perhaps it was the danger he represented, or the fact that he was different from the men she knew.

Luke stirred and sat up, stretching and yawning. When he saw that Shadowhawk had returned, he scrambled to his feet and walked toward him.

The young chief turned to Luke, studying him for a moment before going to his horse and removing something from a leather bag.

"Pemmican," Shadowhawk said, thrusting something at Luke. Then he pointed to Shiloh.

For a moment all Luke could do was stare at the Comanche whom few white men had ever seen. "I sure wish you could speak English," he said. "There's so many things I want to ask you."

Shadowhawk nodded at the pemmican, indicating the boy should share it with his sister.

"Are we to eat this?" Luke asked, glancing down at what appeared to be some form of dried meat.

Again Shadowhawk motioned toward Shiloh.

Luke rejoined his sister, handing her half the dried meat. "What do you suppose this is?"

"If it's what I think it is, Moon Song told me it was delicious. Eat, Luke—you need your strength."

Luke wrinkled his nose. "We don't know what's in it."

"I don't care," Shiloh said, raising it to her mouth. "I'm hungry enough to eat anything." Taking a small bite, she smiled at her brother. "It's not bad—it tastes like some kind of meat with a wild berry flavor." She took another bite. "It's nourishing, so eat it. There is no telling when we'll have our next meal."

Her brother was a bit more cautious as he took a bite. Then his mouth slid into a grin as he chewed. "I like it better than your mush," he said, wrinkling his nose.

"Scoundrel," she said laughingly.

Seemingly satisfied the brother and sister were eating, Shadowhawk moved to his horse, loosening the reins.

"He watches you a lot," Luke observed, taking another bite and chewing.

"He probably thinks I'll try to escape." Shiloh sighed. "Even if we could get away, I wouldn't know which direction to strike out." Her gaze swept to Shadowhawk, who was watching her. "Remember his skill at tracking? I have a feeling we wouldn't get far before he'd overtake us."

Shadowhawk observed the brother and sister. They cared deeply about each other, and they could laugh even when the world around them was crumbling. He liked the boy.

Luke didn't show fear. Shadowhawk's gaze moved to Shiloh and he felt his chest tighten. Sunlight fell on that wonderful hair curling about her face. He ached to touch her, and have her smile at him as she now smiled at her brother.

"She is worried," he observed to his friend, noting the frown that creased Shiloh's forehead. "But she hides it from her brother." Shadowhawk's gaze went to her feet, and he saw they were bleeding from walking across sharp rocks. There was also a burn on her cheek that must be painful. Yet he had heard no complaints from her.

He turned away, pushing all thoughts of Shiloh from his mind. The Apache had been on their trail last night, but they had given up and headed toward Mexico this morning. He didn't expect any more trouble from them. He would allow the brother and sister to rest until sunset, then they must resume their journey.

They would reach his village the next day before the sun was high in the sky.

Antelope Wells

Charley bounded off his horse, moving with a quickness that drew several curious stares from the people in front of the general store. The foreman of the Crooked H Ranch had just emerged from the Texas House Saloon, and paused to watch the old man enter the local Texas Rangers' office.

Taking a bag of tobacco from his pocket, Rawlins shook a liberal amount onto a paper, curled it over, licked the ends, and struck a match. Smoke curled about his head as he pulled his hat low over his forehead, heading toward the stable. His boss would want to know Charley was involving the Rangers in his feud with the Bradens. Most probably he was reporting the barn burning.

Charley found Captain Gunther with his booted feet

propped on his scarred desk, sipping a cup of strong coffee. One look at the old man's face and the Ranger swung his feet to the floor and stood.

"What's happened?"

It took a moment for Charley to catch his breath. Shaking his head, he finally said, "Someone burned our barn last night—it was Tyree—I saw Rawlins riding away."

"Well, if that's true, we can arrest him now," Gunther said, setting his coffee cup on the desk and easing the overwrought Charley onto a straight-back chair. "Tell me everything."

Captain Gunther listened carefully as Charley explained to him about the fire. He fired questions at the old man when he heard the Bradens had been taken by Shadowhawk.

"It could be that Tyree is behind the fire, but it could also be that this Shadowhawk burned the barn as an excuse to kidnap Shiloh and her brother," Gunther observed, anger growing inside him.

"No, sir, he didn't burn the barn. I've known that Comanche was watching the place, but it was to protect Miss Shiloh and Luke."

"So you say."

"It's true. He told me himself he was taking them to safety." Charley explained to Gunther about the elk and the other gifts, and about the lance.

"Did you try to stop him from taking them?"

"I tried to talk him out of it, but he would have his own way. You might've stood there and argued with him, but I'm just not that ready to die. Leastwise not 'til I see Miss Shiloh and Luke safely home."

"Are they in any danger from him?"

"No, sir. To Shadowhawk's way of thinking, he is protecting them against whoever set the place on fire. You gotta understand, Tyree is becoming more dangerous. He wouldn't stop at hurting Miss Shiloh or the boy."

Gunther reached into his desk drawer, took out his holster, and buckled it about his waist, then took a rifle, opening it to make sure it was loaded. "As far as I'm concerned, my first duty is to find and free the Bradens."

"That's kinda what I hoped."

Gunther took several boxes of shells and shoved them into a leather satchel. "Charley, nothing you've said here today has convinced me that Shadowhawk didn't start the fire."

"I told you what I saw," Charley ground out. "What do you think Rawlins was doin' at Estrella in the middle of the night—having a picnic?"

Gunther moved about the office, gathering supplies for the trail and shoving them in his satchel. "I'm going after Miss Braden and her brother. At the moment, I don't care who burned their barn. I just want to get to them before something happens to her."

"I'm going with you."

"No, you're not. I'll need to ride hard, and I don't want you slowing me down, Charley."

"You'll be eating my dust most of the way."

Gunther took an agitated breath. "Look, every moment is precious. Miss Shiloh is a beautiful young girl—Shadowhawk saw her, wanted her, and took her. And I aim to get her back."

The old man's jaw tightened. "You have to take me with you. You don't know which way they rode. And if you think you can track a Comanche without help, you don't deserve to wear that badge."

"Which direction did they take?" Gunther asked.

"South."

Gunther headed out the door, toward the stable, while

Charley gathered the reins of his horse and hurried along beside him. "You'll need my help to find 'em. And 'sides, if you do catch up to 'em, you don't speak the Comanche lingo, but I do."

Gunther threw the saddle blanket over the back of his horse, and then the saddle, fastening the cinch. "I can always ride to Austin and get Jimmy Tall Tree to track for me."

"You could, but you'd lose too much time."

At last Gunther relented. "You can come with me. But you'd better keep up or I'll leave you behind."

"I ain't asking your permission, I was tellin' you I'm goin'."

Gunther didn't seem to hear Charley as his gaze swept over the countryside. "If he harms her—"

"You can put that notion outta your head—Shadowhawk ain't gonna harm 'em."

Gunther's gaze became hard as he thought of gentle, sweet Shiloh in the hands of that savage. "Shadowhawk will regret this. So far we have left him and his people alone because they haven't caused any trouble. But now I'm going to bring the full force of the Rangers down on him."

"You'd better think this through. The Comanche might let me into their camp without takin' my scalp, but they damned sure won't let you go bustin' in with a bunch of Rangers. 'Sides, you'll be outnumbered, and they don't like you Rangers much."

"Don't get in my way, old man. This is Ranger business, and it doesn't concern you."

"It ain't just Ranger business. I promised Miss Shiloh and Luke I'd find 'em, and that's just what I intend to do."

Chapter Eighteen

Blue sky stretched endlessly across the heavens. Although a heady wind blew unceasingly, it did little to alleviate the blistering heat.

Shiloh was so bone weary she wasn't sure she could go much farther. From the looks of Luke, he was every bit as tired as she.

When they finally stopped to rest the horses, Shiloh went quickly to her brother, who leaned heavily against her. "Luke can't take much more of this," she said angrily, glaring up at Shadowhawk. "Look at him, he's exhausted."

Shadowhawk's gaze settled on Shiloh, and she quickly turned away. "I know what you're thinking—you think if he was a Comanche, he wouldn't need to rest. Well, he's not a Comanche!"

That was not what Shadowhawk was thinking at all. He was mesmerized by the flash of Shiloh's blue eyes when she was angry. She loved her brother, and she was fighting for him. She had not mentioned that she was tired, but Shadowhawk could see she was.

Shadowhawk stood silently beside Shiloh, and she was forced to meet his gaze. She was once more made aware that she wore only her nightgown, and it made her feel vulnerable. To cover her embarrassment, she turned to her brother.

Running Fox had given Luke a waterskin and some pemmican, and Luke was feeling better. "Shiloh," he said, holding a strip of pemmican out to her, "I don't think you should talk that way to Shadowhawk. If you think about it, he's been good to us."

"I know," she agreed, unable to make her brother understand how responsible she felt for his well-being. "If Shadowhawk could understand me, I would apologize. But since he doesn't, he doesn't even know why I was angry with him."

Shadowhawk sat nearby, sharpening his knife. To his way of thinking, Shiloh coddled the boy too much. Luke needed a man to guide him. He admired the boy, and if he ever had a son, he would want him to be like Luke.

Luke took a sip of water and smiled at his sister. "You like Shadowhawk, don't you?"

Shiloh frowned at him. "Why would you say that?"

"That's not an answer, Shiloh," Luke said teasingly.

"Of course I like him. He has helped us in many ways, and I believe he thinks he's helping us now. But if he could understand me, I would tell him he's mistaken."

Running Fox knew a little bit of English, and he understood much of what the brother and sister were saying. He looked at Shadowhawk, who seemed to be concentrating a little too much on sharpening his knife. "Do you want this white woman for yourself?" Running Fox asked.

Pausing for a moment, Shadowhawk frowned. "You ask me this when you know how I despise the white race?" Standing, he shoved his knife into its sheath, then gathered the reins of his horse and mounted. The spirited animal shied, tossing its head. Placing his hand on the horse's neck, Shadowhawk spoke quietly and the animal immediately calmed.

"There is no need to remind me of your hatred for the white eyes," Running Fox said, moving away from the brother and sister and catching up with Shadowhawk. "What puzzles me is why you have made this woman's troubles yours. Do you not consider your debt to her paid?"

"Do not ask me to place a price on my sister's life."

Running Fox took a drink of water from his waterskin and wiped his mouth. "Something puzzles me about you—I have two wives, yet you have none." Running Fox's dark gaze drifted to the white woman. "Do you think I have not seen the yearning in your eyes when you look at her?"

Shadowhawk glared at his friend. "You see nothing. It is for honor that I protect her—nothing more."

Running Fox hid a smile. "I say to you, if you do not care for her, perhaps I could take her for my third wife."

Shadowhawk stared angrily at his friend and said in a quiet voice that signaled danger, "If you value your life, you will not go near her. She is mine to protect."

Running Fox shook with laughter. "I do not want her— I was merely testing you to see if you are aware that *you* do. Do not say to me that you want only to protect her. She with the flaming hair has found a way to your heart when others could not."

Shadowhawk guided his horse toward the river. "I will hear no more of this."

With a grin, Running Fox followed him. "It is strange that the white woman does not cry and complain about her capture. Could it be that she wants to be with you?"

Shadowhawk was getting angrier, and he did not understand why Running Fox continued to pester him with questions. "She does not say anything because she is as brave as any Comanche woman. Her hands have been burned, her feet injured, and her face is sunburned because of her light skin, yet she says nothing about it. In any race, she would be considered courageous."

Running Fox looked at him slyly. "I have noticed that

two of your eagle feathers are missing. To which maiden did you give them?"

Shadowhawk's jaw tightened. "While you are my friend, and I share many thoughts with you, I do not tell you everything." Shaking his head in disgust because he had revealed too much, Shadowhawk turned his horse toward Shiloh. "It is time to ride."

Running Fox grinned as he watched Shadowhawk tenderly lift the woman onto his horse. He had known Shadowhawk since they were boys, and he knew his friend had deep feelings for the woman—no matter how he might deny them.

Shiloh tightened her grip on Shadowhawk's waist as they crossed the river. When they rounded a bend, she was surprised to see an Indian village. She might have been frightened if she had not heard the sound of happy children splashing and playing in the river. When the children spotted Shadowhawk and Running Fox, they came out of the river, running alongside the horses, their dark gazes curiously settling on Shiloh and Luke.

Shiloh counted more than thirty tipis scattered throughout the village. Each tipi appeared to be decorated with its own brightly colored markings. There were hides drying on wooden frames, and women going busily about their chores. One woman was scraping a deerskin with what appeared to be a sharpened stone. The women stopped their work when they caught sight of their chief and clustered before a huge white tipi to wait for his approach.

Shiloh watched the smoke from many campfires that drifted upward to merge with an azure-colored sky. Her stomach tightened in hunger when she smelled the delicious aroma of meat cooking over an open pit. She was glad their long journey was at an end.

As they descended into the valley, the children still

clambered after them, laughing and shouting at their chief. Shiloh wondered if any of the children belonged to Shadowhawk—and if one of the young women was his wife. That thought was somehow painful to her.

As they entered the edge of the encampment, a number of fierce-looking warriors joined the women. They all silently watched and waited.

Shadowhawk halted his horse and grasped Shiloh's arm, helping her to the ground. She and Luke drew many curious stares, but there didn't seem to be any hostility in the Comanches' expressions.

Waiting for Luke to join her, Shiloh saw a familiar face in the crowd. Moon Song smiled as she rushed toward them.

The young Indian girl touched Shiloh's arm affectionately. "I am glad you and your brother are not hurt. A rider reached us with word of what happened." Sadness poured into her eyes. "I feel your hurt that someone is trying to do you harm."

Shiloh was glad to see her little friend, but she also wanted answers to her questions. "Can you tell me why your brother had brought us here against our will?"

Before Moon Song could answer, Shadowhawk spoke to his sister, then turned away, leading his horse.

"My brother has told me to make you comfortable. He says you are to meet our mother and that you will be our guests." She gestured for Shiloh and Luke to follow her inside the big white tipi. "You must not fear anyone here—you are both under my brother's protection."

When Shiloh stepped inside the tipi, she was surprised by how spacious it was. A cook pot hung over a pit fire, its smoke rising through the smoke flap at the top of the tipi. Soft-looking skins were stacked against the wall, and the floor was covered with what could only be buffalo hides. Feathered lances, bows, and arrows decorated the walls.

The tipi was certainly not as primitive as she had imagined it would be.

But it was the woman who stood silently watching her that drew and held Shiloh's attention. She was tall and slender, her dark hair braided and interwoven with beads. Her face was lovely, her skin smooth and youthful.

"This is my mother, Vision Woman," Moon Song said. "She speaks your tongue."

With a welcoming smile, Vision Woman moved gracefully toward Shiloh, her dark eyes searching. "It warms my heart to receive you into my home, Shiloh." She nodded at Luke, who was watching her wide-eyed. "And your brother as well. Because of you, I have my daughter back with me."

Shiloh had the feeling she was standing in the presence of great power. "Thank you, madame. Moon Song and I became friends while she stayed with us. I'm happy to see her again."

"While you are with us, you must consider this your home," Vision Woman said.

Nothing Shiloh had heard about the Comanche had prepared her for such graciousness. "Madame, may I ask when my brother and I will be allowed to return to our home?"

Vision Woman looked troubled for a moment. "This I do not know. Here, we honor the decisions of my son. What I know is this—Shadowhawk brought you here to remove you from danger."

Shiloh felt Shadowhawk's mother examine her for a long moment. "Forgive me if I stare," Vision Woman apologized. "But I have seen your likeness before." She smiled. "One day I will tell you about it."

Luke had lost interest in their conversation and was inspecting one of the lances, but not touching it.

Shiloh turned her attention to Moon Song. "What will happen to us?"

"This I do not know," Moon Song replied earnestly. "It is for Shadowhawk to say."

Vision Woman motioned for Shiloh to be seated beside her on a soft robe. "You must be weary. Rest yourself."

After she was seated, Shiloh turned to Moon Song. "How did you know we would be arriving in your village today?"

"Our advance scouts told us." She smiled sweetly. "Knowing you would be hungry, and knowing your love of stew, I made it for you and Luke." Moon Song glanced at Luke and smiled. "But if you would rather have mush?"

Luke returned her smile. "Stew will be fine with me," he told her. "And plenty of it. I'm hungry."

Shadowhawk was seated in his grandfather's tipi, waiting respectfully for the peace chief to speak. At last Red Elk's gaze settled on his grandson. "Why did you bring the white woman and the boy to our camp?"

"You know they saved my sister's life. I say to you, Grandfather, someone wants them dead, and I could not leave them in danger. They will be safe here in our village."

"I speak now as the peace chief, and not your grandfather. In bringing them here, did you think about the safety of your own people?"

Shadowhawk was thoughtful before he spoke. "I could not find it within me to leave them to the danger that stalks them."

"Could you not have guided them to a white settlement?"

"Grandfather, how could I take them to a white settlement when those who wished to harm them could be among that number?"

The old man studied his grandson with intensity. "There is more that you are not saying. I have never known you to walk around the truth. Tell me why you did this."

Shadowhawk stood, gazing at the top of the tipi, where he could see flashes of blue sky. "How can I tell you the truth when I do not know it myself? I can tell you this woman has eyes that are bluer than the sky. I can tell you her hair is the color of fire. I have seen her kindness when she tended my sister and saved her life. I know my gaze finds her wherever she is and lingers much too long on her face." He looked down at his grandfather. "I do not know why she is always in my thoughts. If you know, I would have you tell me."

Red Elk was lost in thought for so long Shadowhawk thought he would not answer. At last he raised his head and said with gravity, "I have watched for years as young maidens placed themselves in your path, but you took no heed of them. I always thought you were too aware of your duty to the tribe to think of your own needs. I fear now you have not considered the tribe enough. You look to a woman you cannot have, and it saddens me."

"Why would you say this? Speak to me now as my grandfather, and not as the peace chief."

"Did this woman come willingly with you?"

"She did not," Shadowhawk admitted.

His grandfather drew in a long breath. "If I thought it would wipe her from your mind, I would say to you, 'take her to your mat.' But that would only make the fire inside you burn hotter."

"What do you advise, Grandfather?"

"You must look at your choices: you can keep her, but that would bring the white men down on us, for they will surely come to take her back. Even now they may be on their way here. Your other choice is to return her to her people, but you say there is danger for her there. This is what I recommend: discover where that danger comes from—get rid of it, and then take her back to her own people."

"Is there not a third choice?"

The old man shook his head. "Not that I can see." Then Red Elk noticed the flash of pain in his grandson's eyes. "When this is done, you must tear her from your heart."

Shadowhawk weighed his grandfather's words. "I do not know how to stop my feelings for this woman."

"You are a leader of men. You must look to your people and cast this woman out of your heart."

Shadowhawk looked troubled. "I shall look to her enemies for answers. I will only return her when I know she will be safe."

"While you were away, the Apache encroached on our lands. They mean us harm, and you must guard against them before you look to this woman's troubles."

"This I already know. On our journey home we encountered Apache advance scouts. They went to Mexico, but they will be back, and we will be ready for them. Do not think because I watch over the white boy and his sister that I will neglect our own people."

"I know this." The old man suddenly looked tired. "It is not for me to tell the war chief what he must do. As peace chief, I can only lay a path for you. It is up to you to follow or not."

"You have always taught me that a debt must be paid."

Red Elk nodded. "My own words come back to unsettle me. Go now, and do what you must."

Chapter Nineteen

Captain Gunther dismounted and studied the ground. Bending down, he frowned, sifting the dirt through his fingers. "What do you make of it, Charley? We saw the place the two unshod horses went into the river. Could they have come out here?"

Charley bent to look at the signs. "These here are Indian ponies right enough, but there's more like seven—no, eight." He stood and searched the horizon. "I don't have any reason to make this claim, but I'd say these here are tracks left by those Apache we sighted a while back. Shadowhawk's too smart to leave any sign we can follow."

Gunther snatched his hat off his head and threw it down in frustration. "Damn it, we've ridden up and down the river for miles, with no trail to follow. Is this Shadowhawk a ghost that he can just disappear without leaving any sign?"

"Some would say he is." Charley gazed toward the west, where the sun had gone down behind a mesa. "It'll take more than you and me to catch Shadowhawk."

Gunther drew in an intolerant breath. "What do you suggest we do?"

"Keep following the river. You take one side and I'll ride the other. One thing's for sure, he had to come out of the water someplace."

"Tell me everything you know about this Comanche chief. And I do mean everything."

"No one knows much 'bout him. I was once told by a trader down in Nogales, who said he did business with Shadowhawk's Comanche, that he got his name not because he had a vision quest as a young man, but because his mother told him to take his name from her vision. It's said Shadowhawk can disappear like a shadow, and has the eyes of a hawk."

"Do you believe such nonsense?"

"Well, sir, it don't matter much what I believe—it's what the Comanche think. Course, I've learned lately if Shadowhawk don't want to be seen, he's near invisible. If you find any sign that he's passed this way, I'll reconsider."

Gunther gripped his horse's reins. "I've always prided myself on my tracking ability. But this Comanche just disappears like a puff of smoke on a cloudy day."

"As for me, I promised those two I'd find 'em," Charley said, bending to examine a blade of grass and finding no sign that a horse had come this way. "I ain't gonna quit 'til I know where they are."

Gunther stared into the distance. "She'll be ruined by now and no decent man will want the leavings of a Comanche."

Charley bristled. "Don't you go talking 'bout Miss Shiloh like that. I'll shoot any man straight through the heart who tries to sully her good name."

Although Shiloh had railed against it, Luke, who was considered too old to remain with the women, had been taken to a tipi occupied by two young Comanche near his age. Although there was the barrier of language, he found he liked them very well. He was allowed to accompany the young men of the tribe to a practice field, where they honed their skills with the bow and arrow.

Shiloh was seated on a buffalo robe while Vision

Woman applied medicine to her hands and her sunburned face. Then Vision Woman placed a cool poultice on the burns; the smell made Shiloh wrinkle her nose.

"Thank you. I believe I feel better already."

Vision Woman touched Shiloh's hair, her eyes narrowing. "Were you born with hair of flame?"

Shiloh smiled at the gentle woman who was now wrapping her hands in soft cloth. "I have been told that my hair was as yellow as corn when I was born, but it changed when I was two years old."

"Your mother had the flaming hair."

"She did."

"Yes. I have seen you in a dream." Vision Woman lowered her head as if it was too heavy for her to hold up. "I knew you were coming, I just did not think it would be this soon."

Shiloh frowned. "I don't understand."

"My son was destined to walk beside you. To what end, I do not know."

Shiloh was confused. "I don't know what you mean. Can't you convince Shadowhawk that my brother and I don't need his protection?"

Vision Woman stood. "It is not for me to tell the chief what he must do, even if he is my son."

"I have heard the Comanche do not have a high regard for women."

Vision Woman smiled gently at Shiloh. "I will say this to you—in the Blackfoot nation, where I was born and raised, a woman is not less than a man. This I have taught my son, although he fights to hold on to Comanche custom. Shadowhawk tries to balance the two paths he walks. One day, he must decide which of those paths he will take." Without another word, Vision Woman left the tipi.

Shiloh turned to Moon Song, who had been sitting

quietly. "What did your mother mean when she said she saw me in a dream?"

"I cannot speak for my mother. She sees that which others do not see. But she does not always share her thoughts with me or my brother."

"Moon Song, I don't even know why I'm here. I don't belong with your people, any more than you belonged with mine." She took Moon Song's hand. "Remember how badly you wanted to go home?"

Moon Song's eyes widened. "I do remember."

"That is how much I want to return to my home."

The young Comanche girl looked sad. "I would help you if I could."

Unwelcome thoughts swirled through Shiloh's mind. What had Vision Woman meant by her cryptic statement about her and Shadowhawk? "Is your brother married?"

"You mean does he have a woman?"

Shiloh nodded.

"Shadowhawk has not yet found the woman he wishes to walk at his side. Although he is handsome, do you not think?"

"Y . . . es."

"Other women think so too, but my brother has not made a choice."

Luke entered, dropping down beside his sister. "You should have been there, Shiloh. The young Comanche can hit a target clear across the field."

"And how did you do?" she asked, smiling.

He looked sheepish. "I learned to string a bow. It's not as easy as it looks," he said in his own defense. "It takes strength."

Shiloh laughed and ruffled his hair. "I'm sure it does."

Luke turned his attention to Moon Song. "Tomorrow, the others are riding out to find the buffalo. Will I be allowed to go with them?"

"You must seek my brother's permission. Until you have it, it would be better if you remained in camp."

"Does everyone have to answer to Shadowhawk?" Shiloh asked heatedly.

Moon Song nodded, not even understanding why Shiloh would ask such a question. "It would be folly if anyone ignored his commands."

Luke looked at his sister. "I'm going swimming with the other boys," he said excitedly. Then he looked guilty for a moment. He was allowed the freedom of the village, while Shiloh had to remain inside Vision Woman's tipi.

"Go, go," Shiloh said, reading his thoughts, and shooing him out of the tipi. It was good that one of them could enjoy themselves, she thought crossly.

Moon Song reached behind her and produced a fringed gown much like the one she wore. "My mother has given you this fine doeskin gown and moccasins. Will you wear them?"

Shiloh was curious, and touched the beaded gown. It had elaborate fringe and beadwork at the bottom. "I can't very well go about in my nightgown."

"Then you will wear it?"

Shiloh nodded. "I will." She turned her back and pulled the doeskin gown over her head. The garment fell softly over her head, and Shiloh wished she had a mirror to see what it looked like on her.

"Why do you wear your nightgown beneath the gown?" Moon Song wanted to know.

"It just wouldn't feel right without an undergarment, and the gown is all I have." She wrinkled her nose. "However, as soon as I'm able, I would like to wash this nightgown." Sitting on the buffalo robe, she slipped her feet into the moccasins. Standing, she turned around in a circle, enjoying the freedom the garments provided, and feeling practically decadent because her ankles showed above the low moccasins.

"You look lovely, Shiloh."

Shiloh arched her eyebrow and lifted a tress of her red hair. "But not like a Comanche." She ran her hand down the softness of the gown. "This is beautiful, with such fine beadwork."

"It is my mother's work."

"Then I will have to thank her."

Two days passed and Shiloh had not seen Shadowhawk since he had brought them to the village. She had questions that needed answers, yet she was kept secluded, probably by his orders.

Moon Song entered the tipi, her face flushed with excitement. "Shadowhawk has given permission for you to walk about the village."

"His permission!" Shiloh ground out. "Does your brother think I am one of his tribe that he can say I may do this but not that?"

There was a hurt expression in Moon Song's eyes. "I thought you would be happy to be given the freedom of the village."

Shiloh looked at her friend apologetically. "Moon Song, I am grateful for your thoughtfulness, but freedom to roam around the village is not what I want. I want answers from Shadowhawk. Tell him that."

Moon Song nodded. "I will see if he will speak to me."

After Moon Song left, Shiloh paced back and forth in front of the tipi opening. Finally, she decided Shadowhawk wasn't coming. She sat upon her buffalo robe, trying to work the tangles out of her hair with a comb made out of buffalo horn. After she had done her best, she braided her hair and wrapped a leather strip around it.

When Shiloh heard the tipi flap open, she looked to

see Moon Song enter, followed by Shadowhawk, who was so tall, he had to duck his head to enter.

His presence seemed to fill the whole tipi.

Shiloh had asked to see him, but now that he had come, she was nervous. Standing, she waited to hear what he had to say.

Shadowhawk was pleased to see Shiloh had agreed to wear the doeskin gown. Turning to his sister, he said, "Tell her to be seated. There are questions I would ask of her."

Moon Song translated what her brother said.

Shiloh went down on her knees, her gaze on Shadowhawk's face. He looked at her intently, and she stared back at him. Now that she saw him here with his people, he seemed different from the man she had come to know. Everyone revered him and obeyed him without question. But she wouldn't.

"Ask her if she has been comfortable here," he said to his sister.

Moon Song frowned. "Why do you not ask her yourself? You speak her language."

"I would be at a disadvantage because I have not spoken English since I was a youth. Ask her if she speaks Spanish."

"I do not believe she does."

"Ask her."

"*Usted habla español?*"

Shiloh looked puzzled.

"My brother wanted me to ask if you speak Spanish so he can speak with you himself."

"Other than English, I speak only a schoolgirl's inadequate French."

Moon Song shook her head as she looked back at her brother.

He seated himself on a robe and though he spoke to

Moon Song, he was looking at Shiloh. "Ask her if she knows the name of the man who burned her barn."

When Moon Song translated his words, Shiloh, looking directly at Shadowhawk, said, "The man responsible is Surge Tyree, the same man you rescued me from the night of the rainstorm."

Shadowhawk's eyes narrowed. "Ask her to tell you all she knows about the man."

After listening to Moon Song translate Shadowhawk's words, Shiloh explained about her encounters with Surge Tyree. "We are not the first people to have suffered from Mr. Tyree's brutality, but my brother and I will not be driven off our land." Still facing Shadowhawk, she addressed him through Moon Song. "You must understand how important it is for Luke and me to return home. If we are not there, Mr. Tyree will eventually find a way to take our land."

When Moon Song translated her words, Shiloh watched Shadowhawk's eyes darken.

"Explain to her that she and her brother will remain here, until I say otherwise."

Moon Song had scarcely finished the translation before Shiloh reacted angrily.

"No! We don't belong here. Luke and I have a home, and land that belongs to us. You have no right to keep us here."

Shadowhawk stood, and for a long moment, he stared into Shiloh's eyes, then motioned for his sister to follow him outside.

Shiloh had not had a chance to ask her questions. Tears blinded her and a feeling of helplessness swamped her.

After speaking to her brother, Moon Song returned to the tipi. "I am told to say to you this land belongs to the buffalo, the hawk, and the wolf, and that we are merely caretakers while we walk among them."

"I will agree with that. Shadowhawk is the caretaker of this land, and my brother and I are caretakers of Estrella. Go and say this to your brother."

Moon Song was shocked. "I dare not. Shadowhawk would take it as an offense. In our village, his word is law. He is a just and wise chief, and will always do what is best for us, and it is my belief he will do what is best for you and Luke as well."

Shiloh sighed. "It is not best for us to remain here as captives. This is not the life our father would have wanted for us."

"You are not a captive, Shiloh. If you were, you would be forced to work with the women, and Luke would train to become a warrior."

"Then what are we?"

"I do not know."

Shiloh suddenly wanted to feel the sun on her face and the wind in her hair. Perhaps if she looked about the village, she might find a way to escape. "I am ready to go outside," she told Moon Song.

Moon Song held the tipi flap open. "I will go with you and introduce you to my world, and if you would like, there is a secluded place where we can swim."

"I can wash my hair and undergarments," Shiloh said with relief.

Chapter Twenty

It was in the cool of the evening when Shiloh walked toward the riverbank. Dark-skinned children were playing nearby, their happy squeals filling the air. A young girl, who could be no more than four years old, ran up the hill and slipped her small hand into Shiloh's.

Shiloh was captivated by the lovely Comanche child. She bent down to her. "If you could understand me, little one, you would know I think your eyes are beautiful, and that you are a sweet child."

A shadow fell across her path and Shiloh glanced up to see Shadowhawk. He spoke to the young girl, and she scurried off to join her companions.

"I wonder what you told her," Shiloh said aloud.

His speech was halting, as if he grasped for each word. "I said to her . . . you found her eyes pleasing. I told her to . . . go to her mother."

Shiloh's mouth flew open in astonishment. "I didn't know you spoke English."

"Not well."

As Shiloh continued toward the river, Shadowhawk fell into step beside her. She stared at the rushing water, trying to remember all she had said about him in his hearing. "You should have let me know you understood English," she accused.

"It did not seem . . . important." He looked at her, frowning. "Did I say the right word?"

Her laughter took him by surprise. "This is the first time you have asked my opinion on anything."

"I once spoke your language well. It comes back to me in . . . pieces."

He seemed to be getting a better grasp of English, and Shiloh suspected that with a little practice he would be speaking it as well as his sister. "How did you know we needed help the night our barn burned?"

"I watched . . . over you."

Her heart leapt into her throat. "Why would you do that?"

"To pay a debt."

She turned to him. "Shadowhawk, you owe me nothing. What I did for your sister, I would have done for anyone."

"It is still a debt."

She looked at him quizically. "Can we say it's met, and you take me home?"

His jaw hardened. "You will stay here."

She had the feeling no woman had ever questioned Shadowhawk, much less won an argument with him, but she was determined to be the first. "Shadowhawk, if you are honest with yourself, you will admit that I do not belong in a Comanche village. September is approaching. On Estrella, we would be stocking hay to feed our animals during the winter months. Slaughtered meat would be hung in the smokehouse to dry. Charley told me the Comanche go on raids in September. My people live by the plow and the sickle, and your people live by the lance."

Shadowhawk studied her for a long moment before answering. "Tell me this—are you not angry because this . . . person, Tyree, tries to take your land?"

"I am angry with Mr. Tyree," she admitted.

"Your race has a habit of taking without asking. They kill the buffalo, taking only the hides and leaving the meat to rot. They will hunt them until they are no more. The Comanche cannot survive without the buffalo, so we fight for our lives and for our children's lives."

Shiloh wanted to defend her people, but she hesitated. Shadowhawk had challenged her beliefs. She had never looked at life from the Comanche's view. But she still wasn't totally convinced he was right. "Many of the people your Comanche kill are law-abiding citizens who have never harmed you."

"When we cannot tell the difference between friend and foe, we must punish them all, lest they think us weak."

"My people do not think you are weak; they believe you are pitiless."

Shadowhawk took a step closer to Shiloh, as if he were compelled to do so. "What do you believe?"

She raised her head, her gaze searching his. "I cannot speak of all Comanche, but I know you to be a man of honor," she acknowledged.

He glanced away quickly, unable to meet her eyes lest he reveal too much of himself to her. It pleased him that she thought well of him. "You will find others here who are also honorable, Shiloh."

By now they had reached the river and he knelt down, cupped his hand, and offered her a drink. Shiloh bent to take a sip and her lips touched the palm of his hand. She pulled back, trembling. She felt much more than respect for Shadowhawk, but she didn't know what it was. Something called her to him—something wild and beautiful— but she would not answer that call.

Shiloh's gaze moved from Shadowhawk's wide shoulders to his narrow waist. She gave an involuntary gasp when she noticed his leggings showed a fair amount of bare thigh as he bent to the river.

Shooting to her feet, Shiloh felt as if a hand had squeezed

her heart. "Shadowhawk, you must let me and my brother go," she whispered. "We had a life—Luke needs me to give him his school lessons every day. We cannot stay here."

Shadowhawk stood, his gaze boring into her. "I have already said you will remain here until I decide you can return to your home."

"Shadowhawk, my people will come after me. They will hunt you down and destroy this village. Your people must not suffer for what you have done."

Shadowhawk realized that Shiloh had come to the same conclusion his grandfather had. Not wanting to think about it, he turned away from her. "I will speak no more of this with you. I will say to you that the old man and the one who calls himself a Ranger are even now searching for you. But take no hope that they will find you."

Shiloh reached out to him. "Please do not hurt either of them. They are only doing what you would do in like circumstances—what you did when Moon Song was missing. You heard Charley say he would search for my brother and me."

"If I had wanted them dead, they would be dead. I had the Ranger in my sights, yet for you, I allowed him to live." He turned back to her, recognizing that jealousy burned in his heart. "Do you care for the man?"

"Of course I do. Charley is like family to us."

"I speak of the Ranger."

She reached inside her mind to find words to explain her feelings for Gunther. "He came to me at a time when I needed a friend. I will always remember his kindness."

Shadowhawk stared at Shiloh for a moment, then abruptly moved away, his long strides unhurried, his back straight, his head held at a proud tilt.

He was so different from Gunther, or any other man she'd ever known. Shiloh knew he could be cruel, but he was strangely gentle with her. When he took a wife, she would be a very fortunate woman.

Shiloh remembered the child who had held her hand; she thought of Moon Song and Vision Woman, and it hurt to imagine this village being destroyed and its people killed. But that was what would happen. She had no doubt that Gunther and his Rangers would eventually locate this village, and that would be a tragedy for all concerned.

Evening shadows lengthened and Shiloh stood by the river, deep in thought. At last, she knew what she had to do. When she reached Vision Woman's tipi, she found Luke waiting for her outside.

Luke began speaking excitedly about how he had joined a deer hunt with the boys his age. "I'm learning to use a lance, and tomorrow, Running Fox said he would teach me to shoot a bow."

"Luke, listen to me," Shiloh said, lowering her voice. "Shadowhawk told me Charley and Captain Gunther are searching for us. Do you think there is a way you can escape?"

He frowned. "I don't know. The Comanche allow me freedom, but I get the feeling they're still watching me."

"If you find a way, you must take it."

Luke was lost in thought for a moment. "Do you mean leave you behind?"

"You have to. My absence would be discovered right away. If Charley and Gunther find this village, they will bring more men. I don't want anyone to die because of me. You have to get to Charley and convince him we have not been harmed. If you can, lead them in a direction away from this village. Do you understand?"

Luke nodded. "But I don't want to leave you."

She took his face between her hands to stress her point. "You must! You have been around the camp, think about the best way to escape."

"I suppose if I could get close enough to the horses, I might be able to make a run for it."

"If you do, lead the animal away from camp before you mount. These Comanche hear every little noise. Go back the way we came, and follow the river. Be sure to take a waterskin, and food, if you can find any. And, Luke, be careful."

"But—"

"You have to try, Luke. For both our sakes, and for the sake of the people in this village!"

Surge Tyree was thoughtful. He had already learned Shiloh had somehow escaped the Indian that had attacked them at the river. And now Rawlins was telling him Shiloh and her brother had both disappeared. "How do you know this?" he asked his foreman.

"That's what it looks like, boss. They ain't around Estrella, and no one's seen them in Antelope Wells since before the fire."

Tyree stared at the Texas map on his wall. "You see this?" he asked, tracing the land belonging to the Crooked H. "I own everything between here and the Masterson place." He hit one point with his finger. "Except for the most desirable parcel in the area—this right here along the Brazos."

"I know, boss."

Tyree spun around to Rawlins. "Find the Bradens. I'm not going to play nice with them any longer. I want that land!"

To Rawlins's way of thinking, they hadn't exactly been playing nice with the owners of Estrella. "I'll get back to town and find out what I can about them."

"Do that."

"Boss, you want me to bring 'em here if I find 'em?"

Tyree took an intolerant breath and let it out slowly. "Sometimes I don't think you've got the gumption God gave a gnat. Now, why would I want you to bring them here?"

Rawlins stared down at the tip of his dusty boot so Tyree couldn't see how angered he was by the insult. "I'll ride to town as soon as I get a fresh horse."

Tyree called out to the foreman before he reached the door. "I want Estrella no matter what it takes to get it. Is that understood?"

Shiloh could see the starlight through the opening at the top of the tipi. A dog barked somewhere in the village, and she wondered if Luke was trying to escape. She glanced over at Moon Song, who appeared to be sleeping along with Vision Woman. Quietly, she rose and tiptoed out of the tipi.

It was dark as she stood beneath the stars, searching for Luke. Suddenly he was beside her, and she quickly hugged him to her. "Go," she whispered. "Follow the river, like Papa always told us to if we were ever lost."

Luke paused for a moment, reluctant to leave her.

"Go now," she urged. "Make them understand I am in no danger and they are to break off the search."

"If I can."

Shiloh gently brushed a lock of hair off his forehead and kissed him on the cheek. "You can do it, Luke. I know you can."

He turned and looked at Shiloh once more before he faded into the shadows.

She was afraid for Luke to strike out, not knowing his way. But they had no choice. She glanced quickly about the village and saw no one about. It would be hours before she knew if he had gotten away safely.

For fear of drawing attention to herself, Shiloh returned to the tipi and curled up on her buffalo robe, praying with all her heart that Luke would make it safely to Charley.

Night shadows surrounded her, and Shiloh shivered, trying to overcome her fear for her brother.

Squeezing her eyes tightly together, Shiloh felt her pulse race. If she had sent Luke to his death, she would never forgive herself. But too many lives depended on his finding Charley and making him understand they must halt their search.

Chapter Twenty-one

Shiloh hadn't slept all night, for worrying about her brother. What if he'd been devoured by a pack of wolves—what if he'd met up with a hostile Indian tribe? She imagined all sorts of dangers he could be facing.

Vision Woman had left early to aid one of the women who was giving birth, and Moon Song had joined the other young girls to pick berries.

Shiloh paced the tipi, waiting to hear if Luke had made his escape. If he had, it wouldn't be long before someone raised the alarm.

Dropping down on the buffalo robe, she buried her face in her hands. If Luke *had* managed to get away, it wouldn't be long before Shadowhawk would seek her out, demanding answers. He would be angry until she explained she had urged Luke to leave to prevent bloodshed between their people.

Moon Song entered, smiling, holding out her basket of berries for Shiloh to see. "The bushes were full today."

Shiloh ducked her head on the pretext of lacing her moccasins, fearing her little friend would read the distress in her eyes.

"I was told that Luke didn't join the hunt with the young warriors this morning."

"Oh."

Shiloh was startled when the tent flap was thrust aside and Shadowhawk appeared. One look at his face told her he was furious. His dark gaze swept the tipi, settling at last on Shiloh. Shadowhawk spoke rapidly to Moon Song, the fury in his tone apparent.

Moon Song shook her head, and turning to Shiloh, said, "Shadowhawk demands to know where your brother has gone."

Shiloh was careful not to meet Shadowhawk's gaze. "Then let him ask me himself."

Shadowhawk grasped Shiloh's arm, jerking her around to face him. "One of my horses is missing. Did your brother take it and leave?"

Shiloh threw her head back. "I hope so. I told him to escape if he had the chance. I only pray he got away and you can't find him."

Shadowhawk gave Shiloh a shake. "Did you not think of the danger he would meet? You saw for yourself how the Apache were following us. Do you know what will happen to your brother if they find him before I do?"

Tears gathered in Shiloh's eyes. "I considered all the dangers my brother might meet, but it was a chance we had to take." She met his gaze. "You know what will happen if my people discover this village in their search for me."

Shadowhawk gave Shiloh another shake. "You sent a boy to stop a war between our people!"

She shoved his hands away and stepped back. "You left me no other choice. And if *I* get the chance to escape, I will take it." She tossed her head. "I will!"

Shadowhawk stared at Shiloh for a long moment, and then spoke quickly and forcefully to Moon Song before he turned abruptly and left.

Moon Song shook her head, tears gathering in her eyes. "Shadowhawk is gathering warriors to hunt for Luke. I have never seen him this angry. He says you are to be watched at all times, and you will share his tipi when he returns."

Shiloh's legs gave way and she sank to her knees. "I will not stay with him." She met the young girl's gaze. "Never!"

"It is not for you to say, Shiloh. My brother is the law here, and his word will be obeyed."

"Why must that be? Why must Shadowhawk think for everyone else?"

Moon Song dipped her head in thoughtfulness. "It was what he was born to do."

A short time later Shiloh heard riders leaving the village. She hoped with all her heart that Charley and Captain Gunther would find Luke before Shadowhawk did.

Throughout the day Shiloh paced, imagining all sorts of things that could go wrong. When Moon Song tried to get her to eat, Shiloh refused.

At sunset, Moon Song led Shiloh to her brother's tipi. Pausing at the entrance, Moon Song tried to comfort her friend. "Do not worry about Luke. Shadowhawk will find him."

"What will he do to me?"

"I do not know."

Shiloh watched the young girl leave, then went inside and dropped to her knees, burying her face in her hands and crying bitter tears.

When her tears were spent and exhaustion weighed heavily on her, Shiloh stood, examining the interior of the tipi. Shields and lances were displayed on both sides of the entrance. Bedding was folded and placed near the back. Shiloh saw moccasins and fringed trousers—a man's domain. She backed toward the entrance. How could she be expected to remain here alone with Shadowhawk?

Hearing a man clear his throat just outside, she knew Shadowhawk had set one of his warriors on guard to make sure she didn't leave. Defeated, she dropped onto a buffalo robe. All that really mattered was Luke finding Charley. She was not sorry for what she'd done. It would be far worse if the Comanche in this village were to die because of her.

Totally exhausted, Shiloh unfolded the robe and lay down upon it, listening to every noise outside the tipi, not wanting to be taken unaware when Shadowhawk finally returned.

But despite her resolution, she was asleep when he finally entered the tipi.

Shadowhawk propped his lance against the wall of the tipi and removed his bow and quiver of arrows. He saw Shiloh huddled as far from the opening as she could get, her body pulled into a tight ball.

As she slept, he stood over her for a long time, staring down at her in the dim moonlight that penetrated from the overhead opening.

Quietly, he undressed down to his breechcloth and unrolled a robe. Stretching out before the tipi opening, he would make certain Shiloh did not attempt to leave during the night.

But Shadowhawk did not sleep. He was too aware of the woman who lay nearby. He could hear her soft breathing and watched the rise and fall of her breasts with every breath she took. He ached to hold her and take her to his body. Turning his back to her, he tried to close his mind to such thoughts.

But even as weary as he was, he found no reprieve in sleep.

Shiloh jerked awake when she heard a dog barking. It took a moment to remember where she was, and then it all came back to her.

She was in Shadowhawk's tipi!

The interior was softly lit by the sunlight that poured through the opening, and she saw Shadowhawk stretched out near the entrance. Her eyes widened and she felt her face redden when she saw that he wore only a breech-cloth.

Easing to her feet, she wondered if she could step over him without waking him. His voice stopped her in her tracks.

"I would not try that if I were you."

She froze. "I did not hear you when you came in."

"I heard every move *you* made."

"My brother?"

Shadowhawk sat up and looked at her. "Had I not found him, I would not have returned."

She felt her heart lurch. "Where is Luke? Did you bring him back with you? I want to see him now."

"I did not bring him with me. Luke met up with the old man and the Ranger."

Unconsciously, Shiloh took a step toward him and asked, "Did you harm them?"

Shadowhawk studied her for a moment. Her hair spilled down her face in curls, and he wanted more than anything to pull her into his arms and hold her. "Because it was what you wanted me to do, I let them go."

With her heartbeat drumming in her ears, Shiloh stared at him, careful not to look below his face, since he wore so little. "I don't understand."

"I saw your brother was safe, and I let the Ranger and the old man take him with them."

Shadowhawk and his warriors would have outnumbered Charley and Gunther, and could easily have overcome them in a battle, but he'd let them live, and he said it was for her sake. "Where are they? Please let me go to them."

"They will not find you. For some reason, Luke is leading them in the wrong direction."

"I know. I told him to."

"Why would you do that?"

"So they would not find this village. I don't want your people or mine to die."

Shadowhawk frowned as if he were trying to understand her reasoning. "You sent your brother to mislead the Ranger?"

"Yes."

He was quiet for a long time as he pondered her words. "I did not expect this."

"Why would you not? Do you think my brother or I could live with ourselves if we caused even one death?" She shook her head in anger. "Of course, this whole incident is your fault. If you had not brought us here, Captain Gunther would not have been searching for us."

A glint of pain flashed in Shadowhawk's eyes, then disappeared so quickly she was sure she had imagined it.

"But I did bring you here, and here you will remain until I decide otherwise."

Shiloh stepped around him, tossing the tipi flap aside, and walked into a day washed with sunlight.

She was still a prisoner, but at least Luke was safe.

Heart heavy, she made her way toward the river and dropped down on the bank. By now, the Comanche were accustomed to seeing her about the village and paid her little heed. After washing her face and hands in the cool water, she cupped her palms and took a drink.

Shiloh heard someone behind her and she didn't have to look up to know it was Shadowhawk.

"I was told you did not take nourishment while I was away."

She saw he still wore only his breechcloth, and felt a blush steal up her face. "It is none of your concern."

"If you become ill, it will be my concern. You will go to my mother's tipi and eat."

"I will not."

Before Shiloh knew what was happening, Shadowhawk

gripped her by the arms and pulled her to her feet. "I am accustomed to being obeyed. I have allowed you to speak to me as no one ever has before, but you test me with your—" He paused to think. "What is the word?" Then he nodded as he remembered. "Stubborn. You are a stubborn woman."

"You may be chief of these people, but you are nothing to me. Why should I obey you?"

With anger burning inside him, Shadowhawk propelled her before him, keeping his grip on her arm. "You will eat whatever my mother sets before you."

On entering Vision Woman's tipi, Shiloh expected Shadowhawk to remain, but he didn't come in with her, and she was glad.

Vision Woman looked at the white girl for a moment and then motioned for Shiloh to sit. "I have heard your brother is unharmed."

Shiloh pointed toward the tipi flap. "Your son orders me around as if he thinks I'm a member of your tribe. I don't like him in the least."

Vision Woman said kindly, "I can understand how you might feel that way. That is because you do not yet understand my son thinks he is doing what is best for you."

Shiloh seated herself on a robe and reached for the dried meat Vision Woman handed her. She paused with it halfway to her mouth. "He doesn't know what is best for me, and he never will."

Vision Woman merely smiled.

Later in the morning Moon Song walked with Shiloh through the village. Shiloh was surprised to be greeted by smiles and friendly nods from the other women. She paused to watch one of the women as her skilled hands worked deftly at the buffalo hide stretched before her. The woman scraped the hair off with a sharp implement that seemed to be made of bone, or perhaps flint.

The serenity of the morning was suddenly disrupted as Shadowhawk and his warriors rode into the village. To Shiloh's dismay, she saw that all of the men wore breech-cloths and nothing else.

Dipping her head to the ground, she refused to look at them.

Moon Song touched Shiloh's arm. "My brother motions that he wants you to go to him."

"Not until he puts on some clothing," Shiloh stated.

Moon Song looked puzzled. "But he wears clothing, Shiloh."

"He and the other men are half naked," Shiloh argued. "I am not accustomed to seeing a man's bare legs and chest."

Laughter spilled from Moon Song's lips. "And the Comanche think the white eyes wear too much clothing."

Shiloh sighed. "This is not my world. I need to go home."

Not knowing how to comfort her friend, Moon Song merely said, "You must go to my brother, and after that, my grandfather will see you."

Shiloh gritted her teeth. Comanche men never asked, they demanded. Not my grandfather would like to see you—or my grandfather wishes you to visit him—but my grandfather *will* see you.

With a determined stride, she approached Shadowhawk. His long hair hung like black velvet across his shoulders. *Handsome* was too mild a word for how he looked. There was an untamed beauty about him. Shiloh directed her gaze to the ground while she waited for him to finish speaking to his companion and notice her.

Shadowhawk saw that Shiloh was uneasy. "What has upset you?"

She slowly raised her head and met his eyes. Shiloh

didn't know how to express her embarrassment, so Moon Song answered for her.

"My brother, Shiloh has never been around men who wear only breechcloths."

Shadowhawk's expression was inscrutable. "Take her to our grandfather," he said at last, then wheeled his mount and rode away.

Moments later Shiloh was seated in a huge tipi staring at Red Elk, thanking her lucky stars he was fully dressed. Moon Song sat beside Shiloh in silence while they waited for Red Elk to speak.

The old man took several puffs on his pipe and studied the girl with the flaming hair who had upset his grandson's balanced world. Red Elk looked past her beauty and gentleness to the strength of character that had captured Shadowhawk. This woman was dangerous—she was upsetting the stability of the tribe. He wanted her out of the village as soon as possible.

He took another puff on his pipe. The way he saw it, the only way to speed her departure was to put an end to whomever was threatening her.

Red Elk spoke to his granddaughter for some time and Moon Song finally turned to Shiloh.

"My honored grandfather, the peace chief, apologizes to you because he cannot speak to you in English. He wishes me to ask you, if the man who is a danger to you and your brother is eliminated, will it be safe for you to return to your home?"

Shiloh was horrified by what Red Elk was suggesting. "What does he mean by 'eliminate'? You just can't go around killing people because it would make life easier!"

Red Elk's hand stilled on his pipe and he stared, startled, at the young white woman. He had not understood her words, but he clearly understood her anger.

Moon Song's face turned pale when Shiloh stood, and she cast her gaze downward to hide her horror. "You must be seated until my grandfather gives you permission to leave," the young girl warned.

"Tell him I do not condone the death of anyone. Where I come from, we have laws to protect us from men like the one who threatens my brother and me."

Moon Song turned quickly to her grandfather and translated what Shiloh had said. Instead of being angry, the old man gave a deep laugh. After a time he spoke to his granddaughter.

"My honored grandfather says Shadowhawk has his sympathy if he thinks he can tame . . . the flaming hair."

"Tame!" Shiloh said. "No one is going to tame me—least of all Shadowhawk."

Moon Song began speaking to Red Elk, but he waved her to silence, telling her he needed no translation. Then he pointed to the entrance of his tipi, indicating his granddaughter and Shiloh should leave.

Once he was alone, the peace chief broke into another laugh. When his wife came to him, he was wiping his eyes on his sleeve. "We have waited long for our grandson to find a woman so our line would not die out. Do not be surprised if your grandchildren are born with flaming hair."

"The white woman is not here by her own wish, my husband. And I have heard it said, although Shadowhawk took her to his tipi, he did not make her his woman."

"Who can resist Shadowhawk when he wants something?" Red Elk laughed and nodded to himself. "Our grandson cannot be having an easy time with the flaming hair."

"I was always against our son marrying Vision Woman. Although she is of great wisdom, she puts thoughts in Shadowhawk's mind that now tear at him. As for the white woman, our grandson merely feels obligated to her," Soaring Bird said indignantly. "He will forget she ever existed when he has satisfied his responsibility to her."

"I do not think so." A grin cracked the old man's face. "I recall how our son made a fool of himself when he first set eyes on Vision Woman. After she became his woman, he never knew another day of sorrow, or so he told me before he left this land to walk with the spirits."

"What you say is true, but Vision Woman is not of the white race—our son's wife is Indian."

"I do not think this woman knows how difficult she is making life for Shadowhawk. I foresee he will not have a peaceful day until he lets her go, or makes her his own."

Chapter Twenty-two

Moon Song walked an agitated Shiloh back to her brother's tipi and left her there.

It was no more than an hour before Shadowhawk entered, his hard gaze settling on Shiloh, his silence disclosing his displeasure.

Although he was still bare chested, he at least wore his leggings, Shiloh noticed with relief.

She was still angry from her meeting with Red Elk. The old chief's words had made it clear to Shiloh how powerless she was. Oblivious at the danger of speaking her mind, she berated Shadowhawk. "How dare you treat me like a prisoner to be summoned by you or your grandfather as you please!"

Ignoring her outburst, Shadowhawk shoved a bowl of food at her. "Eat."

She turned away. "I don't want it. I eat when I want, and not when you tell me to."

He did not raise his voice, but there was a threat in the quietness of his tone. "You will either eat, or I will feed you myself."

She stepped away from him. "You wouldn't!"

"I always do what I say."

Their gazes clashed in a silent battle of wills, and Shiloh blinked first. Taking the bowl, she dropped down on a robe and picked up a piece of meat. She chewed angrily, glaring at him all the while.

Shiloh expected to see satisfied triumph in Shadowhawk's expression, but he merely removed his leather pouch of arrows and dropped them near the door.

"We will be leaving tomorrow," he announced.

"Why?" she asked, fearing he would be taking her deeper into the wilderness. "Where are we going?"

Shadowhawk took in a deep breath. "Woman, no one questions me but you. Why is that?" he asked bluntly.

"Because," she said, tilting her head up to him, "I am not bound by your laws or impressed by your illustrious self."

"What does this word 'illustrious' mean?"

Shiloh thought for a moment, then shrugged her shoulders. "Glorious, magnificent."

Shadowhawk could not suppress a smile. "And you do not see me in this way?"

"I don't. But these Comanche certainly do. In my society, we have a name for people like you, and we deal with them decisively."

He stared at her, waiting for her to enlighten him.

"Rulers or potentates—call them what you will. Sam Houston led a war that threw off the shackles of the dictator who ruled Texas before the revolution."

"I do not understand you."

Shiloh shook her head with a sigh. "I don't suppose you do, or ever will." The meat was quite good, and she took another bite. "You haven't told me why we are leaving tomorrow."

"I will tell you what I think you need to know," he said, lifting the tipi flap and leaving abruptly.

Her hands were trembling and her heart was thumping inside her. She knew it was dangerous to keep arguing with Shadowhawk, but he brought out the worst in her. She was honest enough to admit that she was probably making his life difficult. It was easy to see he was as bewildered by her as she was by him.

* * *

Moonlight poured through the top of the tipi as Shiloh lay on the buffalo robe, feeling lost and alone. She was homesick, and she missed Luke. Even though Shadowhawk might say she was not a prisoner, she certainly felt like one.

It was only a short time later when the tent flap was jerked aside and Shadowhawk entered.

Shiloh quickly closed her eyes, pretending to be asleep. She could hear him removing his weapons, and she stiffened uneasily when she heard him remove his leggings, knowing he would be wearing nothing but his breechcloth. Relief washed over her when she heard him move to his robe and lie down, turning his back to her.

Taking a shallow breath, Shiloh felt some of the tension leave her body. Like the night before, Shadowhawk ignored her. Then her eyes flew open when she had a troubling thought. Perhaps Shadowhawk was leaving her alone because he didn't find her attractive.

She remembered the night he had come to her at her father's grave site. He had been gentle, and had even conveyed his sorrow for her father's death. Now, among his own people, he was cold and indifferent.

"You should sleep," Shadowhawk told her, turning in her direction. "Tomorrow we travel."

The sound of his deep voice sent butterflies fluttering in her stomach and she pressed her hand there. Shiloh edged closer to him. "Are you taking me where no one will be able to find me—is that what you're doing?"

Shadowhawk resisted the urge to reach out and touch her. It was a punishment to lie so near her and yet pretend he did not want her.

He was quiet for so long Shiloh didn't think he would answer, and when he did, it was in a whispered tone. "I want to make your enemies go away so you will no longer need to fear them."

His words tugged at her heart. He wanted to help her. "Take me home and allow the Rangers to punish my enemies."

Her hand brushed his arm and he closed his eyes. "Shiloh," he said, as tenderness swept over him like waves in a flooded river, "get some sleep."

"It's difficult when I don't know what you plan to do."

He wasn't going to get any sleep tonight if he did not satisfy at least some of Shiloh's concerns. "I intend to do to your enemy what he did to you."

"Shadowhawk, it isn't up to you to protect us. Captain Gunther will take care of Mr. Tyree."

"Where was the Ranger when your father was slain?"

Shadowhawk was sure Shiloh did not realize what she was doing to him, when her hand closed around his. "I don't know," she admitted.

With no will to fight against the need in him, Shadowhawk drew Shiloh closer, and she melted against him.

His tenderness tapped into all the sorrows she had kept inside. "Everything changed when my father died. I don't know what to do anymore."

Shadowhawk could not seem to stop himself as he gathered her closer, wishing he could heal her pain. "You are young to have such cares." He stroked her hair, reveling in the riotous curls that tangled in his fingers.

As if it was the most natural thing in the world, Shiloh pressed her head against his bare chest and Shadowhawk felt his heart almost stop. "Shiloh, I do not know what it is I feel for you."

Shadowhawk's words didn't penetrate Shiloh's consciousness because she was overcome with tender feelings for him. Her hand moved to his shoulder as she put herself in his keeping. The hand that he ran up and down her back, pressing her still closer to him, brought her a sense of comfort she had not felt since her father's death.

"I don't understand why you've become my guardian. Although it was wrong of you to take my brother and me away from our home, I am beginning to be glad you did."

His cheek nestled against hers. "I do not understand myself why I became entangled in your life. I only know that I would keep you from all harm."

Shiloh sobered and swallowed deeply as a jolt went through her body. She was hit by new emotions and could not imagine what her life would be like without Shadowhawk. She turned her face against his neck, feeling the pulse beat there. "I'm not thinking clearly."

Smiling at her honesty, he placed his hand beneath her chin and watched as moonlight from the opening at the top of the tipi cast soft light on her face. "My mind is open and clear." He traced her jawline with his finger. "I know what I want, and what I cannot have," he said regretfully, "and they are the same." A soft moan escaped his lips as he laid his face against hers. "I can never have any more of you than I hold at this place, at this time."

Shiloh felt the pain of his words. He was putting distance between them. Raw emotions she couldn't suppress poured into her heart—she loved him. She didn't know how it had happened, but it had.

Shiloh pulled back, staring into his dark eyes. "I have the feeling you are saying good-bye to me."

"It is as it must be."

"Will you kiss me once, before we have to part?"

Shadowhawk released her abruptly. "What is a kiss?"

She looked at him in amazement. "Don't the Comanche exchange kisses as a sign of affection?"

"I do not know this custom."

"Then I will show you."

There was wariness in his tone. "If it is your wish."

Shiloh moved her head so her mouth was very near his.

Boldly, she touched his mouth with her fingers. "I will press my lips to yours."

She felt his heartbeat accelerate, and hers did as well. Slowly Shiloh leaned forward, gently brushing her mouth against his. She had meant to give him only a chaste kiss; she had *not* expected the emotions that poured through her as their lips touched. Never before experiencing such a thing, she was taken completely by surprise.

At first, Shadowhawk stiffened. Unfamiliar with such an intimacy, he felt his whole body being rocked. His breath came out in a gasp and he could not find his voice. The kiss, as Shiloh had called it, opened his mind to sensations he had never imagined. He waited in anticipation, not knowing what Shiloh would do next. When she moved her head back, looking at him in bewilderment, he had a burning desire to feel her mouth against his once more.

He held his trembling hand out for her inspection. "See what you have done to me."

She would have pulled away, but he took her face in both his hands. Then his head slowly descended and he brushed his mouth against hers, as she had done to his.

When Shadowhawk felt Shiloh's lips tremble beneath his, wild desire seared through him, and male instinct took over his reasoning. He pressed his mouth tighter against hers, and she melted against him. He touched her lips with his tongue, savoring the passion that ran hot in his veins.

Shadowhawk felt Shiloh's breasts press against his bare chest, and almost lost control. He wanted to strip off her clothing, take possession of her sweet body, and make her his woman.

More than anything, he wanted his lips on hers again, but Shadowhawk knew he had to be strong and let her go, for both their sakes. Tomorrow he would be taking her back to her home. He could no longer bear the torment of having her so near, when she would never be his. Moving Shiloh out of his arms, he rolled to his feet and turned away from her.

"This must not happen again." Shadowhawk's voice was unsteady, and he could hardly speak above a whisper.

Shiloh shrank back, suddenly ashamed of her actions. She knew nothing about how a Comanche male and female interacted, but she was sure in any culture, her bold actions would be considered disgraceful.

Shadowhawk had not initiated what had happened between the two of them—it had been her doing.

Quietly Shiloh watched him leave, feeling crushed. What had she been thinking? Shadowhawk was a man like any other—well, she reminded herself, not exactly like any other. He had merely responded to her forwardness as any man would have done.

She dipped her head into her hands as shame washed over her. How disgusted he must be with her—so much so, she had driven him out of his own tipi.

Although she waited, wanting to say how sorry she was for what had happened between them, Shadowhawk didn't return all night.

Shadowhawk stood atop a hill that gave him a wide view of the land in every direction. He closed his eyes and held his arms toward the sky. "I want her with everything in me. My heart cries out to her, and my body desires her. Yet, I would not have you take this torment from me, for I would be lost without having loved this woman."

He lowered his head, thinking how near he had come to taking her innocence. He trembled, recalling the touch of her lips, the softness of her skin.

He had little doubt that Shiloh would still reside in his heart when he drew his last breath upon this earth.

* * *

It was nearing morning when Shiloh finally fell asleep. It seemed only a short time later when Moon Song entered the tipi. "My brother has asked that I help you load the travois and the packhorse."

Blinking her eyes and sitting up, Shiloh tried to come fully awake. "Will you be going with us?" she asked hopefully.

"Shadowhawk is allowing me to accompany you for the first part of the journey." Moon Song smiled. "I am glad we have a few more days before we must say good-bye, Shiloh."

Shiloh knew exactly why Shadowhawk was taking his sister along. It was to make sure she didn't repeat her actions of the night before. Most probably he felt he needed protection from her.

After eating, Moon Song showed Shiloh how to pack robes, blankets, and food on the horse-drawn travois. As the morning progressed toward the noon hour, Shadowhawk still had not appeared, and Shiloh was glad, because she expected their meeting to be awkward for both of them.

When the horses were loaded to Moon Song's satisfaction, she turned to Shiloh. "My mother has asked if you would go to her before we depart."

Vision Woman greeted Shiloh when she entered the tipi. "I am sorry to see you leave," she said kindly. "I look forward to the day your path brings you back to us."

Shiloh felt sadness at parting with Shadowhawk's mother. "I don't think I will be returning to the village. I would like to thank you for tending my wounds, and for all your kindnesses."

Vision Woman gestured toward a buffalo robe. "Shiloh, will you not be seated for a moment? There are some things I would like to say to you."

Shiloh dropped down beside Vision Woman and waited for her to continue.

"When I was but a maiden, not much younger than you, a band of Comanche came to my Blackfoot village. One of them stood out from all the rest. His name was 'He Who Stands Tall.' When first I saw him, I was struck to the heart, although it did not seem he even noticed me." Vision Woman smiled. "Later, I learned He Who Stands Tall felt the same about me. I was heartbroken when he left, for we had not exchanged more than a few glances." Vision Woman frowned as if she was reliving something painful. "A season passed before He Who Stands Tall returned to our village, but he brought with him many horses for my father as a bride-price. My heart sang when I rode away as his woman, and not one day have I regretted my decision to go with him. He was a great chief, and a caring husband. He knew of my gift of visions, and trusted my advice, although it went against Comanche traditions for a warrior to consult a woman on important matters. Though I had many adjustments to make, for this land was harsh to me, and the Comanche are more warlike than the Blackfoot, I have lived more fully than most women I know. My son and daughter are my joy, but I wait for the time when I will be reunited with my husband."

Tears glistened in Shiloh's eyes. "Thank you for sharing this with me."

"There is a reason I told you about my love for my husband. One day you will have to make a decision, as I once did. Only you can decide if you will choose love over duty."

"I don't know what you mean."

Vision Woman smiled. "I do not suppose you do. But one day it will all be clear to you. On that day, think back to when we had this talk."

With her mind whirling, Shiloh stood. "I will," she

said, but she didn't really understand Vision Woman's cryptic advice.

Vision Woman followed Shiloh outside and watched her mount a horse. She raised her hand to her daughter and Shiloh, and watched them until they rode away.

"Moon Song, has your mother ever told you how she met your father?"

"Only that he came to her village. It is a tale she does not share with anyone."

Shiloh was even more confused. Why had Shadowhawk's mother told a white girl about her husband, when she had not told her own daughter?

They rode out of the village, and the children ran along beside them, as they had the day Shiloh arrived. Shiloh looked for the little girl who had befriended her, and when she saw her among the others, she gave the child a special smile.

When they reached open country, Shadowhawk and a small band of Comanche warriors rode past, hardly giving Shiloh and Moon Song a glance. It soon became clear to Shiloh that they would be forced to swallow the dust kicked up by the men's horses.

Though her throat felt parched, Shiloh found it easier to swallow the dust than her wounded pride.

Chapter Twenty-three

Luke dismounted and threw himself beneath the shade of a cottonwood tree that somehow looked out of place on the stark prairie. It would take only a puff of wind to bring down the roofless, abandoned shack that marred the land. He glanced at the rusted plow, testament to a family's struggle to scratch out a living in this harsh country. Luke wondered about the people who had lived there. Had they been chased away by Comanche, died of a fever, or just given up and abandoned the homestead?

Charley took a drink from his canteen and joined Luke beneath the shade, while Gunther looked through his field glass.

"It's a mystery to me how a tribe of Comanche can cross this land without leaving a sign that they passed this way," the Ranger remarked in an aggrieved tone.

"The man at the tradin' post done told us the Comanche are out there somewhere, 'cause he's traded with 'em," Charley reminded Gunther.

Gunther turned to the boy. "I know I've asked you this before, but can you think of anything you might have overlooked that could help us find your sister?"

Shaking his head, Luke said, "It's like I told you before, Captain Gunther, they were camped along the bank of a river. When I left the village, I rode through the river so no one could track me." Luke had done as Shiloh had told him and directed the Ranger and Charley in the opposite way from that he'd come. He was not exactly fibbing to the captain, he just wasn't telling him the whole truth.

"What made you do that?" Gunther pressed.

"Because I'd seen Shadowhawk do it to hide our tracks."

"Why can't you leave the boy alone?" Charley said. "He wants to find his sister more'n you do."

"We've followed the Brazos and most of its branches now. If the Comanche are out there, they're well hidden." Gunther blotted sweat from his face with his sleeve. "There are a dozen or so creeks and washes we could search, but it would take us months to get around to them all." His eyes hardened as he looked at Luke. "Surely there's some detail you've missed."

Luke avoided Gunther's eyes. "I can't help you. All this country looks the same to me."

Gunther stared hard at Luke. "If we don't find your sister soon, one of them Comanche bucks'll take her for his woman. You don't want that to happen, do you?"

"Now, hold on there, Gunther," Charley said, patting Luke's arm. "There ain't no call to talk to the boy like that. Why don't you leave him in peace? You've been hammerin' away at him for days."

Gunther whirled around to say something to Charley, but the look in the old man's eyes stopped him.

Luke shook his head. "Shadowhawk's not going to hurt Shiloh, and he won't let anyone else hurt her either. I already told you that."

There was a look of disgust on Gunther's face. "I don't think you are an expert on how Comanche treat white women. I won't spoil your illusion about your hero by telling you about the women I've rescued from the Comanche. I will say the women are never the same. Every one of them has been mistreated in some way or other."

Luke clenched his fists. "Don't say that! You don't know Shadowhawk."

"I've gotta agree with Luke," Charley interjected, trying to defuse the situation. "To Shadowhawk's way of thinkin', he took Miss Shiloh away to keep her safe. Once the danger's gone, he'll bring her home—that's what I'm sayin', and that's what I believe."

Gunther stared across a deep canyon. "It would be out of character for a Comanche to release a captive." He nodded at Luke. "He escaped. They didn't let him go."

Luke stood. "I miss my sister and I want to see her."

Gunther jammed his foot in the stirrup. "Let's head out. We surely won't find her lolling around here. I'm going to take you back to Antelope Wells," he told Luke. "Mr. and Mrs. Curruthers will look after you for a spell."

"I'll go home with Charley," the boy said stubbornly.

Charley shook his head. "I won't be goin' back to the ranch, Luke. Not 'til we find your sister."

Gunther capped his canteen after taking a drink. "Tomorrow I'll set out again with more Rangers. I'll get Jimmy Tall Tree to track for me."

Luke stared into the distance—Shiloh was out there somewhere, and she wanted to go home as badly as he did. Had he done the right thing in misleading Gunther?

Charley pulled Luke aside. "What ain't you tellin' Gunther?"

"What do you mean?"

"You're holdin' something back."

Luke lowered his voice when he said, "If I am, it's for a good reason."

Dark clouds gathered in the north, and Shiloh wished it would rain to cool the temperature. Her doeskin gown was plastered to her skin. Glancing about her, she noticed none of the Comanche seem to be bothered by the heat, not even Moon Song, who was dressed just as she was.

To make matters worse, Shadowhawk had not even

glanced in her direction since they'd set out the day before. She could feel his coldness, even from a distance.

Shiloh was grateful when they stopped to set up camp alongside a river. The travois was detached from the horse and unloaded. Since Shiloh and Moon Song were the only women traveling with the warriors, they would sleep apart from the men.

Shiloh watched Shadowhawk and three of his braves ride away—she assumed to backtrack, making certain if anyone was following, they wouldn't be able to pick up their trail.

"I'm hot and gritty, and I want a bath," Shiloh told Moon Song, pointing toward a place where the river curved around a bend and disappeared among a grove of scrub brushes. "It's secluded enough down there so no one can see us if we bathe."

"I will first have to ask permission of my brother when he returns," Moon Song said, compressing her lips in a worried line. "Shadowhawk may not allow us to wander that far from camp. Can you not see the river is swollen from rain farther upstream? The currents would be dangerous, even for a strong swimmer."

Shiloh walked toward the river bend, with Moon Song hurrying after her. "I don't need your brother's permission to bathe, and as for danger, I'm a strong swimmer. Why don't you go in the water with me?"

"Shiloh, you should not—"

Holding her hand up to silence the girl, Shiloh said in aggravation, "Enough. I intend to bathe in that river, and no one is going to stop me." She thought longingly of the lilac-scented soap she bathed with at home. "Will you come with me, or not?"

"Not without Shadowhawk's permission."

Shiloh stepped around one of the warriors who had been set to watch her. When she glared at him, he looked as if he'd like to stop her, but he moved aside, allowing her to pass. Shiloh imagined the poor man had been warned not to touch her.

As Shiloh hurried over sharp rocks and past thorn-bushes that tore at her bare skin, Moon Song scurried after her. When they had disappeared around the bend, where the warriors could no longer see them, Shiloh breathed a sigh of relief.

"See?" she said. "We are well hidden here, so we can undress." She sat down and began unlacing her moccasins. Next she lifted the doeskin dress over her head and draped it on a mesquite tree branch.

Wearing only the nightgown she used as a shift, Shiloh waded into the water while Moon Song looked on worriedly.

"You should not do this," the young girl warned.

Ignoring Moon Song's protests, Shiloh dove into the water, relishing the feel of the coolness against her skin. Surfacing, she realized the strong flow of water had swept her some distance from the shore, but she was unconcerned.

Moon Song was calling out to her, but Shiloh had drifted too far to hear her words. Turning onto her back, she floated along with the flowing water, freeing her mind of all troubles. She was aware that the current had become stronger, but she still was not worried. When Shiloh turned back to her stomach, she could no longer see Moon Song. Nor did Shiloh see the uprooted tree that bobbed swiftly behind her. She felt the branches snag her hair, and she was dragged beneath the water.

Shiloh was struggling to reach the surface when Shadowhawk dove into the water, lifting her upward, and carrying her ashore. Laying her on her stomach, he applied pressure to her back to expel the river water.

Coughing and sputtering, Shiloh fought her way out of

a fog. Gasping for breath, she rolled over and looked into Shadowhawk's angry eyes.

Shadowhawk had returned to find Shiloh and Moon Song were not in camp. Climbing a butte, he had seen Shiloh and the uprooted tree heading in her direction. He had been afraid he would not reach her in time. Sweeping his wet hair out of his face, Shadowhawk found Shiloh watching him expectantly, her lower lip trembling. Now that he knew she was unharmed, he gave vent to his anger.

"You are the most disobedient woman I have ever known."

"Are we on the other side of the river?" Shiloh asked between coughing spasms, knowing he had every right to be angry.

"We are."

A high canyon wall was behind them, its rock cliffs impossible to climb.

Shiloh hugged her arms about her as chills shook her body. "Will we have to swim back to the other side?"

Shadowhawk stood with his back to her. "No. Because of your foolishness, we cannot make it back before nightfall."

"Why not?"

He turned to her with a scowl on his face. "There is flooding farther upriver and the water rises swiftly."

Shiloh had not yet realized that her wet garment was transparent, and that Shadowhawk could clearly see her nakedness. Need slammed into him like an arrow when he saw the rosy tips of her breasts. Indian women had dark nipples—Shiloh's were the color of a prairie rose.

Shadowhawk could not seem to look away. His hungry gaze moved over her soft curves and he felt his world spin out of control when he saw the tangle of red hair between her thighs. Trembling with a passion he had never felt before, he forced himself to turn away from her.

"We camp here tonight," he said, not daring to turn back to her.

"Your sister will worry."

"You should have thought of that before you acted so foolishly."

"I'm sorry."

The little hellion had never apologized before, and her words took Shadowhawk by surprise. He could never stay angry with her for long. "Moon Song knows you are with me," he admitted. "She will not worry."

Shiloh had finally realized her wet undergarment did little to hide her nakedness. Slumping forward, she drew her knees up and locked her arms about them. "We must swim back! My clothing is on the other side of the river."

He stared into her eyes. "I said 'no.'"

Shadowhawk's arrogance annoyed her. "I can't go around without clothing. I'm wet to my skin and it's cold with the sun going down."

His mouth curved into a frown. "My warriors are on the other side of the river; do you think I would allow them to see you as you are now?"

"I . . . hope you wouldn't."

He grasped her wrist and swung her into his arms. "You cannot even walk lest you injure your tender feet on thorns and stones."

Shiloh gazed into dark eyes that seemed to blaze like molten flames. Shadowhawk's mouth was near hers, and she was unaware her lips parted in invitation.

She felt the very moment his body tensed. "Do not think you can make me press my mouth to yours again."

"I never . . . I would not—"

"You would," he muttered, carrying her up the bank and depositing her none too gently on the grassy slope. "I will build a fire so you can warm yourself."

Feeling embarrassed, Shiloh rose to her knees. "I don't mean to cause you trouble."

"Yes, you do."

Shiloh watched Shadowhawk stalk away with all the grace of a panther. "I don't like you," she called after him, but he had already disappeared on the other side of a thornbush.

When Shadowhawk returned with an armload of dry wood, the sun had dropped behind the canyon wall, and it was almost dark. Shiloh watched him strike flint and fan sparks, igniting a flame. Shivering, she gravitated closer to the warmth.

"I'm hungry," she said, glancing up at him.

"I have nothing to feed you."

Since Shiloh's shift was still damp, it chafed her skin and made her colder. She wondered how the weather could be so scorching hot in the daytime and so cold when the sun set.

Shiloh glanced up and found Shadowhawk staring steadily at her. When she could no longer hold his gaze, she glanced down at her hands. It was obvious he was still angry with her.

She tossed her hair, turning her back to him. After a while she curled up near the fire, resting her head on her folded arm. He had saved her life today, at the risk of his own. Turning back to face him, she found he was still watching her and she gave him a level stare. "Thank you."

He merely turned away, apparently wasting no more of his thoughts on her. He faded into the darkness and she wondered where he'd gone.

She sighed, watching the crackling fire. She was cold and uncomfortable, but there was nothing that could be done about it.

A short time later Shiloh heard the cry of a wolf, and an answering cry just across the canyon. Glancing up at the rim of the canyon, she saw the outline of the animal. Now she was not only miserable and cold, but she was afraid she was about to be devoured by a wolf.

"Shadowhawk!" she cried out. "Where are you?"

Chapter Twenty-four

Shadowhawk heard Shiloh's cry for help and raced toward her. When he broke through the scrub brush into the clearing, he stopped, staring at her. She had picked up one of the flaming logs and held it out like a weapon. Glancing about, he found nothing to indicate she was in danger.

"What has happened?" he asked, withdrawing his knife, his dark gaze penetrating the shadows. "What has frightened you?"

"I . . . heard a wolf."

Shadowhawk swung around to stare at her. "You heard a wolf?"

"Yes, I did." She pointed to the top of the canyon, where the outline of a wolf stood out against the night sky.

Shadowhawk put away his knife. "I have never heard of a lone wolf attacking anyone."

She stepped closer to him. "What if this one is hungry?"

He hid his smile by turning to stare in the distance. Shiloh would not take it kindly that he found her fear laughable. "Should the animal come after you, I will protect you."

Tossing the burning log back on the fire, Shiloh inched her body closer to his. "Give me your word you won't leave me again."

Shadowhawk wished he never had to leave her, but the time would come when he must. "Seek sleep. I will be nearby."

"You'll watch out for the wolf?"

She was watching him with the expression of a frightened child. He said with as much sincerity as he could summon, "I will."

Shiloh lowered her head. "Luke would laugh at my fear of wolves. But I once saw a pack of wolves take down a newborn calf. The memory of their fierceness has remained with me." Shiloh was tired, hungry, and cold. She was living in a world vastly different from the one she was accustomed to. The only stabilizing force in her life was the dark-eyed Comanche, who at the moment watched her with puzzlement. "I truly am sorry I went into the river."

"It is all but forgotten." Shadowhawk motioned to a place near the campfire. "Sleep. I will watch over you."

Obediently Shiloh curled up on the grass near the fire.

Shadowhawk watched her brace her head on her folded arms and close her eyes. In truth, he could have safely swum her back across the river—why had he not? The answer was clear. Even as angry as he had been when he saw her swimming in the river, he had wanted to be alone with her.

As he dropped down beside her, thoughts of his future tumbled through his mind. It was a bleak, empty prospect. For so long there had been an aching void in his heart—that space had now been filled by Shiloh, but to what end?

He watched her long lashes close to rest against her pale cheeks and felt a now familiar yearning. On the day he set her free, he would die a little inside.

He wondered what man would someday win Shiloh's heart, and the pain of that thought was almost unbearable.

Shiloh challenged him at every opportunity, yet tonight she had turned to him for protection. Noticing that she was shaking from the cold, he placed more wood on the fire. His buckskins were wet, so he stripped down to his breechcloth. Lying down beside Shiloh, he pulled her into his arms. Her eyes fluttered open and when she saw that it was he, she snuggled close to his warm body.

He had won her trust.

For long moments Shadowhawk held her to him, gazing up at the star-strewn sky. He would not sleep this night; instead he would savor this moment with Shiloh in his arms.

He dipped his head, his mouth resting against the top of her head. Warmth spread through Shadowhawk as her soft curves settled against him. His thoughts turned to desire, but he would keep those feelings under tight control.

Shiloh stirred, blinking her eyes. Realizing she was nestled in Shadowhawk's arms, she hesitated to move away from his warmth. The campfire had died down to smouldering ash, but she was no longer cold because she drew warmth from his body.

Dark hair fell across Shadowhawk's cheek and Shiloh wanted so badly to touch it. His face, even in half-light, was beautifully sculpted. His mouth was so near her own. Remembering how it had felt when she kissed him, she wanted to press her lips to his once more. Her hand trembled as she reached out and touched his cheek.

Shadowhawk stared straight into Shiloh's eyes. For a long moment neither of them moved.

"You touched me," he whispered, not realizing he had spoken in Comanche.

Still she did not move out of his arms. "I don't understand what you said."

Speaking in English, he said, "Shiloh, I believe you do." Slowly, he drew her closer, pressing his cheek to hers. "I truly think you do."

All the longing Shiloh had kept locked in her heart burst forth. When he drew her to him, she melted inside.

She wanted to throw her arms around him, to absorb him into her body. Her hand slid across his chest, and she gloried in the feel of his smooth skin.

Shadowhawk nuzzled her ear while his hands moved down her back, pressing her to the swell of him. "I have wanted in my time, but not like this, Shiloh. Never like this."

Shiloh couldn't think straight. She felt feverish, her body ached, and she wanted something from him that she could not ask for. Instinctively her mouth moved over his cheek and found his lips.

With a sharp intake of breath, Shadowhawk stilled, afraid to move, lest he lose all control over himself.

Her lips were soft, and the feel of them against his sent yearning thundering through him. "Shiloh, I desire you," he said, tearing his mouth from hers. "You fire my blood."

Somewhere in the back of her mind a small voice warned Shiloh of the danger in tempting this man, but that did not stop her. "You make me feel . . . I don't know how to explain—" Whatever she'd wanted to say went out of her head because Shadowhawk pushed her garment off her shoulders and stared at her breasts. Gently he caressed one and then slid his hand to the other.

Shiloh gritted her teeth to keep from crying out with pleasure. But more pleasure was to come when he lowered his dark head, pressing his mouth against her breast. She bit her lip and twisted her body to meet his.

"Shadowhawk," she murmured.

"I know," he said, caressing one breast while he sucked on the other.

"Ohhh," Shiloh groaned as pleasure coursed through her whole body. She slammed her fists against the ground, writhing with passion. Newly tapped desire raged through her and she closed her eyes, loving the feel of Shadowhawk's warm mouth on her breasts.

Shadowhawk pulled back. "This has never happened to you before?"

"N . . . no. Never. I have been with no man."

Shiloh's admission pleased him, but it also told him he must stop. Shadowhawk slid his hand beneath her chin and made her look at him. "I am glad I am the first to make you feel like a woman."

His words carried her back to sanity and she stared up at him. "What is happening to me with you?"

Shiloh saw regret in his dark eyes. Then those same eyes hardened and sliced through her like a hot knife through butter, reminding her he was a man who lived by rules far different from any man she had ever known.

Shadowhawk rolled to his feet, and Shiloh heard the anger in his voice when he said, "I should not have touched you."

Shiloh hung her head in shame, burying her face in her hands. "It was my fault again."

Shadowhawk stepped away from her, his gaze tracing the first streaks of daylight that touched the eastern horizon. "Do not take all the blame on yourself. You could not have tempted me had I not wanted you." He turned back to her. "We must return to the others."

Shiloh stumbled on a huge stone protruding out of the ground, and Shadowhawk steadied her, pulling her closer to him. "Once more you have no shoes." He lifted her into his arms, but he avoided looking at her. "You weigh little more than a child," he said, treading through the tall grass.

When they came to a place that satisfied Shadowhawk, he set her on her feet. "The river is still swift. I will take you across."

Shiloh shivered when he led her into the river. He swam alongside her, making certain she could maneuver the swift currents. When they reached the other side,

Shadowhawk took Shiloh in his arms and set her on dry ground. Nodding at her dress, which still hung over the branch of a mesquite tree, he said, "Clothe yourself."

Shivering in the cold morning air, Shiloh yanked on her doeskin gown. Sitting down, she pushed her feet into the moccasins and laced them about her ankles.

Shadowhawk, who had been glancing downstream, turned back to Shiloh and said impatiently, "We have remained too long in this place."

As they made their way back to the others, Shiloh was forced to take hurried steps to keep up with Shadowhawk.

When they reached camp, the Comanche glanced at them with curiosity, but otherwise seemed unconcerned.

While Shadowhawk approached his warriors, Moon Song spoke to Shiloh. "You must be hungry. Come. I have food for you."

When Shiloh watched Shadowhawk instruct his warriors to strike camp, sadness overcame her, and she could not have said why.

"What is Shadowhawk telling them?" she asked Moon Song.

"He is sending out scouts toward Antelope Wells. My brother wishes to know what the Rangers are doing."

Chapter Twenty-five

The sun had just dipped behind the canyon when Shadowhawk's scouts caught up with them.

One of the men, who seemed to be the leader, talked excitedly as he relayed his message. Shadowhawk looked grim.

Shiloh turned to Moon Song to ask her what was happening.

The young girl swallowed deeply. "We are being followed by Rangers and your Charley. Jimmy Tall Tree is tracking for them, and he will soon pick up our trail."

Shiloh felt relief. "Is that all?"

The young girl's dark eyes were expressive. "It would not be good for them to do so, Shiloh. They are many and we are few."

Shadowhawk turned his horse and rode beside them, his gaze sweeping Shiloh's face. "You will come with me now."

"Shadowhawk," Shiloh said, "it's really quite simple. Let me ride toward the Rangers so they will no longer follow you."

Shadowhawk controlled his prancing horse with ease. "No," he said emphatically.

"I don't want to cause you more trouble. Just let me go."

His jaw hardened. "No."

Shiloh realized if Gunther caught up with them, even Moon Song wouldn't be safe. "What will you do?"

Moon Song, who was shocked that Shiloh would question a chief's orders in a dangerous situation, quickly spoke to her brother in Comanche. Then she turned to Shiloh. "I am to return to our village with our warriors. You will continue on with Shadowhawk."

"Why?"

"Shadowhawk does not tell me his plans." Her large eyes held a sad light. "This is the second time we have said good-bye, Shiloh. It makes me unhappy to leave you."

Shiloh smiled sadly and reached out to clasp Moon Song's hand. "May God keep you safe."

Moon Song listened to her brother speak to the warriors that would be her escort; then she spoke to Shiloh. "I leave now. The Rangers are a day's ride behind us. My brother hopes by splitting up, we will confuse Jimmy Tall Tree."

"Who is this Jimmy Tall Tree?"

Moon Song met Shiloh's gaze. "He is a Comanche. At one time he was a trusted warrior of our tribe. He now scouts for the Rangers. There is none better at tracking than he."

"Why are the warriors tying mesquite branches behind their horses?"

"It will cause a dust cloud. Shadowhawk is hoping Jimmy Tall Tree will be fooled and follow us, rather than you."

"Will that not be dangerous for you?"

Moon Song shook her head. "I do not think they will be able to catch us."

Shiloh dismounted and stood beside her horse, watching the dust cloud raised by the departing Comanche. She saw Running Fox break away from the main body and ride in a different direction. As they galloped across the prairie, she was struck by how exciting it was to watch the Comanche on horseback—for they truly were masters of the horse.

Shadowhawk, who had never before explained his decisions once they were made, looked down at Shiloh. "Jimmy Tall Tree will see the dust and think he has found me."

"Won't he know it's a trick?"

He swung onto his horse and motioned for her to do the same. "He will in time. I am hoping it will be too late to pick up our trail when he realizes his mistake."

He nudged his horse forward and Shiloh followed. Soon they were galloping across the prairie, heading for a creek in the distance. Shiloh had seen Shadowhawk's methods enough to know they would be riding through the creek for miles to hide their tracks.

As she rode beside Shadowhawk she glanced sideways at him. He was shirtless, and his flowing ebony hair rippled across his shoulders. His long legs gripped the sides of the horse, and it responded to his slightest command.

He was magnificent—honorable, intelligent, and as gallant as any knight of old. Some Comanche woman would be most fortunate when he chose her for his wife. Her aversion to that thought didn't surprise her.

Shadowhawk raised his head to the sky, and it seemed to Shiloh he was listening to the wind, communing with the hawk that circled above them.

As the sun was sinking low, they reached a creek and just as Shiloh had predicted, they rode for miles through the muddy water, emerging when they reached a rock-faced cliff.

Shadowhawk held up his hand for Shiloh to halt. "Remain here. I will backtrack to make certain I left no sign behind. Do not leave this place."

Shiloh nodded, watching him ride back the way they had come. She saw him ride up the creek bank several times, and knew he was leaving false trails for Jimmy Tall Tree to follow.

The others had taken the pack animals with them. She and Shadowhawk were left with what their horses carried. She dismounted, allowing her horse to drink from the creek. There would be no campfire tonight, which meant they would have no roasted meat.

Darkness fell heavily against the canyon walls and still Shadowhawk had not returned. As full dark fell, Shiloh spread her blanket on the grass and sat down, eating a chunk of dried meat and savoring every bite.

After a while, she lay back, closing her eyes and thinking about hot biscuits with butter and jam. Her mouth watered when she thought about bubbling stew, seasoned just right with huge chunks of savory meat.

The night became chilly, and she pulled the edges of her blanket over her for warmth, waiting for Shadowhawk. When he did return, he seemed tense, listening to the wind as if he heard something she couldn't hear.

Moments later Running Fox rode into camp. The two Comanche conversed for a time; then they both settled on the ground, whittling their arrows.

She raised herself up on her elbow. What were they doing?

Wearily, Shiloh lay back, and was almost asleep when she heard Shadowhawk's voice as he spoke to Running Fox. She was so attuned to him his voice sent shivers over her skin. A dark cloud moved across the moon and Shiloh closed her eyes. If Shadowhawk were a white man or if she were an Indian maiden, would he take her for his woman? She found herself wanting to curl up in his arms, to feel the warmth of his body, to have him touch her as he had done the night before.

But today, Shadowhawk had all but ignored her, acting as if nothing had happened between them.

Half asleep, she heard Running Fox ride away. She was startled when she realized Shadowhawk had bent down to her.

"You are still awake, Shiloh?" he asked quietly.

"How did you know?"

"I knew."

He moved his blanket close to her and sat down. "We are not so far from your home."

She sat up and glanced about. "I didn't realize that. But then, most of this country looks the same to me."

"I want you to know what I plan to do."

She sat up so she could see him better. "What?"

"You suspect the man Tyree is responsible for your father's death."

"I know he is."

"Shiloh, one night I saw men slaughter your cattle using arrows. After they left, I examined the arrows and found they had Kiowa carvings. I did not know who those men were at the time, but now I suspect they were Tyree's men."

"We do not have to look far to know where to place the blame," Shiloh said angrily. "You saw him that night by the river when he was trying to force himself on me."

Shadowhawk's tone was guarded. "He will pay for that."

Shiloh looked at him anxiously. "I don't want you to kill him. Promise me you won't."

He regarded her for a moment. "You ask much of me."

She placed her hand on his arm. "Promise me."

He could not deny her. "I will not draw his blood."

"Thank you," she said, knowing his agreement had gone against his instincts.

Moving away from him, Shiloh stared into the distance. "What now?"

Shadowhawk tried to keep all emotion out of his voice.

"Your brother has been taken to the town called Antelope Wells. I am told he stays with the storekeeper and his wife."

"How do you know that?"

Although she could not see his face, she knew he was smiling. "I know."

"What will happen to me?"

"Soon, I will finish paying my debt to you and your brother."

Emptiness invaded Shiloh's heart. What would she do when she could no longer talk to Shadowhawk? The thought of never seeing him again was unbearable. Frantically she reached for his hand and felt his strong clasp.

There was agony in his voice as he whispered, "Shiloh."

With a cry, she threw herself into his arms, nestling her cheek against his shoulder. "I don't want to leave you." The moon emerged from the clouds as she raised her face to his. His eyes darkened with an expression of regret; then with the flicker of his lashes, it was as if a mask settled over his face.

"It is as it must be."

"Common sense tells me you are right, but my heart won't listen." She stared into his eyes. "Is there another woman who holds your heart?"

His arms tightened about her and he whispered something in Comanche. Then he said in English, as his focus shifted to her mouth, "There can never be another woman to hold my heart because it is too full of you." He brushed her hair out of her face. "Will you touch your lips to mine this one last time?"

Shadowhawk knew it was dangerous, but he had been thinking all day about her tempting lips. He was a leader of men and maintained a strong will over those who followed him, but Shiloh was his weakness. The kiss was a white man's custom that had staggered him and brought him to his knees. The thought of pressing his mouth to any other woman's lips was repugnant to him.

Shiloh angled her head and parted her lips. With a strangled groan, Shadowhawk pressed his mouth against hers, and they clung to each other. They were not a white woman and a Comanche warrior, but merely a man and a woman who had reached across barriers and found each other.

His hands moved over her body, his mouth plundered hers. She could feel his heart racing—it matched the thundering beat of her own.

Shadowhawk tore his mouth from hers, his gaze intense. The breeze in the overhead branches played nature's melody as he huskily whispered against her hair, "When first I saw you, the flame of your hair ignited a fire within me, and I wanted to stare forever into your eyes that reflect the color of the sky."

His confession sent warmth throughout her body, and she touched his cheek. "When we first met, I was terrified of you, and I thought you despised me."

He silently watched her, trying to think how to answer. "I have never despised you, not even when you were at your most stubborn."

Shiloh smiled. "I have often been accused of being stubborn. It is a fault I have tried to overcome, but I have failed miserably, especially with you."

"I would not have you change who you are," he said, lowering his head to nestle his lips between her breasts. "I want to lie with you, but it cannot be."

The impact of his words shot through her body. She was honest with him when she said, "I want that too, and I also know it can't be."

"I would give you something of myself. I hope you will understand what this gift costs me." His hand drifted down her thigh and he slowly raised her gown.

Shiloh drew in her breath when he shoved her shift aside, touching her intimately. Tears gathered in her eyes as he gently caressed between her thighs. A consuming ache rushed through her and she gasped when his mouth found hers.

She could hardly breathe when she heard him moan. There was something powerful between them, and it was almost more than she could endure.

Could anything be more beautiful than the feelings that kept them locked in each other's arms? Shiloh wondered.

Burying her fingers in his dark hair, she gave herself up to him completely.

Shadowhawk slowly parted her legs, hesitated, massaged her in such a way that her breath caught in her throat.

Smothering a groan, he denied the need that tore through his body so he could leave her a virgin. As his hand slid lower, he gave to her without taking for himself.

Shiloh cried out, her hips bucking upward at his expert manipulation of her body. Whimpering, she buried her face against his chest, glorying in the feelings he was arousing in her. She could hear his heavy breathing and knew he was as affected as she was.

Something was building inside her. Her hips moved against his hand as he stroked her softly, speaking in Comanche.

"I don't understand," she gasped as he buried his face against her breasts.

"You are my heart. No matter how long I walk this earth, you will always be with me."

She felt a rush of exquisite sensation, just as his masterful manipulation caused her body to quake.

Shadowhawk held her until her body stilled.

At last she raised her face to his. "What did you do to

me?" She placed her cheek against his chest. "What just happened?"

He said nothing because he was incapable of speech.

Shiloh nestled against him, feeling as if she belonged to him. In Shadowhawk, Shiloh had found the only man she would ever love.

"Close your eyes," he said, pressing her closer against him. "Sleep now."

Long after Shiloh had fallen asleep, Shadowhawk held her close to his heart, staring into the darkness. For the moment she belonged to him—in three days' time, he would let her go.

Only when the first faint streaks of red touched the eastern sky did he lay her gently down, covering her with a blanket. He walked some distance, listening to the sounds about him. The nocturnal dwellers had sought their habitats, and the day dwellers were venturing forth.

"Why must my heart be as one with her?" he asked whatever spirit was listening.

"Why did this happen to me?"

Suddenly as if the wind had whispered the answer to him, Shadowhawk knew what he must do. He was war chief to his tribe, and would act for the good of his people.

He had to let Shiloh go.

Bowing his head, he knew what actions he must take to see that she was safe. The man who was a danger to her must be stopped.

Hearing a rider approaching, Shadowhawk slipped his knife out of its scabbard and faded into the shadows. He dropped his guard when he saw that Running Fox had returned.

"I have been watching the man Tyree, as you asked," his friend said. "He has many men guarding him."

"I have no fear of them."

"What then will we do?"

"To have an enemy and not understand his ways is to lose the battle before it begins."

"Do you want me to go back and watch him?"

"Yes. Note everything he does. I want to know all his movements. But do nothing that will place your life in danger. Never forget for a moment that the Rangers are out there somewhere."

"And the woman?"

"She has no place in this. I will take her back to her home, and that will be the end of it."

Running Fox frowned. "Do you want to take her back to her home?"

Shadowhawk felt the now familiar pain rip through him. "What I want does not matter. What must be will be."

Chapter Twenty-six

As the foreman of the Crooked H walked toward the big house, the sun had just risen. Tip Rawlins dreaded this meeting with the boss. Mr. Tyree wasn't going to be happy when he heard the Bradens had disappeared from sight and Rawlins couldn't find anyone who knew where they'd gone.

Hell, he thought, kicking at a weed that had managed to push its way through the pebble walkway. The boss was becoming obsessed with owning Estrella. That was all Mr. Tyree talked about. Rawlins wasn't sure his boss's mind hadn't come unhinged.

He stopped in his tracks, his eyes widening. "Hell and damnation!" he croaked, gaping at the Indian lance driven into the walkway. In shocked surprise, he circled the lance, wondering what it meant, and who had put it there.

Hurrying up the steps to the house, Rawlins pounded on the door. "Boss, boss, you gotta come out here and see what's in your yard."

Surge Tyree came to the door, scowling, a cup of coffee in his hand. He took a sip before he spoke: "Damnit, Rawlins, the wife and daughter are still asleep. What can be so important—" Tyree's mouth gaped open and he set his coffee cup on the porch railing. Slowly he descended the steps without taking his eyes off the offensive object. "If that," he said, pointing at the lance, "is the work of some jokester, I don't find it funny at all."

"Boss, Bill and Mace are still in town, and I sent the

rest of the men to the north pasture like you told me to. The only ones here is me and Paco, and you know full well Paco wouldn't've done this, no more than I woulda."

"Well, it didn't get here by itself." Tyree bent down to study the markings on the lance, for some reason reluctant to touch it. "I think it's Comanche. What do these black crow feathers mean?"

"I don't know, boss. But Paco might. He learned some Comanche when he was trading with 'em down Mexico way."

"Get him out here so he can look at this thing." With a shiver, Tyree glanced about him as if some unseen eyes were watching him. "And don't say anything about this to my wife or daughter. The wife's jumpy enough as it is about Indians."

Moments later Paco hurried toward the ranch house, his dark face creased with a worried frown. No one knew how old Paco was, but every wrinkle on his face folded onto the next one.

"Señor Tyree," he said, his eyes wide with horror. "This is a Comanche war lance. Very bad—very bad."

"Explain," Tyree said with growing unease.

The Mexican pointed to the carvings near the top of the lance. "I do not know what they all mean, but the crooked arrow you see carved here signifies revenge."

Tyree digested that piece of information. "And the crow feathers?"

"Death." Paco's eyes widened as he glanced over his shoulder. "You have been singled out for death."

The boss of the Crooked H sucked in his breath. "I don't believe you. This is someone's idea of a joke."

"This is no prank. See this figure of a hawk at the top—that's Shadowhawk's mark, *Patrón*. I saw it once carved on a knife, and was told by a friend what it was."

Tyree shook his head in disgust. "There's no such person

as Shadowhawk. He's just a figure of someone's imagination. No one's ever seen him."

Paco shook his white head. "I have seen him for myself, *Patrón*. He is real."

"If that's true," Rawlins said, "tell the boss about it."

"I was in Las Candela. There was talk that Shadowhawk was coming and I had no wish to meet him. From my hiding place near the stable, I saw him and three bucks ride in. The streets of Las Candela were deserted, and no one came out of their houses until he left."

Although Tyree felt a stirring of fear, he tried to ignore it. "Was he young, old, tall, fat, short? Surely you saw that much."

"He was young, and mighty, a person revered by the other Comanche, who deferred to his leadership. I can tell you he stood out among his warriors."

"Well," Tyree said, "I've never seen him, never did anything to him, so he can't have a grudge against me."

Tyree's face suddenly whitened. "Wait a minute! I think maybe I did see him." He nodded at Rawlins. "You recall I told you about that Comanche, the one who threw me to the ground the day of the flood. I was lucky to escape with my life. It was so dark I couldn't see him clearly."

"If it was him, why would he let you go, boss—and why didn't he harm the Braden gal?" Rawlins questioned.

"It's all nonsense," Tyree said, going up the steps and hooking his hand around his coffee cup. "Utter nonsense."

He stopped at the door and turned to Rawlins. "Get rid of that thing!"

Shiloh awoke to find Shadowhawk watching her with tenderness in his eyes. When she reached out her hand to him, he rolled to his feet.

"We must leave this place."

Had she not seen the way he had looked at her, Shiloh would have been hurt by the harshness in his tone. Shadowhawk was no longer the gentle lover he'd been the night before; he was the Comanche chief.

They rode for most of the day in silence, and Shiloh knew something was troubling Shadowhawk.

Once, she turned her head to find him watching her, but he quickly nudged his horse into a faster gallop.

It was late afternoon when Shadowhawk halted, pointing across the prairie. "There is something of beauty here you might like to see."

She saw nothing but prairie.

"Wait," he told her.

Shadowhawk rode ahead and dismounted at the edge of a canyon, motioning for Shiloh to do the same. "This is a sacred place to the Comanche," Shadowhawk told her. "I wanted you to see it."

She heard water trickling from a spring, and traced it to the place where it pooled. "I would never have imagined such a contrast of nature here on the prairie." Where she stood, there was dry prairie grass, cedar bushes, and mesquite trees. She glanced down into the deep canyon at the bubbling spring. Stepping over flint chippings where Comanche must have worked arrowheads for generations, she felt like an intruder.

The setting sun struck the canyon walls, turning them crimson, and she caught her breath at the beauty of it. "Will we spend the night here?"

Glancing at the position of the sun, Shadowhawk knew it would be a few hours before dark; they could still go farther. "If you like." He took the reins of his horse, leading it down a steep path, and Shiloh followed.

When they reached the canyon floor, she turned in a circle, trying to take in the beauty of the place. She was fascinated by the water splashing down the canyon to form a crystal-clear pond. Over untold years, odd formations had been carved into the stone.

"Thank you for showing this to me," she said joyfully.

Shadowhawk was unloading the packhorse, and paused to look at her. "You will tell no one of this place?"

"I never shall."

Shadowhawk stared at her with such longing, Shiloh flew into his arms and he caught her to him. His hungry mouth sought those sweet lips that had tempted him all day. He wanted her, he needed her as he needed the air to breathe.

Tears were streaming down her face and he kissed them away. He backed her against the canyon wall, pressing his body against hers.

"I meant to let you go," he murmured against her ear. Then he spoke softly to her in Comanche. He told her how he hungered for one look into her sky-colored eyes. He pressed his hardness tighter against her, telling her he ached to be as one with her. He brushed his mouth against her ear as he whispered he would never stop loving her.

Shiloh closed her eyes, hearing the intensity and tenderness in his deep voice. Although she had not understood his words, she realized he was baring his soul to her.

Suddenly Shadowhawk stepped back. "This must not happen again."

Seeing desire flare in his eyes, Shiloh wanted to give herself to him. And she would.

Shadowhawk had backed toward his horse by the time Shiloh bent to unlace her moccasins. Although she did not look in his direction, she knew he was watching her. She pulled the doeskin gown over her head and laid it aside. Next she removed her undergarment and tossed it down on the grass.

Shadowhawk felt his breathing stop. He had imagined how she would look without clothing, but he had not been prepared for the sight of her creamy skin, the slimness of her hips. Her glorious hair fell across her breasts, and he felt his knees give way when he saw the same colored hair between her thighs.

Shiloh raised her arms to Shadowhawk. He did not remember taking the steps that brought him to her. He crushed her in his arms, trembling like a young boy with his first love.

"How does a Comanche maiden give herself to a man?" Shiloh asked, pulling back so she could see his eyes. "I mean how does she tie herself to him?"

His voice was husky and deep. "It is not up to the woman. The brave who desires her will bring many horses to her father. If her father accepts the horses, and the maiden wishes to be his woman, he takes her away with him."

"And the woman, what does she do if she has no father?"

"She usually erects the tipi and pledges herself to the brave."

With tears glistening in her eyes, Shiloh said, "I can't build you a tipi, and we cannot seek my father's permission, but this night I do pledge myself to you."

Shadowhawk's throat tightened with emotion; his heart raced so fast he thought it would break out of his chest, and he was lost to all reason. His eyes shut and he allowed his hand to drift over her hips, pressing her closer to him. Her breasts pressed into his chest and he wanted nothing more than to savor the moment.

Yearning and need stabbed Shiloh's body. Shadowhawk's hand closed over her breast, sending quake after quake through her.

His voice became deeper with feeling. "Shiloh. I should not let this happen."

She glanced up at him. "Don't you want me?"

Again his eyes drifted shut for fear she would see how

deeply he was affected by her. "My body knew you were for me the first time I saw you."

She trailed her finger up his smooth chest. "Something strong ties us together."

"Yes." He nestled her against him, his hands moving up and down her back.

Lifting her into his arms, he carried her to the soft grass near the pond. Laying her down, he stood over her as he removed his clothing. She watched him unlace his leggings and toss them aside, all the while his hungry eyes moved over her body. For reasons she did not know, she felt no shyness as she stared at his muscled body. He would be considered splendid by any woman—beautiful in a very manly way.

When he came down to her, bare flesh melted against bare flesh. Where he was hard and muscled, she was softly curved. His mouth lightly skimmed over her breasts, and he hardened more when he heard her gasp.

No words were spoken; their bodies conveyed everything they felt. Shiloh was allowing a man's body to conquer her, and it felt right that it should be Shadowhawk.

Fate had dictated that they should be enemies; that same fate had bound them together with a passion that would not be denied.

A sensation of delight went through Shiloh when she felt the hardness of him slide against her thigh. Instantly she opened her legs to him and he pressed down against her, pinning her to the grass.

Aching, needing, and then pleading with her eyes, she waited for the promise of oneness she saw reflected in dark eyes that flamed with intense passion.

Shadowhawk was poised, ready to enter her, but he stopped. He spoke in Comanche, accepting her as his woman, and slid just inside her. When the heat of her closed around him, he swallowed a moan.

Shiloh twisted her body, wanting to take more of him inside her, but he shook his head, his mouth finding hers. Her fingernails dug into his shoulders as he slid slowly inside, filling her emptiness, and her very soul.

When he slid halfway out of her, she wanted to protest. But she had no breath to say anything when he plunged forward.

To Shiloh, their coming together was intense, proving to her they were destined to be together. She bit her lip as Shadowhawk moved inside her, building her pleasure and causing her heartbeat to race.

Shiloh gasped when ecstasy washed over her. Then she trembled and gasped again.

Shadowhawk grabbed her to him and rolled to his back, holding her as if he would never let her go. "You are mine."

Pressing her head against his chest, she heard the catch in his voice. Closing her eyes, she knew she belonged to him more completely than she could ever have belonged to any other man. Her heart was so full she couldn't give voice to what she was feeling.

He whispered near her ear, "You gave yourself to me as my woman, Shiloh. Answer me this—are you ready to leave your home and live with me?"

She touched her lips to his strong chin and looked into his eyes, feeling the tension in Shadowhawk as he waited for her answer. If she only had herself to consider, she would go with him. But Luke was her responsibility, and she couldn't leave him alone, and she could not take him with her to be raised in an Indian village. They were fighting to keep their home, and she could never walk away from that fight.

"I can't leave Luke," she said, beseeching him to understand.

It was the answer Shadowhawk had expected. His arms

locked around her, and he held her so tight she could hardly breathe. "I am not sorry for what happened between us tonight," he told her, "unless the result ends in your giving birth to my child. Should that happen, you and the child would be despised by your people. You must promise to send the child to me so he will not be ashamed of who he is. I say this because it could happen."

The thought that their lovemaking might produce a baby had never entered her mind, and it stunned her for a moment. "Oh, my love," she whispered, "to have your child to keep and hold in my arms would bring me such joy. I would tell him about his noble father, and make him proud of his heritage."

The anguish that filled Shadowhawk's eyes stabbed her to the heart. "You do not know how a child of mine would be treated in your world. I take the blame for what happened tonight. I will also take the responsibility."

She moved off him, brushing her hair out of her face, knowing he loved her as much as she loved him. But love was not enough.

Shadowhawk rolled to his feet and she stared at him. There was a part of her that wanted to follow him wherever he went, and a part of her that knew she must walk away with dignity.

The two of them stood at arm's length, their eyes revealing the truth of their anguish. "I will always remember tonight," she told him. "I will always belong to you alone."

Gently, he gathered her in his arms. "I will relive tonight every day of my life. I will never forget the woman with hair of flame and sky blue eyes, who gave me her love."

She pressed her face to his chest. "If only—"

He tilted her chin, silencing what she would have said with a kiss. She felt him harden and they both drifted onto the grass, neither able to stop the passion that raged within them.

Shadowhawk made love to Shiloh slowly, gently, as if he were attempting to hold on to her as long as possible.

Afterward, he carried her into the pond and washed her. Then he carried her back to the grass, where she curled up in his arms.

Shadowhawk watched Shiloh sleep, and whispered in Comanche, "My gentle love, I have fought battles all my life, but never like the battle I will fight tomorrow when I let you go."

When Shiloh awoke, the sun had not yet risen. She reached out to find Shadowhawk was not beside her, though he had covered her with a blanket some time during the night.

Hearing a sound, she turned in that direction and saw he was already loading the horses. Shiloh quickly slipped into her clothing and moccasins. Folding her blanket, she walked toward him, wanting to tell him how much she loved him, but he would not look at her, so the words stuck in her throat.

"Here is the blanket," she said, holding it out to him.

He took it and secured it to the back of her horse.

Her voice shook as she said, "Shadowhawk—"

Slowly he turned to her, but was careful not to touch her. "Last night is over. Now we must look to today."

His words cut deep, and she fought against her tears, knowing it would cause him pain to see her cry. Turning to look at the canyon, she said, "Yes. We will look to today."

He handed her a piece of dried meat. "We need to ride hard," he said, swinging onto his horse and waiting for her to do the same. "Jimmy Tall Tree was not fooled by my ruse. He is within a half day's ride. Your Ranger and his men must have traveled through the night to get so near us."

Shiloh climbed on her horse. "Then let us leave."

They rode down a gully and up the other side, where Shadowhawk halted, glancing back the way they had come.

Shiloh's eyes widened as she realized where they were. There was no mistaking the high walls of Wild Horse Canyon, which was on the far western boundary of Estrella. On the other side of the canyon she could see the Brazos River, and beyond that, the pasture land that led to the ranch house.

Shadowhawk dismounted and walked toward her. Before she knew what he was doing, he grasped her waist and placed her firmly on the ground. "I have things to say to you."

"Then say them," she said unequivocally, trying to find the courage for this good-bye. There was a part of her that was glad to be home, but there was an ache deep inside her that would never heal.

"Sometimes words are hard to say, Shiloh. This is one of those times."

She called on all of her strength to speak. What she really wanted to do was to beg him not to leave her. What she managed to say after swallowing several times, was, "When you took us away from Estrella, I didn't understand why. I do now. You did it to save us. If Luke were here, he would add his gratitude to mine."

Shadowhawk stepped closer to her, as if he could not help himself. "You do not need to say this to me."

She was close to tears and she backed away from him, fighting hard not to make a fool of herself. "But I never thanked you properly."

He studied her intently, long enough to make her squirm. "You should go, Shiloh."

Shiloh reached for his hand, and clasped it. "Will I ever see you again?"

"You may not see me, but I will be near you at times." He reached out with his free hand, allowing it to drift down her hair. "Have no fear, your enemy will soon be punished."

"Remember your promise not to spill Tyree's blood."

"I will not touch him."

With sadness dragging her down, Shiloh mounted her horse and guided it toward the river. Without looking back, she rode through the churning water and up the bank on the other side.

She urged her horse into a gallop, feeling the distance between her and Shadowhawk widening.

Chapter Twenty-seven

When Shiloh rode past what had once been their barn, she cringed to see the blackened rubble. Dismounting, she placed the horse Shadowhawk had given her in the paddock, and walked toward the house.

"Señorita Shiloh, you are safe!" Hernando cried, snatching off his wide-brimmed sombrero as he ran toward her. "My prayers have been answered today."

"Yes, Hernando. I am safely home."

Hernando looked at her in shock. "You are wearing Indian clothing?"

"Moon Song gave these to me. I'm sure Charley told you that when Shadowhawk took us away, I wore only my nightgown."

Hernando watched her closely and then nodded. "Your brother is staying in town with Señor Curruthers. Did you escape as he did?"

"No, Hernando. Shadowhawk brought me home." Not wanting to talk about what had happened, she headed toward the house. "I want you to ride into town and bring my brother home."

Understanding her need to be alone, the *gran* vaquero said, "*Sí*, señorita. I will leave right away."

"Is Horace Beck still around?"

"He's riding along the river looking for strays."

"Have him ride east toward Wild Horse Canyon, where he will eventually meet Charley and Gunther. They need to know it's no longer necessary to search for me."

Hernando shook his head in confusion. Señorita Shiloh was safe, but she was not the happy, smiling young woman he had known. His brow furrowed. What had that Comanche chief done to her?

When Shiloh entered the house, she should have been comforted by the familiar surroundings, but she wasn't. She thought of a tipi beside a river where happy children laughed and played. She thought of Shadowhawk, a man who didn't understand deceit or lies in others—a man who spoke the truth and expected others to do the same.

Glancing down at her doeskin gown, she went to her bedroom and put on her own clothes. She gently folded the doeskin dress and moccasins and placed them in a chest. She would put them away as she must put away her feelings for Shadowhawk.

Entering the kitchen, she saw that Hernando had filled the wood bin. Rolling up her sleeves, Shiloh started a fire to boil water and set about cleaning, anything to keep her mind from wandering back to Shadowhawk.

Her body had come home, but her heart was still with the tall Comanche, who even now, watched over her.

On her knees scrubbing the kitchen floor, she thought about her brother—she couldn't wait to be reunited with Luke.

Later she would go to the root cellar for apples so she could make him his favorite pie.

It was midafternoon before Luke returned. Shiloh heard him and Hernando ride up, and she ran out the back door to meet them. Going into her outstretched arms, Luke grinned up at her.

"Shadowhawk let you go."

"Yes, he did." Shiloh glanced up at Hernando and nodded. "Thank you for bringing him home." Then she looked her brother over carefully. He seemed none the worse for his adventures. "You need a haircut."

They walked into the house, and Luke sniffed the air, grinning. "An apple pie!"

"Just like you like it."

Shiloh watched Luke lick apple pie crumbs from his fork. "Tell me what happened after you escaped from the Comanche village."

When Luke finished explaining his adventure, he looked at Shiloh with a serious expression in his eyes. He lowered his head. "I led them away from the village, like you told me to. Captain Gunther is determined to find the Comanches and wipe them all out. Do you think he will?"

"I hope not, Luke."

"Captain Gunther's plenty mad at Shadowhawk."

Shiloh decided not to tell Luke that Shadowhawk was still looking after them. "We'll have to tell Gunther that we came to no harm in the Comanche village. I don't want anyone hurt because of us."

"Shiloh," Luke said, looking at her earnestly, "I like Shadowhawk."

She stood and began clearing the table. "So do I."

Shadowhawk turned onto his back so he could see the stars. He couldn't sleep because his thoughts were of Shiloh. He thought of her flaming hair and soft skin. He had held Shiloh to his heart, and he had let her go.

When this thing was finished with her enemy, and Shiloh was safe, Shadowhawk had decided he would join his mother's Blackfoot family. When he was far away, maybe then he would no longer think of Shiloh. He was strong, he knew that. He would put her out of his thoughts.

He stared at the night sky. He would be a very old man, devoid of sight and thought, before he forgot Shiloh.

Chapter Twenty-eight

Rawlins was riding full out when he reached the ranch house. He slid to the ground and ran up the steps. Not bothering to knock, he hurried inside. Finding the parlor empty, he headed for Tyree's study.

"Boss," he yelled, pausing in the doorway. "You've gotta see this." He held out a bloodstained arrow. "I took this out of a dead bull. Ten head of our cattle was shot with arrows just like this one."

Tyree rose, his face red with anger. "What in the hell are you babbling about? What cattle?"

"The cattle in the west pasture, that's what I'm saying." He handed Tyree the arrow. "Look at the markings."

This time Tyree's complexion became ashen. "Kiowa markings." He glanced quickly at his foreman, his mind whirling. "What does this mean?"

"I can't figure it, boss. We know there ain't no Kiowa in this part of Texas. We also know this isn't one of the arrows we used."

Tyree paced to the window, jamming his hands in his pockets. "Someone's trying to mess with my mind. Who besides you knows I ordered the cattle shot with arrows?"

"Norm, Hank, Tom, and no one else, boss—I swear it." Rawlins shook his head. "It was just the four of us."

"And the arrow that killed Jonathan Braden—who besides you knows about that?"

"I kept the killing to myself, just like you told me to."

Tyree swung his massive head in his foreman's direction.

"Then who is doing this? First the lance and now this. You can't tell me someone doesn't know what we did."

"It can't be any of our men. I trust 'em with my life."

"Maybe you trust them, but I don't." Tyree moved back to his desk, and in his fury, broke the arrow across his knee. "One of them talked, or we wouldn't be having this trouble. Find out who it is and bring him to me. And get rid of those mules you stole from Braden. I want nothing that could link me to his death."

"Okay, boss, but I won't be able to sell them anywhere around here." Rawlins hesitated a moment. "What if the Bradens found out what we did and they're striking back at you?"

"Fool. That brother and sister don't have the means or the know-how to do something like this." Suddenly his eyes widened. "Charley, on the other hand, is no fool, no matter how he might pretend to be. He just might have figured what happened. He might be trying to spook me."

"Can't be him, boss. He's out with the Rangers. Least that's what Willard Curruthers told me. He also said Shiloh and Luke Braden are back on Estrella."

"Round up two of the men and saddle my horse. It's time we paid another visit to Estrella."

Sensing trouble was coming, Horace Beck had lit out, and Charley hadn't yet returned from Antelope Wells, where he'd gone to demand that the Rangers arrest Tyree. That left just Luke, Hernando, and Shiloh to protect the ranch.

The three of them had worked all day rounding up cattle and driving them to the river. It was almost dark now as they headed home. Shiloh frowned as she dismounted, handing the reins of her horse to Luke.

As she walked past the burned-out barn, she could still smell the sickening odor that clung to the air. She had just reached the porch when she heard riders approaching.

Luke and Hernando were leading the horses into the paddock, and they hurried toward Shiloh.

"It's that Crooked H bunch," Luke said. "Should I get
the rifle?"

"No." Shiloh said, placing a restraining hand on his
shoulder. "You aren't to do anything to provoke them."

The boy's chin jutted out in a hard line. "Are we just
going to let them ride up and do nothing about it?"

Shiloh would have liked nothing better than to have a
gun in her hand at the moment—especially when she saw
Tyree riding ahead of three others. "Keep calm, Luke."

"Your sister is right," Hernando stated. "Stay beside her
and let me do the talking."

Shiloh agreed with a nod, as she pulled Luke toward
her. She could feel him shaking with anger. She knew
how he felt because she was angry as well.

When the riders reined in their horses, Hernando went
down the steps to meet them. "Señor Tyree, it is late for a
social call, do you not think? What can I do for you?"

"Out of my way," Surge Tyree said, dismounting and
shoving Hernando aside. "I don't waste my time talking
to peons."

Hernando was not to be deterred. "The señorita has no
wish to talk to you. So you will have to talk to this peon."

Afraid Tyree might hurt Hernando, Shiloh turned to
Luke. She had a bad feeling about this confrontation
with the owner of the Crooked H. She whispered quickly
to her brother, "Get your rifle, Luke. Hurry!"

In no time at all Luke rejoined her, shouldering his rifle.
"It's loaded," he said. "Should I cock it?"

"Give it to me."

"You don't know how to fire it, and I do."

"You know that, and I know it, but those men don't
know it." She took the gun and also took a deep breath.
"Stay on the porch. I don't want you getting hurt."

"I will not!" he said, following her to the edge of the porch.

Shiloh was trembling with fear. But this was a serious situation and she didn't have time to argue with her brother. "Then stay behind me. I'm betting on the fact that even an evil man like Surge Tyree won't shoot a woman."

"I won't do that either," Luke told her. "We'll both face him."

Shiloh drew everyone's attention when she stepped off the porch, the rifle aimed at the heart of the owner of the Crooked H. "I've never killed a man before, Mr. Tyree, but I'll shoot you dead if you don't get off our land."

Something in her voice must have rung true, because Tyree cleared his throat nervously. "Now, now, little gal, don't be hasty. We're just here for a friendly chat."

"We have never had a friendly chat. Ride away. Now!"

"I will if you'll answer me one question." He nodded at the lance that Shadowhawk had driven into the ground near the house. "Why do both of us have a Comanche lance at our places?"

Shiloh's eyes widened. "You have one too?"

"I think you know I do. And, seeing as we've both been visited by Comanche, I thought you might know what it means."

Luke stepped forward. "We don't know why the Comanche paid a visit to your place."

Tyree looked past Luke, his gaze settling on Shiloh. "The lance they left in my yard had black feathers; this one has white. Why do you think that is?"

The gun was getting heavy and Shiloh could feel her arms tremble from the weight of it, but she still kept it centered on Tyree's heart. "You would have to ask the Comanche."

Hernando smiled. "I don't know much about the Comanche, but I do know black feathers mean death, and white means life. It looks to me, Señor, like you've been targeted for death."

Tyree shook his head, his gaze hardening on Hernando. "I think I'm being targeted by someone on this ranch." His gaze became even harder when he looked at Shiloh, and then at Luke. "What about it, boy, do you know anyone who's playing games with me?"

"I know who left our lance. It was Shadowhawk. He wanted everyone to know he was protecting me and my sister."

"Don't take me for a fool, boy. Although some believe Shadowhawk exists, even some on my ranch, I say he's just a legend who was made up to scare little children."

"He isn't either. I know Shadowhawk."

"You have all the answers you're going to get from us," Shiloh told Tyree. "Get off our land before I start asking questions, like why did Charley see Tip Rawlins riding away the night our barn was burned?"

Rawlins grinned. "Now, I was nowhere near this place when your barn burned. Anyone who says they saw me is just plain lying."

Tyree glanced from brother to sister. "I'll be back, and when I do, I won't settle for any nonsense."

Shiloh cocked the rifle. "What do I have to do to convince you that you aren't welcome on Estrella? Don't come back again."

Tyree's eyes were as cold and deadly as a rattlesnake's. "Little gal, don't think your rifle is going to stop me."

Shadowhawk watched Tyree from a distance, ready to make his move if the man tried to harm Shiloh or Luke. He was too far away to hear what was being said, but he saw Shiloh raise the gun to Tyree's chest. After heated words, Tyree and his men rode away.

With his lip curling in contempt, Shadowhawk watched

Tyree ride so close to his hiding place, he could have reached out and touched him.

Shadowhawk frowned, trying not to allow anger to guide his next move.

The following afternoon Charley and Gunther rode in. Shiloh served supper while she told them about Tyree's visit the night before.

"Why haven't you arrested him, Gunther?" she asked. "Charley saw his foreman riding off the night our barn was burned."

Gunther seemed uncomfortable and shoved his plate back. "I need to talk to you in private, Shiloh."

Charley and Luke exchanged glances.

Shiloh expected Gunther to explain some legal aspect of the case to her. "We can go out on the porch. It's cool there."

Once they stepped outside, Shiloh watched Gunther pace up and down. At last he stopped in front of her. His next words were a complete surprise. "It isn't a secret that I have feelings for you, Shiloh. I have from the beginning."

She blinked her eyes. "I like you too, Gunther."

"It goes further than like. I was thinking about asking you to be my wife."

Astonished, Shiloh moved away from him to stand on the top step of the porch. "As I said, I like you, Gunther. But not enough to marry you. It wouldn't be fair to either of us."

He clamped his jaw in anger. "Now, why is that? Has that Comanche devil had his way with you? Are you soiled, Shiloh?"

Her mouth widened in horror. "You have no right to speak to me this way. How dare you!"

He grabbed her arm and jerked her toward him. "That's no answer—he did have you, didn't he?"

"Take your hands off me."

His grip tightened on her arm and she flinched. "You're hurting me."

"I just want to say, even if you've been ruined, I'd still marry you."

"I wouldn't marry anyone who could say such things to me."

She pushed on his hand, but instead of releasing her, he leaned forward and ground his mouth against hers. Shiloh tried to break free of his grasp. At last she turned her head and took a deep breath.

"You take liberties, Captain Gunther," she said coolly.

Luke slammed the screen door behind him. "Let go of my sister."

Gunther ignored the boy. "The town's already gossiping about you. They say you've been with a Comanche buck. Marry me and the gossip stops. You need a man around to keep Tyree away, and I'll take care of you and Luke."

Shiloh spun out of his grasp. "I am not of the mind to be married at this time."

"You're turning me down?"

Luke stepped between his sister and the Ranger. "She already gave you her answer. You'd better be leaving."

Gunther's gaze flicked to the boy. "Do you think you can protect her from the malicious tongues in Antelope Wells?"

"Gunther, I thought you were our friend, but you aren't," Shiloh said. "I don't want you coming here anymore unless you come to tell me you've arrested Surge Tyree."

The Ranger turned and stalked back into the house to get his hat, and a short time later brother and sister heard the front door slam.

"I hadn't thought about gossip, Luke."

He slid his arm about her waist. "We aren't going to worry about that." He listened to Gunther ride into the night. "When he was looking for you, and couldn't find you, he started to get mean."

Shiloh hugged Luke to her. "We won't worry about him." But she did. The man who had been so angry and accusing tonight was not the person she had thought he was.

She was not soiled—she loved Shadowhawk. Shiloh had pledged herself to him, and by Comanche law, she was his wife.

In her heart she felt that she belonged to Shadowhawk, even if they were not together. If only she could leave duty behind and embrace love.

Chapter Twenty-nine

Shadowhawk waited until dark before he crept out of the shadows. He slowly opened the bunkhouse door to find Charley pointing a rifle at him, which the old man lowered.

"What took you so long? I figured you'd be here long 'afore now."

Shadowhawk spoke in Comanche. "I have questions and I believe you have answers."

Charley answered him in the same language. "Ask what you will. I know you have been around pestering Tyree."

"If you know that, you know why."

"I do. You are giving Tyree a dose of his own medicine. You are counting coup—touching Tyree without drawing blood."

"Shiloh made me promise." Shadowhawk waited a moment before he asked, "Do you doubt Tyree killed Shiloh's father?" He would trust the word of this white man above any other.

"In my mind there is no doubt. Not that he did the deed himself, but that he ordered it done."

"Why has the Ranger not arrested Tyree?"

"The law wants proof, and we ain't got it yet."

"Shiloh and Luke do not have time to wait. Tyree is becoming desperate. Desperate men are dangerous. How can I find this proof?"

"There is a way. When Mr. Braden was killed, he had

matching red mules pulling his wagon. I believe whoever killed him took the mules. If there was a way to get into Tyree's barn without being seen, you might find them there."

"Tell me, how will I know these animals?"

"As far as I know, they are the only red mules in this part of the country. They will bear Estrella's brand on their rumps."

"A star."

Charley switched to English. "Yep."

"I will find this proof."

Charley nodded. "When do you figure your debt to this family's been met?"

"I will let you know."

Shadowhawk slipped out the door without making a sound—it was as if he'd never been there.

Tyree slept in a room across the hallway from his wife, Caroline. They hadn't been intimate for over two years— not since some of the fine womenfolk in town told Caroline he was seeing the town milliner, Nancy Taylor. Nancy hadn't meant anything to him, but he'd liked being with her. Now Caroline hardly spoke to him at the supper table. He had tried to make up to Caroline by sending to St. Louis for a fine jade necklace. But she hadn't even worn it. He'd offered to take her to France, but she had refused. Of course, it wasn't the first time in their marriage he'd been with another woman, it was just the only time he'd gotten caught.

As much as he could love anyone, he supposed he loved Caroline. She was still a beautiful woman, small and delicately built. But when she looked at him, there was nothing in her eyes. In the past when he'd tried to make love to her, she would allow it, but cried the whole time. He didn't go to her anymore, but he still visited Nancy when he was in Antelope Wells.

Tyree remembered the first time he'd see Caroline. She had been visiting a cousin in San Antonio, constantly surrounded by men who admired her. Tyree hadn't thought he'd have a chance with her. But in the end his persistence had won her over and she had agreed to become his wife.

At the time, Tyree could not believe his good fortune. He was proud to show her off, and he loved giving her presents. He'd wanted a son, and paid little attention to their only daughter, who had her mother's looks. He supposed he resented the child because she had not been a son.

Now his one passion in life was to own Estrella.

The lamp on the bedside table flickered low, and he closed the ledger he'd been reading. Wearily, his eyes drifted shut.

That was when he felt the covers move. His eyes flew open and he wondered if he had imagined something under the covers with him. Whatever it was, it slithered along the side of his left leg, and he jumped out of bed, slamming his body against the far wall. A shout was choked off in his throat as he picked up the lamp and threw it at his bed.

In moments the whole bed was in flames, and he watched a rattlesnake drop to the floor, slithering in his direction.

With a scream of horror, Tyree ran into the hallway, waking everyone as he shouted, "Get water! The house is on fire!"

Before long his men had formed a bucket brigade and the fire was soon extinguished, but not before his bedroom had been destroyed by fire and smoke. His only satisfaction was in knowing the rattler had died in the fire.

"However did this happen?" Caroline asked fearfully, her daughter clinging to her skirts.

Tyree avoided her gaze because he was wondering the

same thing. He was afraid. Someone was out to get him—someone who knew what he'd done to the Bradens.

"Tyree," Caroline said, looking worried. "I asked you how this happened."

"I was reading in bed and must have knocked the lamp over," he said irritably. "You and the child can go back to bed now. The fire is out."

"You should be more careful," Caroline said.

"Don't worry," he ground out. "I intend to be." He caught Rawlins's eye. "We need to talk."

"Sure, boss."

Tyree led the way into his office and began pacing. "Someone put a rattler in my room."

"You mean like the one I put in the window at the Brandens' ranch house?"

"Yes, that's what I mean."

"But, boss, your bedroom is on the second floor, and we've got guards posted around the place. An ant couldn't get in without our seeing it."

"Well, someone did. And someone shot my cattle with arrows."

"The Bradens wouldn't know how to pull this off. It can't be them."

Tyree turned to his foreman. "Then you'd damned well better find out who it is. Your job as foreman depends on it."

"I'll do what I can."

"Whoever is doing this knows how to come and go without being seen. I want to know who it is."

Rawlins noticed Tyree's left eye twitching and the man's hands were shaking as if he was scared. "You feeling all right, boss? You need a shot of whiskey or somethin'?"

Tyree sank down in a chair and leaned his head back. "I need to know who is doing this."

"Charley might've done it."

"Charley can't climb up to the second story with a live rattler."

"Hernando, then?"

"No. It wouldn't be him." Tyree couldn't quit shaking. He had always been the one in control of any situation. He had built an empire by sheer strength of will, and no one was going to take it away from him.

He flinched. Lurking somewhere in the shadows was a nameless and faceless enemy who was out to destroy him.

Before, the owners of Estrella were just people in the way of what he wanted—that had now changed. He had to destroy the Braden family before whoever was out for revenge got to him again.

Chapter Thirty

Antelope Wells

Shiloh was perched on the wagon seat beside Luke as he drove toward town. Charley was seated on the back spring seat, his rifle on his lap, while he continuously watched for trouble.

The old man took a chaw of tobacco and glanced at Shiloh. "It's been a spell since you've been to town, ain't it?"

Shiloh nodded. "Not since we visited the banker." She also searched the countryside, but for a reason far different from Charley's vigil. She wondered if Shadowhawk was somewhere nearby. If he was, she knew he wouldn't allow her to see him.

The narrow streets of Antelope Wells were bustling with wagons and mounted men. Shiloh began to notice as they neared the Currutherses's store that she and Luke seemed to be the center of attention. Mrs. McNair, the banker's wife, stared with her mouth gaping open, and quickly rushed toward the general store.

When Luke halted the horses, several other women hurried into the store.

"You stay inside 'til I get back, Miss Shiloh," Charley said. "I need to talk to the blacksmith."

Luke set the break and jumped down, then helped Shiloh to the ground. "I'll be in as soon as I secure the horses."

It was a cool, September day, and there was a smell of moisture in the air. Glancing at the gathering clouds, Shiloh feared it might rain before they got home.

Mr. Curruthers met her as soon as she entered the store. "Good morning, Miss Shiloh. It's sure good to see you safe. We all worried about you when we heard you was took by the Comanche. A whole passel of Rangers rode out in hopes of finding you. But you found your own way home." He waited expectantly for her to tell him how she had fared with the Comanche.

Shiloh merely smiled. "I want to thank you and Mrs. Curruthers for looking after Luke. It was kind of you."

"Shoot, Miss Shiloh, he weren't no trouble a'tall. If me and the missus had a son, I'd like him to be just like your brother."

Mrs. McNair poked her head around several bolts of material, then pulled back when she met Shiloh's gaze.

Shiloh heard the voices of the ladies who had gathered at the front of the store. It was clear to her they wanted her to overhear their conversation.

"She ain't no longer fit for one of our white men to wed," Mrs. McNair stated, raising her voice. "And we can't let our daughters around her."

Shiloh recognized Sally Dawson's voice. "Poor thing. No telling what those Comanche bucks did to her. She'd've been better off if they'd killed her outright."

Shiloh's face reddened when she heard the other women murmur their agreement.

Mr. Curruthers touched her arm, his eyes filled with sympathy. "Don't pay no heed to those old biddies. It'll all pass away in time when they find someone else to belittle."

"We both know it won't pass," Shiloh said, refusing to give in to tears. She handed him her list. "Will you please fill this for me?"

"You bet I will, as soon as I give those women what for."

"Don't bother, Mr. Curruthers. No matter what you say, it won't change their opinion of me."

When Shiloh turned to make her escape, she found herself surrounded by the women, all of them staring at her with vicious pleasure.

Nancy Taylor, who owned the millinery, grinned. "You didn't have any choice but to submit, did you? Tell us how it happened."

"Let me pass," Shiloh said with as much dignity as she could summon.

"Now, dear," Mrs. McNair said in a condescending voice. "We're all your friends. We want to help you. Tell us what happened while you was in that Comanche camp."

Shiloh saw an ugliness gleaming in Mrs. McNair's eyes. The woman looked at her eagerly, as if waiting for some juicy tidbit of gossip. Raising her chin, Shiloh faced the woman who seemed to be goading the others on. "I respect your husband, Mrs. McNair. He seems a kind and reasonable man. If I told him the truth, he would believe me. But I will never trust you with the truth."

"Well," Mrs. McNair huffed. "Don't put on airs with me. You are no longer a decent—"

Martha Curruthers suddenly appeared, stepping between Shiloh and the other women. "Leave her alone, Dolly. Don't you think Shiloh's been through enough without you adding to her pain?"

"You defend her actions?" Mrs. McNair asked, her lips drawn up in disapproval.

"Shiloh's good name doesn't need defending. I want you to leave, right now."

Luke and Charley had entered the store. Luke stepped to his sister's side and gripped her arm. "You're all just mean. What did my sister do to you to make you treat her like this?"

Charley stepped up, looking disgusted as he took Shiloh's other arm. "Ain't no sense in talking to a bunch of squawkin' hens," he said, leading Shiloh toward the door. "Miss Shiloh's lost her pa, and faced more danger than any of you'll see in your lifetime. It seems to me, she deserves your understandin', not your mean mouthiness."

When Shiloh stepped out the door, two men were standing near the wagon. One of them she knew, the other was a stranger.

"Get out of the way," Charley said, helping Shiloh onto the wagon seat. "Leave this family be."

"Now, Charley, there ain't no cause to go talking like that," said Sam Higgins, who spent more time in the saloon than he did at home with his wife of twenty years. "Me and Joe here was just wondering if this here little lady would like to know how it feels to do it with a white man."

"Yeah," the stranger said, looking eagerly at Shiloh. "We'd like to hear how we compare with them Comanche bucks."

Before Shiloh knew what he was doing, Luke ran at the man and punched him in the jaw. "You leave my sister alone!"

Charley pulled Luke back and reached for his rifle, pointing it at Higgins. "Say one more word, and you'll be sorry."

Shiloh could do no more than bury her face in her hands as shame washed over her. "Don't bother about them, Charley," she said, fearing he would actually shoot the man. "Let's go home."

Higgins glared at Charley, then at the rifle pointed at him. "You got no call to pull a gun on me, Charley. You wouldn't kill me over having a little fun, would you?"

"I don't intend to kill you, Higgins. But I'm thinking you could do with one less ear."

Higgins covered both ears with his hands, and backed toward the store. But Mr. Curruthers was there, blocking his way. "Get on out of here until you sober up, Sam, and don't come into my store before you do. You're not fit to be around decent folks."

Charley climbed into the driver's seat and headed the horses out of town at a fast pace, causing others to dodge out of the way.

Shiloh didn't dare give in to tears. Luke was patting her arm, and she realized how hard it had been on him to hear the vile things the town folks were saying about her.

"It's all right, Luke. I don't care what they say." She wanted to hide her hurt from him. The people she had known most of her life had turned on her, trying to make her feel defiled. She thought of the Comanche, who had taken her in to their village; none of them had been unkind. She had done nothing wrong—in her heart she was Shadowhawk's wife, and she always would be.

Charley glanced at Shiloh worriedly. "I'll come back to town tomorrow and get the supplies, Miss Shiloh. There ain't no cause for you to see those people no more."

But they both knew she would see them again, and she would face the same derision that they had exhibited today.

"Shiloh," Luke said, laying his head on her shoulder. "Maybe it would be best if we sold Estrella and moved back to Virginia."

At the moment Shiloh would have liked nothing better than to pack up all their belongings and leave. But she could never do that to Luke. Besides, as long as she was on Estrella, there was always hope that she would see Shadowhawk again.

Chapter Thirty-one

Running Fox darted into the barn behind Shadowhawk. They had counted six men guarding the house, but it had been no challenge to slip past them. Two of them were asleep at their posts, one passed out drunk, and the other three were talking in a group.

As they waited for their eyes to adjust to the darkness, Running Fox asked, "Why are we here?"

"We search for mules with the star brand," Shadowhawk told him, already moving from stall to stall.

Stopping at the last stall, Running Fox gestured to his chief. "The mules are here."

As he circled the two red mules, Shadowhawk's jaw clenched. "These are the animals from Estrella," he said, tracing the star brand. "The man, Tyree, is the one who killed Shiloh's father."

Silent rage washed over Shadowhawk. Motivated by greed, Tyree had set out to drive Shiloh and her brother off their ranch, and he was getting away with it.

"What do we do now?" Running Fox asked.

"I will take these mules out of here; you must set fire to the barn."

Running Fox did not question Shadowhawk, nor ask how Shadowhawk planned to get the mules past the men on guard. He had every confidence in his chief's ability to slip past the white men unobserved.

* * *

It was late, but Tyree was avoiding going to bed, because he'd only lie awake as he had for the last two nights. Because of the fire in his bedroom, he was forced to sleep in the guest room at the end of the hallway. No matter how hard the servants had scrubbed the bedroom that had caught on fire, it still smelled like smoke, and it reminded him of his fear at seeing the rattler in his bed.

Focusing his eyes on his ledger, he couldn't seem to concentrate. He kept dwelling on the unknown enemy who was out to destroy him.

His hand shook so badly he left a blob of ink on a column of figures. Cursing and throwing the ledger across the room, he watched it slam against the wall.

Hearing shouts outside, and hurried boot steps on the porch, Tyree jerked to his feet. "What the hell is going on?"

"Boss!" Rawlins said, rushing into Tyree's office and bending to catch his breath. "The barn's on fire!"

Hurrying down the hall and out the back door, Tyree stopped in his tracks when he saw flames leap into the sky. His legs gave way beneath him and he fell to his knees. He could do nothing but watch helplessly as hungry flames devoured the barn. Out of control, the wind caught the fire and carried it to the nearby bunkhouse, and it too went up in flames.

Tyree watched as his men scurried around, trying to form a bucket brigade, but it was too late for that. The barn and bunkhouse were gone.

"What about the horses?" Tyree shouted to one of his men.

"You lost the broodmare, boss. Couldn't get her out in time."

Rawlins shook his head. "The blessing in all this, boss, is Braden's mules were destroyed by the fire."

Without a word, Tyree walked into the house, went into his office, and slammed the door. He had some heavy thinking to do, and he didn't want anyone to interrupt him.

No matter who was doing this to him, it was being done for Shiloh and Luke. That meant those two had to die.

It was toward the early morning hours when Charley snapped awake, sensing a presence in the room with him. "Shadowhawk."

"It is I. The red mules were in Tyree's barn," Shadowhawk said, coming out of the shadows and standing next to the old man. "I placed them in the paddock here."

Charley sat up and eased his legs off his bunk. "Now we have the proof we need to go to the Rangers."

"They will not believe me if I tell them the mules were in Tyree's barn," Shadowhawk replied. "You cannot think the Ranger, Gunther, would listen to anything I have to say?"

"I 'spect he wouldn't," Charley admitted. "Gunther's got a personal grudge agin' you. If I was guessin', I'd say it has something to do with Shiloh. It seems to me he's kinda sweet on her."

Shadowhawk stared at the old man fiercely. "Are you saying he wants her for his woman?"

"I figure he did, but she won't have him. Leastwise that's what Luke told me." Charley stood, reaching for his trousers. "Gunther's been dragging his feet, taking too much time to move on Tyree. I've had me a notion to talk to Ranger Briggs and see if he knows why that's happening."

"Could Gunther be in this with Tyree?"

Charley was quiet for a long moment. "A Ranger. I never considered it. But something about the whole situation smells, and it makes my blood run cold."

"Be warned, Tyree is angry. If I have judged him right, he will be coming after Shiloh and Luke."

Charley hooked his trousers. "I'll be looking out for him. Will you be nearby?"

"I will until this is settled."

"Shadowhawk, I know you said Shiloh won't like it if you go outside the law and kill Tyree. But what if it comes to that?"

"He will not die by my hand. I cannot break my promise to Shiloh."

Charley suddenly realized he was alone. Again Shadowhawk had left in his usual silent manner.

All hell was about to break loose, and Charley had to be ready for it.

Through tear-filled eyes Shiloh stared at her father's matched red mules. Her heart swelled with love for Shadowhawk, who had found the proof, while others were too afraid to approach Tyree to gather the evidence to bring him to trial. "Charley, what do we do now—go to the Rangers?"

"I'm gonna ride into town today and put the proof before Ranger Briggs, and see what he makes of it."

Luke reached through the fence and rubbed the neck of one of the animals. "How did Shadowhawk find Papa's mules?"

"Don't know. He didn't talk much 'bout it. Just said to be careful 'cause Tyree was gonna come against us now, hard and fierce."

"You actually saw Shadowhawk?" Shiloh asked.

"Yep. He came to see me twice. I didn't say nothin' to ya before 'cause he wouldna wanted me to. We got a lot to thank Shadowhawk for," Charley said.

Shiloh closed her eyes to stop the flow of tears. Shadowhawk had done this for her. "Do you think Shadowhawk will leave now, Charley?"

"Not 'til this is over, least that's what he said."

She nodded, her mind racing ahead to what her life would be like without the man she loved. People in town had long memories, and the gossiping would never stop. She remembered Gunther's accusation, and it made her cringe. The horrible talk would hurt Luke, but there was nothing she could do about that.

With a heavy heart, Shiloh turned toward the house. "Let me know what Briggs says," she told Charley.

Tyree looked at the man he'd sent for. "Can you tell me what's going on here?"

"Looks like you've been targeted by Shadowhawk, war chief of the Comanche."

"Why would he come after me? I ain't never done anything to him or his tribe."

Gunther shifted from one foot to another. "It seems he's taken a liking to Miss Shiloh. I'd say her troubles have become his."

"Rawlins told me he'd heard she was taken by the Comanche," Tyree said. "But they let her go."

"That Comanche's had her, I know he has," Gunther said venomously.

"Weren't you sweet on her at one time?"

"I don't want to have anything to do with the leavings of a Comanche."

"Is there any way we can pin Jonathan Braden's death on the Comanche?"

"We could have, but you used the markings of the Kiowa on the arrows you used. How can I blame that on the Comanche?"

"Am I in danger?"

Captain Gunther stared at Tyree. "I've kept the law off you, even when all the evidence pointed to you."

Tyree's face paled. "But what about this Shadowhawk? Can't you stop him?"

"I can, but it'll cost you more money."

"Hell, I've already paid you off and that puts you in this as deep as I am. I don't have to give you anything."

Gunther studied his fingernails. "What are you going to do, go to the law and tell them what I've done? I don't think so. No one is gonna take your word against mine. You aren't very well liked hereabouts. You're going to have to come up with more money."

Tyree's face reddened with anger. "How much more money are you asking for?"

"Five thousand dollars."

"How dare you! I've already given you three thousand."

Gunther stood. "Take it or leave it. I got Corporal Briggs looking at me with suspicion. I need a grubstake so I can hightail it out of Texas before he decides I haven't been doing my job."

Chapter Thirty-two

Shadowhawk watched the lights go out, and he waited, knowing Shiloh would come to him tonight. Many nights he had watched her climb up the hill; once she had even called his name. It had been difficult not to make his presence known, but he knew it was for the best.

Today he had intended to leave. But in the end, he had sent Running Fox to the village, and he had remained, needing to see Shiloh one more time.

He did not have to wait long before he heard her familiar footsteps coming up the hill. He moved into the shadows, thinking he would watch her for a moment and then leave, without Shiloh knowing he was there.

Shiloh bent to place a clump of flowers on her father's grave, and knelt for a while with her head bowed.

At last she stood. "Shadowhawk, I know you are here. Talk to me."

He stepped out of the shadows. "How did you know?"

Turning, Shiloh wanted to reach out and touch him, to have him open his arms so she could feel them about her. "I seem to feel it when you are near." She searched his eyes. "Do you feel it when I am near you?"

He hesitated, knowing the admission would strip him bare. But he would never speak an untruth to her. "Yes. I have those feelings and many more."

"Charley told me how you found the mules. It seems I always end up thanking you."

"You will be fine now. Charley will see that justice is done."

"There will be satisfaction in knowing the man responsible for my father's death is punished." Shiloh placed her hand over Shadowhawk's, trying to understand why he must leave. She feared she would never see him again.

"If Tyree had been punished by Comanche law, the deed would be long done. I did not draw his blood because you asked me not to."

Without realizing she was doing so, Shiloh moved closer to him and laid her head against his chest. It seemed the most natural thing in the world when he gathered her close.

"I miss you," she blurted out. "So much."

He tilted her chin. "There will not be a day when I do not think of you."

Shadowhawk's words tore at her heart. "Are you going back to your tribe tonight?"

"For a time. I have decided to take my mother and sister to Blackfoot country."

Shiloh blinked tears from her eyes. "But that is far away, isn't it?"

"It is."

Aching, she tried to speak, but no words passed her lips. At last she swallowed, and said in a quivering voice: "You won't leave without telling me, will you?"

He touched his mouth to her forehead. "You will know when Tyree has been defeated that I am no longer near you."

"If only . . . if we . . ." She buried her face against his neck. "Why must we live in a world that will not recognize the bond between a man and a woman who love each other, even though they come from different peoples?"

"The change, if it comes, will not be in our lifetime,

Shiloh." He drew her body close to his. "I want you more than my life. But I cannot come to live with you in your house, and you cannot live in a tipi with me."

"I can't leave my brother. You know that. You of all people should understand duty." In that moment, she remembered Vision Woman's words. Shiloh had chosen duty over love. And it was breaking her heart.

Shadowhawk dropped his arms and stepped back. "You should go in now, Shiloh."

Trying to keep back tears, she hurried down the hill.

Shadowhawk watched Shiloh disappear into the house, feeling an aching emptiness inside.

An emptiness that would never be filled.

Luke was leaving the barn when he saw at least a dozen men approaching the house. They were strangers to him, with the exception of Ranger Briggs, who gave him a quick nod.

"Sir," Luke said, smiling. "It's good to see you."

"I'm here on Ranger business, Luke. Go get Charley and Hernando. I'll get your sister."

Luke frowned. "Is something wrong?"

"Just the opposite actually. Hurry, son. Time's a-wasting."

Shiloh had fed the Rangers. The others had gone outside, but Briggs remained. "Gunther, working for Tyree!" she exclaimed. "But he is a Texas Ranger. Why would he do that?"

"Some men are born bad, and others turn bad—I think Gunther turned bad." Briggs nodded at Charley. "He is the one who set us to watching Gunther."

"Yeah," Charley agreed. "I know'd there was somethin' strange 'bout him when we gave him evidence agin' Tyree, and he didn't act on it."

"Corporal Briggs, what did you do about Captain Gunther?" Luke wanted to know.

Briggs sat forward in his chair and leaned his elbows on the table. "I had Gunther followed, and Charley, here, let me know Shadowhawk was also following him. Shadowhawk sent word to us through Charley that he'd find out what happened for us."

Luke studied the Ranger for a moment. "You mean the Texas Rangers were working with a Comanche?"

Briggs nodded out the window at an Indian, who hung back from the others. He wore white man's attire, with a hat pulled low over his brow. If one could not see his bronzed face and his long braids, he might be mistaken for white. Shiloh knew who he was before Briggs said his name.

"Jimmy Tall Tree told us we could trust Shadowhawk. We saw him bring the mules home, and I knew then Tyree had killed your father. That was the final clue we needed to arrest Tyree. The man fought us all the way— ordered his men to shoot us, but of course they didn't. We also arrested Rawlins, and several others."

Shiloh had always thought Tyree's arrest would bring her joy, but it didn't. Relief, of course, but not joy. Nothing could ever bring her father back. "Thank you, Corporal Briggs. Luke and I are indebted to you."

He smiled and opened his vest. "It's Captain Briggs now."

Luke smiled widely. "Congratulations!"

Briggs grinned. "Thank you, Luke."

"What about Tyree?" Shiloh asked.

"We sent him up to San Antonio to stand trial. He'll be hanged, no doubt about that."

Charley spoke up. "Where's Gunther?"

"Behind bars, in Antelope Wells. No one likes a Ranger gone bad. Most likely he'll spend the rest of his life in prison for his part in helping Tyree."

"In the beginnin', I trusted Gunther," Charley said. "But thinkin' back, there was always somethin' I couldn't figure about him."

"It's called greed, Charley." Briggs stood and tipped his hat. "We'll be going now. If you ever need us, you know where to find us. But I don't think you'll need us anymore. I'm glad things worked out like they did for you."

Shiloh and Luke walked the Ranger to the door and watched him mount his horse.

"It's thanks to Shadowhawk they made the arrests," Luke said.

"Yes," was all Shiloh could get past the tightening in her throat. She felt in her heart, Shadowhawk was gone.

It was early evening when Shiloh walked up the hill, her footsteps guided by the full September moon.

Shadowhawk was not there.

But there were fresh wildflowers on her father's grave, and she knew he had placed them there.

"Shadowhawk," she called longingly.

There was no answer.

Chapter Thirty-three

Estrella was a beehive of activity. The barn had been rebuilt, and Shiloh had hired five new hands to work the hundred and fifty cattle that now grazed in the pastures.

Shiloh removed her hat and blotted her forehead with her neckerchief. It was an unusually hot day for November. She stared up at the storm clouds gathering in the east, wishing for rain.

Dismounting, Shiloh led her horse into the barn. Lifting the saddle, she tossed it over a stall gate. She went through the motions of day-to-day living, but she felt as if her heart had been ripped out. Every day she watched for Shadowhawk, and every night she walked up the hill to see if he would be there.

He never was.

Removing her gloves, Shiloh leaned her head against the stall, stroking the long sleek neck of the pinto Shadowhawk had given her. She felt in the deepest part of her heart, she would never see Shadowhawk again. He was proud, and she had hurt him when she had chosen to stay with Luke instead of going with him.

With the heat bearing down on her, Shiloh walked toward the house. Pausing on the porch, she watched the activity going on around her. A hammer striking an anvil reverberated through the air as one of the new hands worked on a horseshoe. Hernando's wife, Juanita, was hanging her wash on a clothesline, while her two sons were in the paddock grooming horses.

Shiloh closed her eyes, absorbing the sounds of a thriving ranch. Her father would be proud of what she and Luke had accomplished. Of course, they couldn't have done it without Charley and Hernando.

And Shadowhawk.

On entering the house, she went straight to the kitchen. Filling the blue galvanized coffeepot with water, Shiloh added two scoops of coffee. Ducking her head, she felt tears close to the surface. None of the neighbors had been around, and Shiloh refused to go into town after the ugly incident that had happened at the Curruthersses's store. She touched her stomach. It was still flat, but would soon be swelling with Shadowhawk's child.

The neighbors would never understand that Shadowhawk was Shiloh's husband, and even if they did, it would only give them more reason to gossip. For herself, their talk didn't matter. But it would hurt Luke and she did care about that.

Drawing in her breath, she knew she had to tell Luke about the baby, and soon. She wasn't sure how he would take the news.

When she heard Charley knock at the back door, clearing his throat before entering, Shiloh quickly wiped her tears away.

"I'd take me a cup of that coffee if'n it's ready."

Knowing the dear old man was worried about her, Shiloh put on a smile before she turned to him. "It's perking now, so it won't be long until it's ready."

There was another knock at the door and Hernando entered, snatching off his sombrero. "I thought I smelled coffee, Señorita Shiloh."

Shiloh heard the front door open and Luke's footsteps in the parlor. He stuck his head into the kitchen. "You got any coffee?"

Shiloh sat down at the table and glanced at the three

of them. "Luke, you don't drink coffee. The three of you have something on your minds, don't you? Why don't one of you tell me what is going on here?"

Hernando nodded his head to Luke, deferring to him, and Luke nodded to Charley, deferring to him. "We got us company, Miss Shiloh."

Shaking her head, Shiloh blurted out, "I don't want to see anyone."

"You'll want to see this person," Charley said, edging onto a chair. "Luke asked her to come in, but she chose to remain outside 'til we spoke to you."

Shiloh looked concerned. "Why?"

"Well, we've been talkin' among ourselves and we got a few questions to put to you."

Shiloh was completely puzzled. "All right . . ."

Hernando took a chair across from her and watched her carefully.

"I've heard you crying during the night," Luke said, scooting his chair close to her. "Most every night."

Shiloh lowered her head. "I'm sorry. I didn't know you could hear me."

"It's Shadowhawk, ain't it?" Charley asked, getting to the heart of the matter.

She pressed her hands against her eyes, trying to stop the sudden flow of tears. "I can't help it—I think about him all the time. I said the words that made me his wife." She glanced at Luke, and then at the other two, saying in a whisper, "I am going to have Shadowhawk's child."

Luke frowned, Charley nodded, and Hernando looked worried.

"I didn't mean to tell you like this, but you will soon find out anyway."

Luke bent down beside his sister, and saw her lips tremble. "Why didn't you tell me sooner?"

"I wasn't sure at first." She laced her fingers though his

and looked into earnest blue eyes. "I didn't want to hurt you, Luke. And I couldn't go with Shadowhawk, as he wanted me to. I couldn't leave you to run Estrella alone."

Tears gathered in Luke's eyes. "Don't you know I would have gone with you?"

Shiloh lowered her head as fresh tears washed down her face. "I couldn't ask you to do that."

Charley awkwardly patted her on the shoulder. "Don't carry on so," he said, his voice trembling with emotion.

Luke brushed the tumbled hair out of his sister's face. "Johnny Tall Tree is outside. He's brought someone who wants to see you."

Shiloh was astounded that the Comanche tracker was there. "Who?"

Luke met his sister's confused gaze. "It's Vision Woman. She wants to talk to you."

Shiloh shot to her feet so fast she knocked over her chair. "Why would she come here? Has something happened to Shadowhawk?"

Charley stood and calmly poured himself a cup of coffee, while Hernando picked up the chair Shiloh had knocked over. "Shadowhawk's fine, far as I know. I 'spect if you talk to Vision Woman, you'll find out why she's here."

Hernando held his cup out for Charley to fill. "You should talk to her, Señorita Shiloh," he urged.

Overcome by uncertainty, Shiloh looked at each of them in turn. Without a word, she hurried outside.

When she stepped onto the porch, the first person she saw was Johnny Tall Tree, who regarded her with marked interest. Several of Estrella's hands had gathered to watch the Indians with suspicion.

Shiloh's attention turned to Vision Woman, who had dismounted, and was moving toward her with easy grace, the fringe on the bottom of her doeskin gown rippling as she walked. Shadowhawk's mother stopped in front of her, looking her over carefully.

"You have been sad, my little friend."

"I have," Shiloh admitted. "Will you come into the house so we can talk where it's cooler?"

"Can we not sit on the porch?" Vision Woman asked. "What I have to say to you will not take much time."

"You must be hungry," Shiloh insisted. "Surely I can offer you something to drink."

Vision Woman held up her hand. "I want nothing."

Shiloh made a gesture toward the steps, watching Johnny Tall Tree dismount to stand beside his horse.

Once they were settled, Vision Woman took Shiloh's hand. "You carry my grandchild in your belly."

Meeting the older woman's eyes, Shiloh was glad to share her secret again. "You must not tell Shadowhawk."

"My daughter," Vision Woman stated, "my son hears nothing anyone says to him. His love for you torments him so. He suffers in silence, but he suffers."

Shiloh's hand went to her heart. "Why did you come here to tell me this?"

"My son told me you gave yourself to him as his wife." Vision Woman's eyes were probing. "If that is so, why are you not with your husband?"

Shiloh's hand went to her stomach, where Shadowhawk's child nestled. "I . . . don't . . . know. I can't leave Luke."

Her brother stepped onto the porch and she realized he'd been listening. "You gotta go to him, Shiloh, and I'll go with you," he told her, nodding at Vision Woman. "Charley and Hernando can run things on Estrella until I come back."

"Luke," she said, fighting against fresh tears. "Will you?"

"Of course I will. If Shadowhawk's your husband, he's my brother."

Shiloh's heart was beating so fast, she could hardly speak as she grasped Vision Woman's hand. "Where is Shadowhawk?"

"He has gone to the Sacred Place, because his heart was troubled. When he returns, we will be leaving this land."

Charley and Hernando came out the back door. Hernando spoke. "We have been shamelessly listening to what was being said," he admitted. "With the new hands to work the cattle, we will have no trouble on Estrella."

Charley's troubled gaze settled on Shiloh. "You ain't happy here, Miss Shiloh."

Looking into the two men's faces and then at Luke, who nodded, she asked, "Would . . . it be wrong for me to leave Estrella and go to Shadowhawk?"

The old man carried his coffee and took a sip before answering. "Only you can say."

She loved the two men who had stuck with her and Luke even when it was dangerous to do so, and her heart overflowed with gratitude. "I want to go to him and live as his wife."

"Then what's keepin' us?" Charley asked, taking another sip of coffee. "It won't take long for me to load a packhorse with my belongin's. Hernando, here, don't need me, so I'll be goin' with ya."

Vision Woman, who had been following the conversation, stood. "Jimmy Tall Tree will take you to Shadowhawk."

Joy burst through Shiloh's heart and she knew what she must do. "That will not be necessary. I know where to find him."

Chapter Thirty-four

Shiloh dismounted at the top of the mesa and glanced down at the Sacred Place. This was where she had become Shadowhawk's wife, and it was right that she should reunite with him there. Tying the reins of her horse to a mesquite branch, she gathered her courage.

As she made her way down the steep embankment to the valley below, her heart was thundering. She was plagued by doubt. What if Vision Woman was wrong, and Shadowhawk didn't want her?

She had taken care to walk softly, but when she stepped from behind a scrub brush, strong arms reached for her and pulled her tight against a hard body.

Astonishment was written on the stark planes of Shadowhawk's face as he turned her to face him.

"Shiloh? I did not know it was you." He saw she wore her doeskin gown and moccasins, and it pleased him. "I am sorry if I hurt you."

Shiloh managed to smile. "If you give the same greeting to those you call friend, how must you greet an enemy?"

He turned his back to her, staring out on the land as if he was seeing it for the last time and committing it to memory. "You should not have come."

"Shadowhawk, I became your wife in this place. Should not a wife be beside her husband?"

He turned back to her, and she could read the question in those wonderful dark eyes.

Shadowhawk feared the hard life in an Indian village

would be too difficult for Shiloh. "I do not accept you as my wife."

"Then you deny the child I carry is yours?"

His throat constricted, his chest tightened, and he dropped his head. "Then the worst has happened. I have done you harm, when I want only the best for you."

"You are the best for me."

He took a step toward her. "You will have this child?"

She placed her hand on her stomach. "I love this child. If it is a girl, she will bring joy to your heart, and if a boy, he will need his father to guide him through life."

Shiloh cried out when she saw tears gleaming in Shadowhawk's eyes. "I want you so, I can think of nothing else. But will you give up your life to live with me in a tipi?"

She lovingly touched his face. "I would live with you anywhere. There has not been a day that I didn't hope you would come back for me."

Shadowhawk jerked her into his arms, burying his face in her hair. For a long moment, they stood locked together. Shadowhawk was the first to pull away.

"Life will not be easy for you."

"Without you, I have no life, and neither will this child."

His hand drifted down her hair, to rest on her shoulder. "Will you come to Blackfoot land with me?"

"I will."

"Your brother?"

"Luke is young. He still needs family to guide him. He could have no one better to teach him about life than you." She raised her eyebrow. "Charley will be coming with us. He will not be left behind."

For the first time she saw the flicker of joy in his eyes. "I have thought of you as my wife since the night we spent here. I loved you from the first time I saw you. It gladdens my heart that you are willing to sacrifice your way of life to live with me."

Shiloh smiled. "It is no sacrifice. With you, I will have everything I want."

He went down on his knees, touched her stomach, and pressed his lips there. "The night you gave yourself to me, my heart knew you as my woman."

He stood, lifting her into his arms, and smiling. "I have hungered for your lips. Kiss me."

Her mouth parted in invitation, and he lowered his head to partake.

Chapter Thirty-five

The Land of the Shining Mountains

Winter stayed long beyond the Wind River. The Blackfoot village was obscured by a thick layer of snow, and plump flakes continued to sift earthward.

A group of warriors had gathered in the lodge of Vision Woman's brother, White Owl. The chief smiled at his nephew. "Do you think your woman is the only one ever to give birth?"

"As far as I am concerned, she is, my uncle."

"You will have both sons and daughters from the redhaired one. Although she is small in stature, she will bear you many children," his uncle assured him.

Luke sat alone, his eyes going often to the lodge opening. He was upset because Shadowhawk was obviously concerned.

Shadowhawk moved close to Luke and bent to him. "Little brother, we will see this through together."

Never having regretted his decision to accompany his sister and Shadowhawk, Luke had accomplished many things most white boys would never know. He learned to become as one with his horse when he was riding. He could throw a lance and shoot an arrow straight and true. He had been surprised how readily the Blackfoot tribe had taken him into their circle. He and Shiloh now had a new family.

But at the moment, Luke was worried about Shiloh. "Charley, do you think my sister is all right?"

"Why, shoot, Luke. Babies are born every day. This one's got a strong bloodline from its ma and pa."

Vision Woman appeared in the lodge. "The child is delivered. My son has a son!"

Shadowhawk took a deep breath, looking anxiously at his mother.

"They are both well," she told him, smiling.

The men who had gathered with Shadowhawk to await the birth of his child grinned, congratulating him on the birth of a son. Good-natured laughter followed Shadowhawk as he hurried out of the lodge to the birthing tipi.

He hesitated before entering, then stepped inside, closing the flap behind him. Shiloh lay upon a buffalo robe, her long hair hanging over her shoulder. The smile she gave him went right to Shadowhawk's heart.

Going down on his knees, he touched her face. "Are you no longer in pain?"

"I am not," she answered, speaking in Blackfoot, although she still had a limited knowledge of the words. Shiloh smiled down at the tiny bundle she held against her. "Your son wants to know his father."

Shadowhawk's throat clogged when she held the baby out to him. Without hesitation, he took the child and stood. The child's skin was not as dark as his, but not white either. Looking down at the tiny face and mop of dark hair, Shadowhawk felt love and pride swell within him.

"My son!" He glanced at Shiloh, who was smiling tenderly back at him. "Thank you for this gift."

Her laughter made his heart even lighter. "It seems to me you had something to do with the gift. I remember well the night you planted this child in my body."

Moon Song had just entered the tipi and Shadowhawk handed the baby to her, then watched her leave to take the child to show the others.

Dropping down beside Shiloh, he said, "When you first

came to me at the Sacred Place, I thought my way of life would be hard for you. But you are always joyful as you go about your day, and you love my people as much as they love you."

She stared into his handsome face, and thought how wrong her own people were in their perception of the Indian. The Indians she knew were hardworking, loyal, and honorable. To have one for a friend was to have a friend for life. They had a great capacity to love.

Shiloh touched her husband's cheek. "You never told me why you wanted to leave Texas and come to Blackfoot territory."

"I could no longer be at war with your people, and my son carries the white blood of your people. We know not the future, or how our people will deal with each other as the years pass. As for me, I shall spill no more white blood."

Epilogue

1855

Although Shadowhawk was only half Blackfoot, he was well respected in the tribe, and was chosen chief when his uncle died.

With the wind blowing through his hair, he stood on a mountaintop, gazing down at the valley below. He glanced at the far mountains that were still snowcapped, thinking his heart belonged in this land of his mother's people.

Shiloh came up beside him, and he reached out for her hand. "Joy sings through me this day."

She had finally mastered the Blackfoot language. "And me as well," she told him. "Although I will miss Luke when he leaves in the spring for Virginia, he is ready to attend William and Mary as our father always planned. Though what Luke really wants is to return to Estrella."

Shadowhawk placed his hand on his wife's swollen stomach. Already she had given him two sons, and his mother said this child would be a daughter. "Luke is a young man of eighteen years. His path will eventually lead him back to Texas."

"Yes, it will."

Shadowhawk held her to him, loving her more deeply with each passing year. "We shall visit our brother often, and he will come here." Shadowhawk laughed. "It seems Charley will be around for a long time. He will not be parted from you and the children."

"I love that dear old man."

"Are you content with our life together?"

Shiloh rested her head against his shoulder. "More than I ever thought possible."

Shadowhawk had been a Comanche chief, and now the Blackfoot looked to him for leadership. He was an extraordinary man, and Shiloh felt most fortunate that he had chosen her to love.

Savage Fantasy
by
Cassie Edwards

Savage Fantasy

Tah-hay-chap-shoon-wee—Moon of Dropping Deer Horns

Wildflowers dotted the land in a tapestry of colors. It was a beautiful country, where the high hills were covered with lush, green grass and verdant trees.

Yvonne Armistead rested on her knees as she puttered in her flower garden. With gloves to protect her hands, she swept mounds of dirt around the roots of her rosebushes.

She smiled down at the snapdragons that were just revealing their faces to the sun. She shifted her gaze and sighed in pleasure. Her azaleas were the brightest pink this year that she had ever seen.

And the jonquils! They were so large and such a deep shade of yellow.

Yvonne wiped a bead of perspiration from her brow and paused to savor the satisfaction she felt. She had been married to Silver Arrow for six years now, and she was completely content with her life as wife of the powerful Ottawa Indian chief.

The people of his village, who had welcomed her as one of them, were busy at their chores. The warriors who were not in council with her husband in the council house were out on the hunt. Some women worked in their vegetable gardens, planting seeds, while others sat outside their lodges preparing hides for various uses.

She gazed over at her own vegetable garden, glad that

she already had her family's seeds in the ground. If she looked close enough, she could see the faintest of tiny sprouts shoving the dirt aside.

Later today, she planned to join the women in the larger fields, where corn, used by the whole village, would be planted.

But it was her flower garden that Yvonne cherished. It reminded her of many things, some sad, some happy. Her sad thoughts were of the times when the only money that her widowed mother could earn was from the sale of fresh flowers from their Saint Louis garden.

She chose to think of the happy times of her life, when her mother had remarried, and her flower garden was a source of joy rather than income. Her mother had brightened every nook and cranny of their large stone home in Saint Louis with flowers.

The sound of a horse and buggy approaching drew Yvonne's attention. She stood up. Shielding her eyes from the sun with a hand, she peered in the direction of the buggy.

Recognizing it, she smiled. It was her stepfather, who was a Methodist minister. Over the years he had taken the place of the father she'd lost. She adored him.

And everyone in the Ottawa village loved him, for he had given their children opportunities no other white man had ever offered. When Anthony had moved to the Ottawas' homeland of Wisconsin, he had not only brought himself and his family, but also plans to build a schoolhouse so that the Ottawa children could have the same book knowledge that white children had.

With assistance from the United States government, the school had been built, and now it had been operating for seven years. Side by side with the white children of the community, the Ottawa children attended her father's school.

Yvonne and Silver Arrow's son, Black Crow, was among the children at the school today, as well as Yvonne's thirteen-year-old brother Stanley, and Silver Arrow's sister Rustling Leaves.

Smiling at Anthony as he drew closer in the carriage, Yvonne slipped off her gloves and thrust them into the pocket of her denim skirt.

When her father reined in the horse and buggy beside her, she walked briskly to the other side of the buggy and waited for him to step down to the ground.

The wind had picked up. It whisked Yvonne's long, flowing chestnut hair back from her shoulders. Dust particles stung her hazel eyes.

"Let's get inside quickly," Anthony said, his hat flying from his head. He looked heavenward and peered through his thick-lensed glasses at the clouds overhead. The beautiful day had turned suddenly dark, and lightning forked across the sky.

"I'll get your hat," Yvonne said, running after it as the wind tumbled it along the ground.

Anthony reached inside the back of his buggy and lifted a small, golden chest into his hands.

When Yvonne returned with his hat, they hurried into the longhouse where a fire in the large, stone fireplace greeted them. It cast its magical, golden light all around the room, revealing Yvonne's tasteful choice of plush armchairs arranged before the fire, and braided rugs made by her own hands on the wood floors. Flowers graced the tables, alongside kerosene lamps.

Farther still, where the kitchen was visible from the central room, a wild turkey roasting in the oven wafted its tantalizing aroma throughout the house.

Anthony spied a cherry pie sitting on his daughter's kitchen table and freshly baked bread cooling on a windowsill.

"I see you've been as busy as usual." Anthony chuckled as Yvonne laid his hat on a chair. Loving her deeply, he watched her rake her fingers through her long hair to untangle it. "I would ask for a piece of that pie, but, alas, I have a meeting soon at my church with the deacons."

"You can take the pie home with you, if you wish," Yvonne said, taking off her apron. Her eyes were on the small chest held between her father's hands. "I can bake another."

"My wife is home baking pies even now," Anthony said, seeing how Yvonne stared down at the chest.

Yvonne lifted her eyes to his. "What is in the chest?" she asked softly. "It looks vaguely familiar. Should I know what it is? And why you have brought it to me?"

"It was your mother's," Anthony said, his voice drawn with melancholy at the mention of his first wife, whom he'd adored, and whom he missed dearly. "I'm not sure if you have seen it before or not, for I am not even sure when it came into your mother's possession. She always meant for you to have it, Yvonne. But I was so upset by her death, and then our move to Wisconsin, I absolutely forgot about it."

"Did you bring it with you from Saint Louis?" Yvonne asked, taking the chest as Anthony gently placed it in her hands. She stared down at it. The handmade wooden chest had been intricately inlaid with gold, which gleamed bright in the firelight.

Yvonne gazed at it a moment longer, then questioned Anthony with her eyes. "Have you had it all this time since our move from Missouri?" she blurted out. "What is inside the chest? Why do I feel there is some mystery to your having it?"

Anthony shuffled his feet nervously. His gray eyes wavered. He leaned over, grabbed his hat, and placed it on his thick gray hair. "I really must be going," he said, turning to walk toward the door.

"Father, what is there about this chest that causes you to behave so . . . so . . . strangely?" Yvonne asked, her breath catching in her throat when he slipped a hand in his coat pocket and retrieved a tiny golden key.

"You will need this," he said thickly. "It unlocks the chest."

His eyes held hers as he handed her the key. "Yes, I guess I must tell you all about it," he said, sighing heavily.

He regretted having to bring up a sensitive subject. He knew Yvonne had struggled long and hard learning to read and had never succeeded. Even he had puzzled over her inability to master the skill. He was a scholar himself, and had never been able to understand her difficulty.

Because of her humiliation at not being able to read, Anthony had allowed her to quit school. He knew that, when she saw the book inside the chest, she would feel humiliated all over again.

Yet he had no choice but to tell her about the book, and implore her not to allow its presence in her life to make her feel inadequate. There were so many things she had mastered. Being unable to read was a small lack in comparison.

It wouldn't be fair to Yvonne to withhold something as precious as this from her—an heirloom which had been handed down through generations of her mother's family, a book, something which held her own mother's signature along with the personal annotations of the other daughters and mothers who had once had the beloved book in their possession.

It had been meant for Yvonne to own, and her daughter after her. It would have been wrong not to have brought it to her. In fact, he should have remembered it earlier. He never should have left Saint Louis without it.

Anthony removed his hat. "Yvonne, inside the chest is a book that belonged to your mother," he said, turning his hat nervously around between his fingers. "It is a copy of an ancient, treasured book, passed down from generation to generation, from mother to daughter, for centuries. Your mother told me the original book is in the Library of Congress. This copy was made for her when she was just a girl, but when she died, it was forgotten. The Smiths, who now live in our house in Saint Louis, found it and shipped it to me. It was delivered today."

"A . . . book?" Yvonne said hesitantly.

"Yes, a book, Yvonne," Anthony replied, his voice drawn. He was the only one who knew that she couldn't read. He had guarded the secret well for her, to hide her embarrassment.

"I see," she murmured, her fingers trembling as she held the chest, staring down at it.

"Your mother always kept the chest well hidden. In our Saint Louis home, she hid it in the attic. While renovating the home, the Smiths found the chest beneath some loose floorboards. They knew it had to be ours, since we were the only previous owners."

"I do recall seeing this once," Yvonne said, thinking back to the time she had come upon her mother reading the book. "It was before she married you."

Unable to read, Yvonne had crept away from her mother without asking her about it. She had never liked any reminders of her inability to read, especially in front of her mother, who was so skilled with book learning.

"Yes, your mother did have it before we were married," Anthony said as another rumble of thunder seemed to shake the ground.

He gazed out the window. "I must leave now," he said. "If I hurry, I might get to the church meeting without being soaked to the bone."

A smile quivered across Yvonne's lips. "Thank you for bringing this to me," she murmured. "Anything that belonged to my mother is precious to me, even . . . even . . . if I'll never be able to know what is written in the book."

"If you wish, I shall come from time to time and read it to you," Anthony said, reaching a hand to her cheek.

A quick panic filled her. "No, Father," she said, her voice breaking. "I would never want to risk Silver Arrow finding you reading to me, when I should be able to read it myself. Silver Arrow doesn't know of my affliction. I have ways to hide that dark side of myself which I hate. At least I can write my name. Thank heavens you and mother were able to teach me that."

"Darling, darling," Anthony said thickly. "There is not one inch of you that can be described as dark. But I do understand how you feel, and I shan't cause you any more anxiety over this book. The main thing is that it is in your possession, where it should be."

"You are always so understanding," Yvonne said, following him to the door.

He gave her a quick kiss on her cheek, placed the hat on his head, and hurried through the blustery wind to his buggy.

Yvonne stood at the door and waved, then watched him ride away.

She turned and walked back inside the longhouse, slowly closing the door behind her.

She kept glancing toward the door, and then down at the chest. "Do I have time to open the chest to see the book before Silver Arrow comes home, or should I wait until later?" she whispered, anxious, yet in the same breath apprehensive, about seeing what had been so important to her ancestors.

One thing for certain, she didn't want Silver Arrow or her son to see the chest. Just as her mother had kept the chest hidden, so would she . . . but for different reasons!

Her urge to see the book sent her to her bedroom, where

she would have time to shove the chest beneath her bed if she heard the door open when Silver Arrow arrived home. Their son, Black Crow, would not be home for hours, for the school day had only just begun a short while ago.

Swallowing hard, Yvonne rushed to her bedroom and closed the door behind her. The sky dark with the impending storm made it necessary for her to light a lamp.

She laid the chest on her embroidered, lace-trimmed bedspread and struck a match to the wick of a kerosene lamp on the table beside the bed.

After the flickering light flooded the walls and ceilings of the room, Yvonne sat down on the edge of the bed and rested the chest on her lap. Putting the key in place, she slowly turned the lock until she heard a low clicking sound.

"It's unlocked," she whispered, laying the key aside. "Now . . . to see the book."

A musty smell rushed from the chest as she slowly opened it, the small rusted hinges squeaking ominously. She sighed when she saw the beautiful book, where it lay on a bed of maroon crushed velvet.

From her first glance she knew that the treasured book was special and unique. Gilded in gold, it was exquisitely bound in doeskin.

Lifting the book into her hands, she squinted as she tried to decipher the letters that had been stamped in gold on the doeskin cover so many years ago, when her mother was just a girl.

Slowly she opened the book, taking care while doing it, for the pages were yellow with age. When she had the book all the way open, she gasped softly. Her mother's signature was inscribed on the inside page. Although she could not read, she knew her mother's signature.

Tears flowing from her eyes, Yvonne softly ran her fingers over the faded ink. Touching the spot where her mother's pen had once rested was almost the same as having her there with her now.

And if Yvonne inhaled deeply enough, somewhere amidst the musty smell of the book was a faint fragrance of her mother's perfume. It smelled of lily of the valley, the perfume her stepfather had given her mother the first year of their marriage. Never, from that day forth, had her mother gone anywhere without the perfume dabbed behind her ears and on her wrists.

The sound of the door in the living room closing made Yvonne jump. It had to be Silver Arrow. Panic grabbed her as she glanced down at the book and then at the closed bedroom door. She must get the book hidden quickly!

Fearful that her secret might be uncovered, Yvonne hurriedly placed the book back inside its chest. Falling to her knees, she shoved the chest far beneath her bed, then rose quickly when the door opened. Silver Arrow stood looking questioningly at her.

"Ki-mi-no-pi-maw-tis-noo?" he asked. He stepped into the room in his fringed buckskin attire. "Are you not well? Your face is flushed, yet beneath your eyes there is a strange paleness."

He swept his arms around Yvonne and drew her close to him. He gazed into her eyes as she looked meekly up at him. "My wife, there is something else about you that is different," he said. "You look guarded, as though you might be uneasy about something. Would you like to tell me what causes this?"

"I'm tired. That's all," she murmured, swallowing hard. "I guess I did too much this morning." She forced a laugh. "I not only baked a pie and a loaf of bread, but I also worked long hours in the garden."

"Did I not warn you against trying to put too much into one day?" Silver Arrow scolded. "And it is only midmorning." He gazed past her at the bed. "Were you in here to rest? Did I disturb your nap?"

Seeing his innocence, his gentle understanding and caring, Yvonne felt guilt rise inside her. She placed a gentle hand on his copper cheek, loving him so much her heart ached from the intensity of it.

Not only was he a man of wonderful compassion, but he was also handsome. His face was finely chiseled. His midnight-dark eyes were penetrating, as though they could look clean into a person's heart and soul. His coal black hair hung to his waist, a band at his brow holding it in place.

Yvonne's gaze lowered, marveling anew at the width of his shoulders, the power of his bulging muscles.

He had swept her off her feet the very first time she had seen him. She had gloried in the moment she discovered that he had fallen just as deeply in love with her.

Theirs was a lasting love. And she never wanted to jeopardize it, or disappoint him.

She had never wanted to live the lie that she had been forced to live. But how could she explain to him that when she tried to read, she saw the letters backwards and out of order? Such letters as *d* and *b* were reversed. Something inside her mind kept her from sorting the letters of the alphabet out and placing them as they should be to form a word.

Even her very educated stepfather hadn't been able to discover the cause of her problem. If he couldn't, surely no one else could.

She had given up trying long ago.

And so now she had two secrets to keep from her beloved husband—her inability to read, and the book that she had inherited. The latter would be the harder to keep from him, for someday in the future she would be handing the special book down to their own daughter if they were blessed with one.

"No, you didn't disturb my rest," Yvonne said softly. "I . . . I . . . just came into my room to . . ."

Silver Arrow interrupted her as his gaze shifted to the vase of flowers on the bedside table. "You brought flowers to scent our room for our time together tonight," he said. He smiled slowly down at her. "What talents you have. You have such skill in gardening." He chuckled. "I am sure there are many more hidden talents that you have not told me about."

Yvonne paled. The conversation was coming too close to the secret that troubled her to the core of her being. She took him by the hand and walked him from the room. "My darling, how is the weather?" she asked, peering toward the window. "Do you think it will be too nasty for the spring celebration? I plan to cook many wonderful dishes before sunup tomorrow for the celebration."

Silver Arrow gave her a puzzled gaze, then shrugged off the thought that she seemed to be trying too hard to make conversation. He still saw something about her that troubled him. There was something different in her eyes today. He had seen her stepfather arrive while he was in council. Perhaps . . .

"Why was your stepfather here?" he asked, watching her expression.

Yvonne knew that his question was causing the color to drain from her face, yet she could not help her reaction any more than she could help the fact that she could not read.

"He . . . he . . . just came to tell me that Black Crow was adjusting well to school," she said, wanting to bite her tongue as the lie slipped across her lips. She never liked to lie to anyone, especially her husband. But she knew now that lies were sometimes necessary, especially when the truth might cause a husband to lose respect for his wife.

"*Ni-wob.* It is good that Black Crow is doing well," Silver Arrow said. He went to the kitchen and pinched off a flake of piecrust. "But it was not necessary for him to come all this way just to tell us that." He turned to Yvonne, again questioning her with his eyes.

"Darling, look. The sun is out again! It's not going to storm after all. It's passed on over us," Yvonne said, ignoring his stare. She took the loaf of bread from the window-sill and wrapped it in a towel. "Tomorrow will be such fun, don't you think?"

Silver Arrow slowly nodded. "Yes, *ka-ye-ti*, truly so. The ceremony of spring will renew my people's faith for an-other summer," he said.

Yvonne gave him a slow stare, smiling sheepishly when she found him studying her as she never remembered him studying her before. Knowing that he had cause to ques-tion her, she lowered her eyes.

The weather had been beautiful for the long day of the Ottawas' spring celebration. Much food had been con-sumed and there had been many games and merriment.

Even now, as the sun was lowering in the sky, Yvonne sat beside Silver Arrow on a raised platform covered with rich pelts. They were watching their son, Black Crow, as he played *paw-baw-da-way* with the other children. Yvonne had learned from her husband that *paw-baw-da-way* was a ball game the young braves played.

"The day has been good and you have had much time to relax while watching the children play their games, yet you look so tired," Silver Arrow said as he swept an arm around Yvonne's waist, to draw her close to his side.

His eyes moved over the beautifully beaded white doe-skin dress she had worn for the celebration. It matched his own special white attire.

Yet no matter how much he wanted to look past the weary look in his wife's eyes, to see her total beauty, he could not. Ever since yesterday she had not been herself.

"Remember, darling, I *did* get up quite early today to prepare my share of the food for the celebration," Yvonne said, trying to hide her true feelings of despondency.

She was thrilled to have the special book that had belonged to so many women of her family, yet it had also brought the recollection of her dreadful inability!

She wanted to be as cheerful as she had been before yesterday, but it was impossible. She hid a lie beneath her bed, and by doing so, she felt as though she was betraying her beloved husband, who had always been nothing but good, gentle, and truthful to her!

"You have awakened early many mornings and prepared food for various celebrations of my people," Silver Arrow said, placing a gentle hand on her cheek, caressing her soft, silken flesh with his thumb. "Today is different. There is something wrong. Would you not feel better if you confided in your husband? Can you think of a time we kept secrets from one another? It is not a natural thing between us, my sweet wife."

"I'm sorry," Yvonne said, swallowing hard. She turned her eyes from him, fearing he would be able to see within her very soul and read her thoughts. "The celebration was wonderful this year, Silver Arrow. I love the ways of your people."

"You are one with us," Silver Arrow said, smiling at his son as Black Crow cast him a winning smile after having made another point for himself in the ball game.

Yvonne gazed at the large pole in the center of the village, which stood upright in the ground close to the large outdoor communal fire. She watched the fabric that hung from it flutter in the softness of the wind. She would never forget the first time she had seen the pole and had learned its meaning. Each spring the Ottawas gathered all the cast-off garments that had been worn during the winter. They strung them up on this long pole while they partook of a festival and jubilee to the Great Spirit.

These tattered bundles of old garments were a sacrifice to the Creator, *Kit-chi-manito.*

For many hours today the Ottawa people had danced around the pole, beating a consecrated drum and shaking sacred rattles made from the hard smooth shells of winter squash.

The instruments that had been used were very old and kept for that purpose only. They were accompanied by two musicians who sang, "The Great Spirit will look down upon us. The Great Spirit will have mercy on us . . ."

Though the ceremony had fascinated her in other years, today Yvonne's thoughts kept returning to the hidden book. She hated having to keep it secret from her husband. Yet how could she tell him? It would only be natural that he would ask her what the book was about. How could she tell him, when she could not read one line of the text?

Too troubled to sit still any longer while others were carefree and guiltless, Yvonne wrenched herself away from Silver Arrow and ran to their longhouse, where she flung herself across their bed, sobbing.

Stunned by her behavior, now certain that something was wrong, Silver Arrow rushed after Yvonne.

When he found her on the bed in tears, he lay down beside her and drew her to him. "My woman," he murmured, cradling her close. "Free your heart of whatever burden you are carrying by sharing it with your husband. Have I not always been understanding? Why would you think I would not be now?"

The book was so close, beneath this very bed on which her husband comforted her, that Yvonne's betrayal seemed twofold.

Yet still she could not find it in her heart to tell him. She did not want to appear ignorant in her husband's eyes. He had learned long ago how to read, even before the school was erected close to his village. Priests, traders, and past white friends had taught him. It was for certain that he could read as well as any white man.

"Just hold me," Yvonne whispered against his cheek. "Make love to me. While in your arms it is so easy to forget."

"Forget . . . what?" Silver Arrow persisted, framing her face between his hands, drawing her eyes to his. "What are you not telling me?"

"It is truly nothing," she said, blinking her eyes nervously under his close scrutiny. She thought quickly. "My time of month draws nigh. You know how my mood always changes with the moon."

Silver Arrow laughed, partly from relief that nothing so terribly wrong caused her strange behavior, and partly from recalling just how that time of the moon had always caused her to become somewhat of a stranger to him. He had often teased her about becoming a hellion who would snap at him without provocation when that time drew nigh.

"I should have guessed the cause," Silver Arrow said, brushing a soft kiss across her lips. "Your moods *do* change with the moon. But this time, you are more softly emotional than glinty-eyed."

"Glinty-eyed?" Yvonne said, raising an eyebrow at the way he described her. "Do I look and act so bad during my monthly? If so, I am sorry."

"I would not be able to say that you look or behave as gentle as a butterfly," Silver Arrow said, chuckling. He rose from the bed and closed the door, then undressed as his body grew warm with passion. "Seems it is best I love you now, my woman, for perhaps tomorrow night my monthly enemy will keep me from it."

"The children," Yvonne said, glancing toward the door. "Rustling Leaves and Black Crow have learned that when our door is closed, it locks in our privacy," Silver Arrow said, bending to slip off his moccasins.

Yvonne's eyes widened as she watched him removing his moccasins. With him bent so low, he just might see the chest beneath the bed!

She slipped off the bed quickly and began seductively removing her clothes, which she knew would draw his undivided attention.

She relaxed by degrees when she realized that her ploy had worked. Unclothed, he stood close beside her, his passion-filled eyes watching each and every one of her movements.

Yvonne was glad that, for the moment, there would be no more questions. The way her husband was looking at her melted her insides with need. Her need, her want, *his* need, *his* want, took precedence over everything else.

Silver Arrow reached out for Yvonne and gathered her into his arms and led her down onto the bed. He knelt over her as his lips found hers, warm and quivering. His mouth then brushed her cheeks and ears. He tenderly kissed her eyelids.

"I love you so," she whispered.

"You are my everything," Silver Arrow whispered against her lips, then covered her mouth with a meltingly hot kiss.

Yvonne's breath quickened with yearning as he filled her with his heat. She closed her eyes and reveled in ecstasy as their bodies strained and moved rhythmically together. All that she was aware of now was being with him, her golden knight. She was floating, thrilling, soaring. The web of magic was weaving between them, drawing them together as though they were one breath, one heartbeat.

Yvonne twined her arms around his neck, breathless as they continued making love. She sucked in a wild breath of pleasure as his lips swept over a breast, brushing it with a feathery kiss.

A delicious languor stole over Yvonne as rapture totally overwhelmed her.

Silver Arrow moaned as ecstasy leapt through him. Hot, silver bolts of lightning were zigzagging their way through his veins.

And when they floated down from their shared cloud of paradise, lying side by side, only then did Yvonne once again think about what lay so close beneath them on the floor. Tomorrow she would take the book far into the forest. She would study the words. Perhaps if she tried hard enough she could glean the sense of the book so that, if she showed it to her husband, she would be able to answer his questions.

"Again you are pensive," Silver Arrow said as he turned on his side to face Yvonne. He stroked her silken flesh with a hand, running his fingers over the gentle curve of a thigh. "If only it were possible to wish the coming days away so that you would not have to battle the moods that plague you."

"My darling," Yvonne murmured, running her fingers gently over his sinewed shoulders. She laughed softly. "I promise to be better. I shall smile and laugh my own moods away."

He filled his arms with her and held her. "Ah, but if it were that easy," he said, chuckling.

She closed her eyes and sighed as they shared ecstasy's moments again.

After the children had left for school, and Silver Arrow had left for the trading post to do his weekly trading, Yvonne put her plan into motion. Carrying the book, she went far into the forest where she knew she would not be disturbed, not even by her husband should he return from the trading post earlier than usual. To find her place of solitude, she chose the route exactly opposite that which her husband had traveled today.

The scene from the top of the hill where she sat on a blanket was rapturous. The wooded slopes, the meadows of wildflowers, and the rippling river below her took her breath away.

But she had not come to enjoy the view. Yvonne's fingers trembled as she opened to the yellowed pages. She took the time to gaze again upon her beloved mother's signature.

"Mother," she whispered, brushing her fingers across the signature. "If only you were here with me now to read this to me. I know that you read it time and again in the privacy of your bedroom. Why didn't you read it to me then? I would at least know the story enough to tell my husband and child!"

Not wanting to spoil any of the pages with her teardrops, she flicked the tears from her eyes with trembling fingers.

Slowly she studied the words, going from one to the other. She soon became frustrated as she always had in the past when she had tried to read. She still could not make sense of anything on the page.

"What have we here?"

A voice behind Yvonne, deep and mocking, caused her spine to stiffen. She gently laid the book aside on the ground and rose slowly to her feet.

Fear gripping her insides, she turned and stared at the interloper.

She backed slowly away. The man's face was darkly bearded, and his eyes were almost as round as coins, yet bottomless in their empty gray coloring.

Yvonne's gaze swept quickly over the man. His clothes were soiled and smelled of dried perspiration. One side of his jaw was puffed out like a chipmunk's and a stream of chewing tobacco trickled from the corner of his lips as he slowly shifted it inside his mouth. He held a rifle aimed directly at her middle, his leering, crooked smile almost as threatening as his firearm.

"I wouldn't go much farther, ma'am," the man said, chuckling beneath his breath. "You just might fall over the edge of that cliff. I wouldn't want that. You would lose your value."

Filled with a quick panic, Yvonne turned with a start and gasped when she saw how close she had come to falling over the edge.

She turned again.

Now standing her ground, she turned fearful eyes back to the man. "What do you want of me?" she asked, her voice guarded. "What value could I be to you? Who *are* you? Where did you come from?"

"My, oh, my, ain't you jest full of questions?" the man said, taking a slow step toward her. "There ain't no need for me to answer them 'cept to give you a name to call me by. Just call me Owl—you know, as in bird, as in big eyes?" He laughed again, then spit a long stream of tobacco from between his lips. "Come with me, ma'am. I've got plans for you, and your savage husband."

"What could you possibly want with me . . . and . . . Silver Arrow?" Yvonne said, gasping when he grabbed her arm and shoved her ahead of him. Her insides tightened when she felt the barrel of his rifle nudge her in the back.

"Don't ask no more questions," Owl said. "I'll let you in on my plan after I get you tied up in my cabin."

"Your . . . cabin . . . ?" Yvonne said, giving him a quick glance over her shoulder. "I don't remember seeing any cabin."

"Now maybe that's 'cause I built it so safely hidden 'midst a grove of cottonwood trees away from the snoopin' eyes of your savage husband," he said, chuckling. "It ain't far."

"My husband isn't a savage," Yvonne defended, then cried out with pain when she stubbed her toe on a tree root.

"Watch your step now," Owl said. "Cain't hand you

back over to your savage with bruises all over you or he might think I placed them there."

She paused and steadied herself. "Then you mean me no harm?" she asked softly. "You are going to eventually set me free?"

"If your savage cooperates," Owl said, shrugging nonchalantly. He spat over his shoulder. "If he does as I asks him, you'll be as free as a bird."

He took a quick step toward her and gave her another shove. "But not until I get what I'm after," he growled. "Hurry along. You see that cabin up ahead? Head straight for it."

"Why are you doing this?" Yvonne asked, her heart pounding harder the closer she came to the isolated cabin. Once inside, she would be at the crazed man's mercy.

A sudden hope filled her when she saw a piece of cloth tied to a low limb of a sassafras tree. She knew that cloth tied in such a way was how Indians left an offering to the spirits. It made her feel better to know this wasn't an altogether isolated area. The spirit offering was proof of that.

"I'm sure you've heard tell of your husband's grandfather's gold," Owl said, giving her a crooked smile as she sent another quick, alarmed look over her shoulder. "Yes, I see that you have. Well, ma'am, I intend to trade you for some of that gold, *if* your savage cooperates, that is."

"Many have tried to find ways to get at the buried gold and none have succeeded," Yvonne said, a chill racing up and down her spine as she recalled her husband's determination not to give in to past threats.

Many years ago, the neighboring bands of Ottawa Indians had brought their gold coins to Silver Arrow's grandfather for safekeeping. His grandfather had hidden the gold. It seemed now that everyone was hearing about it.

"Have you been used as ransom before?" Owl snickered.

"No, but—" Yvonne stammered.

"Then there's your answer," Owl said, giving her a shove through the open door of the cabin. "I'm the smartest of them all for having thought up a certain way to get my hands on the gold. Your savage will gladly hand it over to me to get you back in his bed."

Yvonne scarcely breathed as she looked around the shadowy interior of the cabin. Except for a table and one chair, it was devoid of furniture. And it smelled of fresh lumber. That had to mean that Owl had only recently built it.

"Sit down on that chair over yonder," Owl said, using the barrel of his rifle to motion toward it.

Knowing that she had no other choice, Yvonne did as she was told. She flinched when a wasp darted out of the shadows and buzzed wildly about her head.

"Damn you. Scat," Owl said, waving off the wasp.

He grabbed a length of rope from another dark space. "Now sit still while I tie your hands and feet, or by damn, I'll grab up my rifle so quick and shoot you, you won't have time to think about escapin' my clutches," he warned.

Knowing that he meant business, Yvonne anxiously nodded. Trembling, she placed her wrists together. Tears spilled from her eyes while she watched him tie the rope around her wrists, and then her ankles.

Then something else came to her which momentarily made her breath catch. "The book!" she cried, eyes wide. "Oh, no, my book! I can't let anything happen to it! How could I have forgotten it?" She glared at him. "You are the cause. You and your schemes made me forget it."

"What book are you talkin' 'bout?" Owl said, stepping away from her and idly scratching his brow. Then his eyes widened in remembrance. "The book you were reading when I came up behind you? Is that what you're fussin' about?"

"Reading?" Yvonne said, the very word causing her

insides to ache. She swallowed hard. "Yes, uh, yes. The book I was reading."

"Why do I get the feeling you are more concerned about that book than you are your very own hide?" he asked, leaning his face into hers. "What is it about that book? Tell me."

"It is very valuable to me," she blurted out. "Please, oh, please go and get it for me."

"Hmm," Owl said, kneading his chin contemplatively. "If it's that important to you, I must at least go and fetch it so I can see for myself why."

"Thank you, sir. Oh, thank you," Yvonne said, sighing heavily.

"*Sir* she calls me!" Owl said, laughing boisterously as he left the cabin.

Yvonne held her breath until he returned. When she saw him with the book, she let out a breath of relief. At least she had done one thing right today. She had convinced him to retrieve the precious family keepsake.

Now to see what he would do with it!

Owl held the book to the light of the door and leafed through the pages. Then he stopped and read some of the passages to himself.

Yvonne watched his expression, seeing a sudden amused glint in his eyes.

"A love story," he said, sending her a quick, teasing smile. "This ain't nothin' but a damn love story between characters with the strangest names I've ever seen. Damon? Angeline?" He held his head back in a fit of laughter, then sobered as he laid the book aside on the table.

He went and leaned over Yvonne, bracing himself with his hands on the arms of the chair. "And so you sneak away into the woods to read love stories, do you?" he taunted. "Well, ma'am, if you need more romance in your life than what your savage is givin' you, I can oblige. Ma'am, I can give you a true lovin'."

The thought so repelled Yvonne she visibly shuddered. "You dare not touch me in that way," she hissed out. "When Silver Arrow catches up with you, he'll hang you!"

A love story, she thought to herself; now at least she knew what the book was about!

"Don't worry yourself about it," Owl said, taking a step away from her. He yanked a piece of paper from his rear pocket. "I don't have time for such pleasures as you. I've more important things to see to while your husband is at the trading post."

Yvonne gasped as she realized that Owl knew so much about both her and Silver Arrow's activities.

"Yes, ma'am," Owl said, as though he had read her mind. "I've been watchin' you for days, hopin' to get the chance to catch you alone. I've been watchin' your savage's daily activities. I knew where he'd be today. And by gum, lo and behold, even you. You served yourself to me today on a silver platter, wouldn't you say?"

"What are you going to do now?" Yvonne asked, working with the rope, trying to get it free at her wrists.

"I'm going to deliver this note, then see if your savage cooperates," Owl said. His laughter trailed after him as he left the cabin.

Yvonne twisted and yanked on the ropes until her wrists were raw. She watched the sun slipping slowly toward the midpoint in the sky, and then its slow descent.

"Silver Arrow . . ." she whispered.

She stared at the book, wondering if she would be the last of her family to have it. Surely this evil man would kill her once he got what he was after. He would probably burn the book, laughing while watching it go up in flames!

"Will Silver Arrow part with his gold . . . ?" she whispered.

She felt guilty for having put her husband in the position of having to choose, and a sob caught in her throat.

Silver Arrow had made a good trade today and done it more quickly than usual; he was anxious to return home to his wife. This morning she had seemed even more moody than yesterday. He knew why and had come home early to see if there was anything he could do to lift her spirits. He was going to suggest taking a long walk in the woods, where they could breathe in the sweet scents of the forest flowers, and the fresh fragrance of the leaves in the trees.

Yes, he would cheer her up, one way or the other!

When he stepped inside his longhouse and didn't find her in the living room or kitchen, he gazed toward the bedroom door, which was ajar. Expecting to find her there, perhaps taking a nap, he walked lightly toward it, his moccasined steps making no more sound than a panther's.

When he opened the bedroom door and didn't find her there, he raised an eyebrow.

"Her garden?" he whispered, smiling as he envisioned her puttering amidst her flowers, a flower herself in her loveliness.

But something captured his attention. When he saw a small chest lying open on the floor beside the bed, he gazed questioningly at it for a moment, then knelt down and picked it up.

Studying the chest, he turned it slowly from side to side. "Where did this come from?" he whispered to himself. "Why did she not show it to me?"

Something else caught his eye. A small gold key, which lay in the folds of the bedspread on the bed. He reached for it and placed it in the lock of the chest. "They go together," he murmured.

He thought long and hard, then laid the chest and key aside.

"I must find her," he said, his jaw tightening. "Something is amiss here. I must find answers."

He ran outside and checked the garden.

She wasn't there.

He asked around, whether or not anyone had seen her. None had.

He checked his horses. They were all accounted for in his corral.

Yvonne's buggy rested beneath a tree where she always left it when not using it.

"Her father must have come for her," Silver Arrow said, swinging into his saddle.

He rode in a hard gallop until he reached her father's cabin.

His hopes were dashed when he found no one there.

He then rode to Anthony's church, where it was normal for the minister to be in the study, preparing his Sunday sermon.

Silver Arrow strolled into the study without knocking. Anthony sat behind his desk, his Bible opened to a particular scripture. He looked up at Silver Arrow, startled by his sudden appearance.

"Have you seen my wife?" Silver Arrow asked, his heart racing when he saw that she wasn't there.

"No, I haven't," Anthony said, rising slowly from behind his desk. "Silver Arrow, why do you ask? Isn't she home?"

"*Kau*, no," Silver Arrow said, kneading his brow. "I cannot find her anywhere."

A thought came to Silver Arrow. The chest. The key. And Anthony's visit the day before yesterday. "Anthony, you came the day before yesterday to see Yvonne," he said. "Did you possibly bring her a chest?"

Anthony's eyes wavered. "Why would you ask?" he said warily.

"Today when I was looking for her, I found a small chest on the floor of our bedroom," Silver Arrow blurted out. "I have never seen the chest. Did you bring it to her?"

Anthony felt torn—between his daughter, who had chosen not to confide in her husband about the book and her inability to read it, and a true friend, Silver Arrow. And he was not even sure if the book had anything to do with Yvonne's disappearance.

Unless she had taken it with her somewhere in private . . .

He hurriedly explained everything to Silver Arrow.

Silver Arrow's lips parted in surprise, not so much at Yvonne not being able to read, but because she had chosen to hide her mother's book from him.

"Please try to understand her feelings," Anthony pleaded. "She has always felt so inadequate because of her inability to read."

"With me, she should never feel inadequate about anything," Silver Arrow said. He turned on a heel and rushed back to his horse, quickly mounting it.

When he returned home, he found a note tacked to his front door—a ransom note. The note told him where to leave a bag of his grandfather's gold, and that soon after, in the gold's place, he would find his wife, unharmed.

Growling as rage filled him, he tore the note in shreds.

Never giving in to threats, and knowing every inch of this land, he gathered many of his warriors and explained to them about the ransom note.

"Fan out!" he shouted as they came to him on their horses. "Comb every inch of this land! Find . . . my . . . wife!"

When the sun was dipping low in the sky, Silver Arrow

and several of his warriors found the cabin. He gave them instructions in sign language since it was the quietest way to communicate. One by one they slid from their saddles.

Rifles clutched in their hands, they crept stealthily toward the cabin.

When they reached it, and no one fired at them, Silver Arrow ran inside.

"Silver Arrow!" Yvonne cried, a sob of joy lodging in her throat. "How did you know?"

"Do you think any white man can outthink and outdo this red man?" he growled as he laid his rifle aside. He slipped his knife from a sheath at his side and sliced the ropes away from his wife's ankles and wrists.

He then drew her into his arms. Over her shoulder he saw the book on the table. He stiffened at the sight.

But he had no time to question her about it now. Gunfire broke out outside the cabin. A shriek of pain filled the air, and then there was silence.

Yvonne went with Silver Arrow to the door and looked outside. "He's dead," she said, staring at Owl, who lay sprawled on the ground, blood seeping from a chest wound, warriors standing over him.

"He was an ignorant man who did not know well the art of planning that which would have placed gold in his pocket," Silver Arrow said, his teeth flashing white as he smiled confidently.

Then he reached for the book. He held it out before him for Yvonne to see. "Your father told me about the book, and . . . and . . . other things," he said, his voice drawn. "My woman, why would you not trust my love enough to confide in me about all things?"

"It was not that I didn't trust your love enough," Yvonne said, swallowing back another choking sob. "It was because I . . . I . . . was so ashamed about not being able to read. I have so often felt not good enough for you. You have mastered the art of not only speaking English, but also reading. How could I feel otherwise?"

"Because of my deep love for you," he said, laying the book aside. He embraced her. "My wife, you do not need to have knowledge of reading. I love you for what you are. You are my everything. Have I not told you that enough times for you to believe me?"

"I so want to believe that," she murmured, clinging.

"If reading is so important to you, *I* shall teach you," Silver Arrow said, his hands framing her face. "Together we shall read the book that was your mother's. Will that make you happy?"

"Father tried often to teach me and I . . . I . . .," Yvonne stopped, grimacing at the thought of Silver Arrow trying and failing, and her feeling doubly foolish.

"Your father tried when you were younger," Silver Arrow said. "This is *na-go*, now. You are older. You *will* learn, but only if you will allow me to teach you."

He placed a soft hand on her cheek. "And did you not quickly learn the art of speaking my language as well as my own people speak it?" he asked.

Yvonne battled feelings inside herself, but knew, in the end, that she must give him the chance or lose a part of him that she might never regain. "*Ae*, yes, I did learn your language well and even how to write it," she said, recalling the ease with which she had done that.

"Then, my wife, I know that you will now be able to learn how to read the words of *your* people," Silver Arrow said determinedly.

"Oh, Silver Arrow, I hope that you are right," Yvonne said, sighing. "I would love for you to teach me how to read. I have wished to know for so long, not only for the knowledge that one gets from books, but also the pleasure. Do you truly think you can teach me?"

"If you have the same faith in yourself that *I* have in you, *ae*, you will read," he said.

He held her close. "Your father says the book is a love story," he said, chuckling. "Will that not make reading it together much more pleasurable?"

"I doubt that it will teach us anything more than we already know," she said, giggling, trying her best to make light of the situation, while deep inside she dreaded these next few days and weeks . . . perhaps even *months*, while she might look like a clumsy fool in the eyes of her beloved husband!

The days passed into weeks. Each day there was a special time set aside when Silver Arrow and Yvonne sat before the fire in their longhouse, the wonderful book shared between them.

Word by word, sentence by sentence, Yvonne learned how to put the letters together to finally form words she had never been able to decipher before.

She beamed as she mastered one page of reading, and then another.

And the story was so romantic, it made their lovemaking even more special each night. In a sense they *became* Damon and Angeline, the hero and heroine of the wonderfully romantic saga.

Then when the last page was conquered, and Yvonne realized that she could finally say that she had read one complete book, she felt as if she were glowing from the pride of it.

She gazed at Silver Arrow. "But why now?" she asked as she clutched the book in her hands. "Why was I able to learn how to read now, but never in the past?"

"Because, my wife, your life is as you wish it to be now, sweet and full of peace, with no worries plaguing you which before clouded your thoughts," he said softly.

"When you were just a child you were thrown into a world where survival each day was more important than reading."

"Yes, when I stood with my mother on the street corners in Saint Louis selling flowers," she murmured, the remembrance so vivid it was as though she were that child of yesterday now.

"Then came your mother's death," Silver Arrow said. "I need not bring more painful memories into your heart. But you see, do you not, how it was that you had many things that made learning difficult for you?"

"*Ae*, so much of my past is steeped in sadness," she said, swallowing hard.

She turned to him and smiled. "But now I am surely the happiest woman on the earth," she murmured. "For I have *you*, my darling."

He took the book and placed it inside the chest, then lifted her on his lap and held her close. "There is one other thing that may have made learning easier now than in the past," he said, laughing huskily. "It was your husband teaching you."

"Yes, my husband," Yvonne said, snuggling closer to him. "Sweet darling, the book has brought so much into our lives."

She gazed over at it; then she looked with wavering eyes at Silver Arrow. "Darling, we have no daughter to pass it on to. Only . . . a . . . son . . ."

Silver Arrow laughed throatily. He swept her up into his arms and carried her to their bed. "My wife, shall we begin now making that daughter?" he said huskily.

"*Ae*, yes, oh, yes," she whispered, closing her eyes with rapture when he covered her lips with a warm, quivering kiss.

SHIRL HENKE

The Cheyenne Seer

Since childhood the amber-eyed, red prairie wolf has filled Fawn's dreams. After being educated in the white world, she returns to the Cheyenne to guide them with her medicine dreams.

The Red Wolf

With his cunning and his Colt, Jack Dillon has become a feared lawman. But he faces his toughest job ever when he agrees to protect Fawn and her people from the scum trying to steal their land.

The Grand Design

When Fawn meets the amber-eyed, russet-haired Irishman, she is both infuriated by his cocky self-confidence and irresistibly drawn to his charismatic charm. He is the wolf totem of her dreams who holds the key to unlocking her visionary powers. Together they can save her people, if only he chooses to love the...

CHOSEN WOMAN

ISBN 13: 978-0-8439-6248-2